WHAT MIGHT HAVE BEEN

A DANIELS BROTHERS ROMANCE

SHERRI HAYES

What Might Have Been

Daniels Brothers Series

Sherri Hayes

ABOUT THIS BOOK

Missed opportunities, unspoken feelings, and the power of second chances.

Trent Daniels is a man plagued by regret. He's spent years watching from the sidelines. Then he gets called to help landscape several office buildings, and he comes face-to-face with the woman who's haunted his dreams since high school.

Abigail Hoffman left her hometown, and the loving embrace of the Daniels family, behind to move to New York City. The weight of her own secrets kept her away for far too long. Now, her job has brought her back to the place she thought she could avoid forever.

Sparks fly as Trent and Abby find themselves working together. The undeniable chemistry between them ignites, and years of unanswered questions come flooding back. With passions running high and old wounds reopened, they must navigate a maze of emotions and confront the painful secret that has kept Abby away.

Will Trent and Abby seize this second chance at love, or will the past be too much for them to overcome?

CHAPTER 1

TRENT DANIELS DOUBLE-CHECKED to make sure he had all the paperwork he might need. He had no idea why Frank and Lillian Baxter wanted to see him. As far as he knew, they were happy with the work his landscaping crew was doing, but the vague call he'd received the day before asking if he could meet with them at one o'clock was ominous. Like it or not, he had to consider that he might be losing his biggest client.

Satisfied everything was in order, he closed his briefcase and straightened his tie. He hated suits and did his best to wear them as little as possible. Give him jeans and a T-shirt any day over the noose he currently had wrapped around his neck.

"Got everything you need, Boss?" He glanced over his shoulder to find his office manager, Trinity, smirking at him.

"Everything I can think of, at least."

She crossed her arms over her chest and leaned on the doorframe. "Too bad Mrs. Baxter isn't twenty years younger. You could charm your way to securing the contract. You're looking pretty smokin' in that suit."

That made him grin and some of the tension dissipated. "Thanks. But I'm hoping talent brings this one home."

"You don't know what it's about, though, right? I mean it could be nothing." Joking aside, Trinity knew more than anyone did how big a blow it would be if they lost this account. She'd been with him since the beginning and had helped him build the company from the ground up. If things went badly with the Baxters, he might have to lay some people off and that was the last thing he wanted to do.

Trent picked up the briefcase and headed toward Trinity. She pushed herself away from the wall and took a step out of the room as he drew closer. The look on her face told him she was as worried as he was. He came to a stop in front of her and did his best to reassure her. "You're right. It could be anything. No reason to think the worst."

She smiled, but he could still see the worry in her eyes.

He placed a comforting hand on her arm. It was bad enough one of them was stressed out over this. "We'll be okay. We always are."

Trinity nodded and took a deep breath. "Go get 'em."

He gave her arm a reassuring squeeze. "Exactly what I plan to do."

As he passed Joss and Kevin, they didn't bother to look up from whatever they were working on. To them it was just a normal day at the office.

The drive to the Baxters' corporate office seemed to take longer than usual. He was sure that was only because of the lead weight that had settled in his stomach. Landing the Baxter account five years ago had put him and his company on the map. Before, he'd had a small crew made up of four guys and himself with a handful of regular accounts around the city. It wasn't bad, but he had bigger plans for himself and his company.

Trent parked in one of the guest spots near the front of the building then strolled up the steps toward the main entrance. As he passed by the flower beds, he couldn't help but take a quick survey of their condition. Everything looked great, in his opinion. The hedges were neatly trimmed and the beds well maintained. His crew did good work.

Shaking his head, Trent pushed everything out of his mind except for the task at hand. He had to be prepared for anything. Even if they lost the account, it wouldn't do any good to leave a bad impression.

A security guard sat behind a circular desk not far from the entrance. The middle-aged man glanced up as Trent walked in the glass doors.

"I'm here to see Mr. and Mrs. Baxter."

The security guard, looking somewhat bored, passed him a sign-in sheet. "Name?"

"Trent Daniels."

Nodding, the man picked up the phone, effectively ignoring Trent as he put his name and time of arrival on the paper attached to the clipboard.

When the man hung up the phone, Trent handed the sign-in sheet back to him. The security guard took it and placed it on the desk without looking at it. "You can have a seat over there. Mr. Baxter's assistant will be down to get you shortly."

Trent had been dismissed. He knew it wasn't personal and went to take a seat on the modern-looking sofa.

Less than five minutes after he sat down, Melinda, the Baxters' assistant, exited the elevator. She had a sly smile on her face as she approached him. "Frank told me you were going to be stopping by today. It's good to see you again. It's been a while."

"It hasn't been that long. I was here last month." Trent stood and followed her as she pivoted on her heel and strode toward the elevator. He didn't miss the extra swing in her hips as she walked that drew his attention directly to her backside. Melinda was a beautiful woman and she knew it.

He'd considered asking her out, but decided it wasn't a good idea. If something went wrong, he didn't want to put himself and the Baxters in an awkward position. However, that didn't mean he couldn't enjoy the view.

The elevator doors closed. She glanced over her shoulder, meeting his gaze.

"Nice dress."

Melinda beamed at the compliment. "Thank you. It's new."

She took a step toward him and ran a hand down the side of her dress in a way that had him wondering what those curves of hers would feel like pressed up against him.

"You don't think it's too much for work? I was thinking of going out later tonight and didn't want to go home first to change."

He grinned, trying to keep it casual. "Not at all. I'd say it's perfect for a girls' night out on the town."

Her confidence faltered a little at his response, but she recovered quickly. When they reached the top floor, Melinda sashayed out of the elevator, giving him another perfect view of her ass. Interested or not, Trent was a guy and it was hard to ignore something like that when it was right there in front of you.

She exaggerated every movement as she made her way over to her desk and sat down. It was like this every time he visited.

Trent cleared his throat. "Should I go in?"

Melinda looked a little disappointed, but nodded. "Yes. He's expecting you."

"Thanks."

Trent paused outside Mr. Baxter's door and took a deep breath. The one thing Melinda's flirting had done was help get his mind off this meeting. If he didn't know she'd take it the wrong way, he'd send her flowers or something.

He raised his hand and knocked.

"Enter." Despite the closed door, Mr. Baxter's voice rang out loud and clear.

Trent straightened his shoulders, opened the door, and walked in.

Mr. Baxter smiled when he saw Trent and waved him inside. "Come in, come in. How have you been?"

Seeing Mr. Baxter's upbeat attitude, Trent relaxed some. Surely if they were going to fire him, Mr. Baxter wouldn't be so welcoming.

"I've been well, Mr. Baxter. Thank you for asking."

He motioned for Trent to take a seat and waited until he was settled before continuing. "I'm so glad you could make it in today."

"Of course." Mr. Baxter was pushing sixty, but it was hard to tell. He dyed his hair and worked out regularly. If not for the lines around his eyes, he could easily pass for someone in his forties.

Hearing a noise behind him, Trent glanced toward the door. A man around his age, wearing a very expensive-looking suit, entered followed by Mrs. Baxter.

"I was beginning to think you two weren't coming," Mr. Baxter said, rising from his seat to give his wife a peck on the cheek.

Mrs. Baxter grinned at her husband, and then lowered herself into the empty chair next to Trent. "Lunch took longer than expected. I do believe the waitress had a small crush on Maxwell."

The other man, who Trent assumed to be Maxwell, took a seat on the couch along the wall and rolled his eyes. "I think you're making too much of it, Aunt Lillian. She was just trying to be nice."

His comment received a look of disbelief from Mrs. Baxter, but she didn't reply.

Mr. Baxter cleared his throat. "Let's get started, shall we?" He turned his attention to Trent. "As you've probably already surmised, this is our nephew, Maxwell Collins."

Trent nodded in Maxwell's direction. The man leaned forward and extended his hand in greeting. Trent took it and smiled politely.

"Good. Now that the introductions are settled," Mr. Baxter said when their handshake was over, "we can get down to business."

"We have something we'd like to ask you," Mrs. Baxter began, before being cut off by her nephew.

"What my aunt means to say is that I'm in need of some help and they feel you might be able to assist me."

"What is it that you need?" Trent asked. He was still trying to shift gears from thinking he was going to lose the account to being asked for help.

Maxwell sat forward, clasping his hands in front of him. "My father was diagnosed with pancreatic cancer and has recently taken a turn for the worse. He kept it from all of us until recently. Now that I know, I've come home to take care of things and to run the family business."

Trent waited for him to go on, since that still didn't explain what they needed from him.

"My father's assistant, Emily, knew about his condition and helped him hide it from the family," Maxwell continued. "As he got worse, she took over more and more of the daily operations."

He stood and walked over to the bank of windows along the wall. When he came into the room, he'd looked to be in his early thirties, the same as Trent himself. But now, talking about his father's declining health, Maxwell seemed to have aged ten years before his eyes.

Stuffing his hands in his pockets, Maxwell turned around to face Trent. "Long story short, some bad decisions were made. One of those was to trim the budget so it didn't include outside maintenance for any of our properties. It's no wonder sales are declining when the grass hasn't been cut in weeks and there are weeds everywhere."

It sounded like a mess. Lawns left unattended that long were likely to have seeded. It would take weeks, if not months to get them back to where they should be. "How many properties?"

"Ten. And I need them looking presentable as soon as possible. I'm willing to pay for overtime or whatever else is needed. My family has put a lot of work into building this company. I won't allow it to crumble under my watch."

Trent needed to see firsthand what he was dealing with. "I would have to take a look at all the properties and come up with an action plan."

"Good. When can you get started?"

"I have some time tomorrow if that would work for you."

Maxwell grinned and handed Trent two business cards from inside his jacket. "I'll have my assistant, Abigail, meet you in front of our corporate office at nine. She can take you around to each of the properties and answer any questions you may have."

Trent glanced down at the two cards. One had Maxwell Collins, Attorney at Law written in fancy lettering along with a Manhattan address. The second card was for Collins and Baxter Property Management Corporation with a local address.

"If you need anything before tomorrow, you can reach me on my cell."

Standing, Trent tucked the cards in his pocket. "If I can get a look at everything tomorrow, I should be able to have some figures for you by the end of the week."

"I look forward to it." Maxwell extended his hand again to Trent.

After a brief goodbye to Mr. and Mrs. Baxter, Trent left the office and made his way back down the elevator. His head was spinning. Not only had they not lost the Baxter account, but it looked as if they were gaining another big client.

Trent strolled past the security guard in the lobby and out into the parking lot. He climbed into his truck, shut the door, and reached for his cell.

Two rings later, Trinity picked up. "How'd it go?"

Trent tilted his head back against the seat and chuckled. "You're not going to believe it."

* * *

Abigail Hoffman took a seat on the stone bench outside the Collinses' corporate office. She glanced up at the sky and frowned. It was going to be hot and humid once the sun worked its way higher in the sky. Just her luck she'd be spending the day driving around town showing the new landscaper all the Collinses' properties. Abby prayed his vehicle had air conditioning.

Max had returned from his meeting the day before and gleefully informed her of how she'd be spending her day today. She was glad he'd solved one of the hundreds of issues they'd inherited upon his return to Cincinnati, Ohio. Instead of spending time with his ailing father, Max was stuck trying to fix the months of bad decision-making his father's assistant, Emily, had made.

Emily had no experience running a business and it showed. She'd cut spending in an effort to save the company money, but she hadn't understood that sometimes you have to spend money in order to make it. Now it was up to Max, and Abby, to get things back on track. If they didn't, Collins and Baxter Property Management wasn't going to last much longer.

She glanced at her watch. It was already five minutes after nine and there was no sign of the landscaper.

Her phone buzzed and she dug in her purse to check the message. It was from Max, of course.

Didn't scare him off, did you? - Max

She rolled her eyes. **No. He hasn't shown up yet. - Abby**

He didn't reply immediately. **Don't worry. He'll be there. Aunt Lillian says he's the best landscaper in town. - Max**

High praise coming from your aunt. - Abby

I know. Call me tonight? - Max

Sure. - Abby

Sighing, she put her phone back in her purse. When Max told her about his dad and asked for her help, Abby couldn't say no. Max was her best friend and he'd been there for her more times than she could count over the years.

That didn't mean she was feeling all warm and fuzzy about being back in her hometown. There were too many memories here. Too many chances of running into someone she knew.

Abby checked her watch again. Ten minutes after nine. Maybe Aunt Lillian had been wrong about this guy of hers.

"Excuse me?"

She looked up at the large figure looming over her. The sun was behind him and she was having trouble seeing his face. "Hi."

"Hi." He sounded amused. "Would you happen to be Abigail?"

Right then he moved a little to the right, blocking the sun, and she got a good look at his face. Abby blinked. She had to be seeing things. It couldn't be—

"Are you all right?" His amusement had turned to concern when she didn't respond.

Abby stood and attempted to hide her unease. She didn't need to be at any more of a disadvantage than she already was. "Yes. I'm fine."

A second later, she saw recognition cross his face. "Abby? Is that you?"

"Hi, Trent." That wasn't exactly the truth, but what else could she say?

"Wow. I can't believe it. When I was told I'd be meeting Abigail, I had no idea it would be you."

"Yep. It's me." She knew what was coming and the last thing she wanted to do was take a trip down memory lane. "And I'm guessing you're the landscaper."

"Landscape architect, actually. But my company does everything from design to implementation and maintenance."

She was impressed, despite everything else that was going through her head at that moment. "Sounds like a lot of work."

"It is. But I love it."

Standing there, Abby realized how easy it would be to slip into the effortless friendship they'd had before. A part of her longed for that, but she had to remember why that wasn't a good idea—why she needed to keep her distance. "Word on the street is that you're the best."

Trent lifted a single eyebrow and one side of his mouth tilted up. "By the street you mean Mrs. Baxter."

She couldn't help the bubble of laughter that escaped. "Max's aunt thinks highly of you and she doesn't dole out praise lightly."

Abby knew that much from personal experience. The first time she'd met Lillian and her husband, Frank, she'd been peppered with questions from the woman. Even though Max had explained that he and Abby were merely friends, Lillian was convinced there had to be more to it. She wanted to make sure her nephew wasn't having the wool pulled over his eyes.

"You must be talking about another Mrs. Baxter. She's always been quite pleasant to me." He was teasing her and it brought back a lot of memories . . . memories she really wanted to keep buried.

"Lucky you." Abby smiled and picked up the paperwork on all the properties she'd brought with her, trying to ignore the churning in the pit of her stomach. "We have a lot of ground to cover today. Are you ready to get started?"

He motioned toward the parking lot. "Ready when you are."

They made their way down the walkway to where he'd parked his vehicle—a silver pickup truck. It looked new, but when Abby climbed inside she noticed a few signs of wear on the interior. There were also several notebooks and a stack of papers on the seat between them.

Trent put the key into the ignition, started the engine, and put the vehicle in gear. "Where to first?"

Abby flipped open the folder in her lap. The first property on the list was another office building. It was as good a place to start as any. "Gavin's Ridge. We'll start there."

"Gavin's Ridge it is."

He backed out and maneuvered his way through the parking lot and onto the main road. Abby told herself to stay calm. It would be okay. This was Trent. Her childhood friend.

While that was true, a lot had changed since they'd sat on the steps outside his home and played *I spy*.

She chanced a glance at him before looking away.

Pressing her lips together, she ordered herself to breathe. It would be okay. She'd do her job, he'd do his, and then they'd go their separate ways.

Yeah. Who was she trying to kid? There was no way Trent would leave it at that. Not with their history.

CHAPTER 2

Abby.

Trent was still trying to wrap his mind around the fact that she was standing only a few feet away from him. Seeing her again had been a shock to his system. It had been more than ten years, but she hadn't changed all that much. Her hair was shorter and she had a few more curves than he remembered, but other than that, she looked the same. That is if you discounted the designer suit she was wearing. The Abby he knew preferred jeans and T-shirts.

"What do you think?" she asked.

He cleared his throat and put thoughts of the past out of his mind. There would be time for that later. "It needs a lot of work. I don't know who was in charge of the landscaping before, but this is in worse shape than I expected. Some of this over here has seeded already. It'll need to be removed and new sod put down. The mulch needs to be replaced. And I'm concerned about those trees over there. I'll have my arborist look at them to be sure, but I think they're going to have to come down."

In his head, he was going over the numbers. How long would it take to do what needed to be done based on the number of guys he could spare? As much as he wanted to make this work, he couldn't sacrifice the needs of his other clients.

Abby walked over to one of the bushes. It was out of control and would need to be cut back considerably. She plucked a leaf off and ran it between her thumb and forefinger. It made him recall sitting in the backyard with her years ago. She used to pick a blade of grass from the lawn and wind it around her finger over and over again.

"Max was devastated when he saw it." She looked around the property with sadness in her eyes. "His dad never would have let this happen if he'd been well."

Hearing her talk so casually of her boss made him wonder what kind of relationship they had. Was it purely professional? He knew he shouldn't care either way, but this was Abby. Even after all the years they'd been apart, he still felt that pull to her. "How long have you worked for *Max?*"

She glanced over at him then quickly averted her eyes. "About five years."

He nodded and went back to inspecting the plants. There were so many things he wanted to ask her, like why hadn't she come back after college, or at least stayed in contact? Trent thought he understood on some level, but it still hurt. They'd been friends. Whatever had happened between her and his brother shouldn't have affected the friendship she and Trent had.

They were both quiet while Trent made his way around the lawn. He made some notes and sketched a rough layout of the property. It would help him later when he was putting together his proposal.

When he was finished, he and Abby headed back to his truck. They drove to the next property on her list. This one was an apartment complex.

He grabbed his notebook and stepped out of the truck. The first thing he noticed was an overgrown garden trellis. It framed the door leading to the office. He imagined it had once been a thing of beauty. At the moment, it was out of control. Trent couldn't imagine anyone would be eager to pass under something that looked as if it wanted to swallow a person whole. He was beginning to understand what Maxwell Collins had meant when he said it was costing them business.

After introducing themselves to the office manager, Trent and Abby strolled through the complex of roughly twenty townhouses. It was more of the same—plants that hadn't been trimmed in months, if not years, and mulch that needed to be replaced. The grass looked as if it had been mowed regularly, at least, but there were quite a few bald spots that would need to be addressed.

Abby followed beside him. If he asked a question, she would answer. Otherwise, she remained silent.

It gave him a lot of time to think of more questions. What had led her to working for Maxwell Collins. When she'd left for college, she'd had plans to become an interior designer. What happened there?

When he was satisfied he had everything documented, they went back to his truck and moved on to the next property. Abby had kept a respectful distance from him all morning. If she'd been a stranger he wouldn't have thought much of it, but she wasn't. They'd been best friends, damn it. She could barely look him in the eye.

They finished up at their fourth property around noon. He pulled out of the parking lot and onto the main highway without asking Abby for the address of their next destination. She didn't say anything. Trent wasn't sure if that was because she trusted him or because she'd already guessed he was headed for food.

He drove for about five miles until he saw one of his favorite food trucks. There was already a line.

After finding a place to park on a side street not far away, he turned off the engine, and unbuckled his seat belt.

Abby glanced over at him then at the clock on the dashboard. "I guess we should probably get something to eat."

"Yep. I'm starving." He palmed his keys, opened his door, and winked at her. "Wouldn't want you to wither away, now would we?"

It took a few moments for her to exit the truck and join him on the sidewalk. She held her hand against her forehead like she was trying to shield her eyes from the sun. It created a shadow over her face, but he still noticed the red on her cheeks. He'd made her blush.

Once they had their food, Trent guided her over to one of the picnic tables beneath a pair of trees. It was a decent day even if it was a little on the humid side, but in the shade there was a nice breeze.

Abby sat across from him and started eating her tacos. She scanned their surroundings, looking everywhere but at him.

Trent devoured three of his tacos before he decided he had to say something. "Last time I saw you, you were headed off to college to become an interior designer."

He let that hang in the air to see if she took the bait.

She sipped her lemonade and shrugged. "Things change. People change."

"True. But I thought you were pretty perfect before." He took another bite of his taco and waited.

Abby grinned. "You haven't changed."

"I'll take that as a compliment."

"Definitely a compliment." She was quiet for a long moment. "It's good to see you again, Trent."

He was tempted to put all his questions on the table, but something told him if he did that she would shut down on him. "Do you know how long you're going to be in town?"

Abby released a deep breath and met his gaze. "I don't know. Max has to get his dad's company back to where it should be before anything can be decided. Plus, there's his father's health to consider."

"And you'll be here as long as Max is." It still felt odd calling him Max, but that's what Abby called him so Trent was going with it.

It wasn't really a question, but she nodded anyway.

Trent finished his lunch and gathered his trash into a pile. "So for a while, then."

"Most likely. Max needs someone here with him that he knows will get things done."

"Which is where you come in." Trent wasn't sure how he felt about that.

"Max is handling as much as he can from here and his partners back in New York are taking care of anything that has to be done in person."

"What does Max do exactly? Back in New York, I mean." Trent knew he was a lawyer, but that was about it. Did the guy defend lowlife criminals, or something more mundane?

"He's a lawyer. Corporate stuff, mostly. Contracts. Mergers. That sort of thing."

"And you're his personal assistant." He tried not to put too much emphasis on *personal*, but when she raised her eyebrow at him, he knew he hadn't succeeded. "Sorry. It's just that you two seem to have a rather . . . casual relationship."

She straightened her shoulders and the little vein in her forehead pulsed—a sure sign she was annoyed. "We're friends."

"Okay." He figured it wouldn't be a good idea to push her.

Abby wiped her hands and got up to throw her trash away. He followed her lead. The walk back to the truck was a quiet one. It was obvious that he'd overstepped.

Trent waited until they arrived at the next property before broaching the subject. He pulled into one of the visitor spots, turned off the engine, and twisted in his seat to face her. "I'm sorry. I didn't mean to offend you."

"You didn't." Her abrupt response told a different story.

"Well, either way, I am sorry if I put my foot in my mouth. Whatever your relationship is with Maxwell Collins, it's none of my business."

She didn't respond.

Trent sighed, picked up his notes, and climbed out of his truck. Whether he liked it or not, he had work to do.

* * *

Abby sat in the cab of the truck and watched as Trent strolled around the property. It was an office building and she knew it wouldn't take him long. When she told him she'd wait in the truck he hadn't argued.

It wasn't as if this was the first time someone had assumed her relationship with Max was of the intimate variety. They were friends —good friends—but that was all. In a lot of ways, he was like her big brother. There wasn't anything romantic about it and there never would be.

So why did it bother her so much that Trent insinuated the same thing so many others had? That was simple. Abby actually cared about his opinion of her. She shouldn't, but it was there all the same.

Forcing herself to get out of the truck, Abby joined Trent along the side of the building. He looked up when he heard her approach.

She stopped several feet away and cleared her throat. "I may have overreacted."

Trent gave her his full attention. "No. You were right. I shouldn't have said anything. It's none of my business."

"You're not the first person to think there's something going on between me and Max."

He glanced at his notebook then back at the bush he'd been examining before she'd interrupted him. "That doesn't make it right."

Abby was frustrated. She shouldn't care this much. The Daniels family was part of her past, not her future. When Max got things turned around, he'd appoint a new CEO and the two of them would be on their way back to New York. Rebuilding a friendship with Trent wasn't smart and her soon-to-be-changing zip code was only one of the many reasons it wasn't a good idea.

"Can we start over?" she asked. Whether she liked it or not, they were going to have to work together for the foreseeable future.

He'd knelt down beside the bush, but he glanced up at her question.

"Please?"

Trent stood and walked over to her. He extended his hand. "Trent Daniels. Nice to meet you."

She laughed. "That's not what I meant."

He smirked. "I know. But it was too good to resist."

As they stood there smiling at each other, Abby felt that old connection returning—the one that made her want to spill all her secrets. The thought brought her up short. She pushed past him and focused on the plant he'd been inspecting. "Do you like being your own boss?"

It took him a second to answer. "I do. Gives me freedom to come and go when I need to."

Abby nodded. Things never used to be this uncomfortable with Trent. He was her rock. The friend she could always count on. Now things were awkward and she knew it was her fault. "I guess I never saw you as the type that would want that kind of responsibility. You were always . . ."

"So laid back?"

"Yeah."

Trent resumed his inspection of the area, making notes as he went. "I still am. Usually. Most of the hardcore stuff I leave for my office manager, Trinity. She's a hardass when she wants to be."

The smile on his face when he talked about his office manager left her feeling irritated. Her reaction didn't make any sense. She didn't even know the woman. "I guess that makes you two a good match."

His cell rang, interrupting their conversation. He dug it out of his pocket and answered the call with a genuine smile on his face. "Hey, Trinity. Not at all. What do you need?"

He walked back toward his truck leaving Abby to stare at his retreating back. She couldn't hear what they were saying and it bothered her that she wanted to know. They weren't even friends anymore. Why did she care?

Needing a distraction, she pulled her own phone out and checked her e-mail. There were twenty unopened messages, half of them from Max. It looked as if she'd be working this evening.

"Everything all right?" Abby snapped her head up to see Trent coming toward her.

"Yeah. Everything's fine. Just checking my e-mail." She waved her phone at him before shoving it back in her pocket. Then she tilted her head in the direction of the cell he still held in his hand. "You?"

Trent glanced down at it as if he'd completely forgotten it was there. He tucked it in his pocket. "One of my crew went home sick. Nothing out of the ordinary, but Trinity wanted me to know she'd had to move a few things around."

"The fun of being a boss." She wanted to ask him more, but knew she shouldn't.

"Exactly." He looked around before returning his attention to her. "We have four more places to hit before we can call it a day. You ready to go?"

"Ready when you are."

It took them another two hours to finish. Trent had pages upon pages of notes. She had no idea what he had in there, but by the sheer volume Abby was guessing things were in worse shape than Max had thought. It wouldn't matter, of course. Max would do whatever it took to get things fixed for his family.

At five thirty, they returned to where their day had begun. Trent pulled into the same spot and put the truck in park. "Thanks for going with me today. Let Max know I'll go over my notes and have a proposal to him by Friday."

"No problem. It was . . . educational."

He grinned. "Just what a man wants to hear after spending the day with a woman."

Abby chuckled and reached for the door. The longer she stayed the more she longed for things to be the way they were before. "Have a good night, Trent."

"Same to you, Abby."

She walked over to her car and unlocked the door. It didn't escape her notice that he was still sitting in his truck, probably watching her. His mom used to stand on the front porch and watch her walk home. Even though Abby's house was only three doors down, Marilyn Daniels would wait until she saw Abby walk through the door to her house before going back inside. The apple didn't fall far from the tree, not with any of the Daniels boys.

Once she was behind the wheel of her vehicle, Abby checked her phone. She had a text from Max.

Call me when you get home. - Max

Abby shook her head. What would she do with all these overprotective men in her life?

That thought made her pause. Trent wasn't in her life. Not anymore. Today didn't count. Chances were she wouldn't see him again after he worked out the contract with Max.

Tears pricked her eyes as she started the vehicle and maneuvered out of the parking lot. She blinked them away. This wasn't something to cry over. It was for the best. They couldn't be friends anymore. Too much time had passed. Too much had happened.

It took Abby almost twenty minutes to reach her apartment. Max had offered to let her stay with him at his parents', but she hadn't felt right about it, so he'd arranged an apartment for her. His father was dying and she didn't want to intrude on their family time.

Abby let herself in, turned on the light, and kicked off her shoes. She crossed the living room to her small kitchen. Lunch had been hours ago and she was starving.

She pulled out of the refrigerator some chicken that she'd made the night before, and popped it in the microwave. While she was waiting for her dinner to heat up, she dialed Max.

"Well, how was it?" he asked. It wasn't unusual for him to forgo a greeting when she called. Max liked to get to the point.

She leaned against the counter and watched as the numbers on the microwave counted down. "Hot. I should have worn something other than a suit."

He chuckled. "I've spoiled you with the air conditioning."

"Is that what you're calling it now? Spoiled? Last time I checked, you enjoyed the same benefits of the air conditioning as I do."

"Yes, but I'm a high-powered lawyer. Perks of the job, you know."

Abby rolled her eyes. "I saw you sent me enough work to keep me busy for the rest of the evening."

"Nothing pressing. It should be fine until tomorrow. Take the evening and relax. I'm sure you earned it."

The microwave beeped, and she took her food over to the table. "That I did. I know we drove by all the properties the other day, Max, but they're worse than we thought."

"How so?"

She took a bite of her chicken and made him wait until she'd swallowed for a response. "Some of the properties need all new sod and mulch. And I think some trees might have to come down, too. Trent said he'll have a proposal to you by Friday, but given all the notes he took and some of the stuff he said, it's going to be extensive."

Max was quiet for too long.

"Max? You there?"

"I'm here." He paused. "Trent, huh? So after spending a day with the guy, you're on a first name basis? He must have made quite an impression."

"Oh. Um. Not exactly. We kind of know each other. We grew up together and . . ." *And he's Chris' brother.*

Of course, Max realized she wasn't telling him everything. "Did he do something, Abby? Do I need to make his life a living hell?"

Abby shook her head and grinned. "No. Not at all. The Daniels family was great to me. Better than I deserved."

It was then that Max seemed to put two and two together. "Wait a minute. Was his brother . . ."

"Yeah."

"I see."

They sat quietly for a long time. She pushed the plate away. Her appetite had completely disappeared.

"Do you want me to find someone else to work with this landscaper? My first choice is you, but I don't want you to be uncomfortable, Abby. That's the last thing I want. If I'd known he was—"

"Max, it's fine. I'm fine. It was a long time ago." It was a long time ago, but that didn't stop her from reaching for the charm that dangled from her neck. She closed her eyes and clasped the tiny lamb in her fist.

"That may be, but you aren't fooling me."

Abby took a deep breath. "Really. I'm good. Trent is a great guy. I'll be fine."

"Okay. Well, if you change your mind—"

"You'll be the first to know."

After they hung up, Abby took her uneaten chicken and put it back in the refrigerator. What she needed was a glass of wine and a good book. That would get her mind off the past. At least, that's what she was hoping.

CHAPTER 3

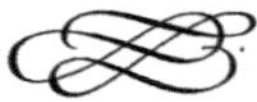

FRIDAY MORNING, Abby sat at her desk outside Max's office trying to weed her way through the purchase orders she'd found the day before. There were receipts for everything from printer ink to comped lunches. Everything was mixed together without any apparent rhyme or reason. They'd all been stuffed in a boxed underneath the desk.

Abby was so absorbed in what she was doing that when the phone on her desk rang she jumped. Taking a deep breath to calm her racing heart, she answered it. "Maxwell Collins' office."

"This is Chuck over at the Perimeter Building. We've got a problem over here. Mr. Collins said he wanted to be notified personally if—"

"Yes, I'm glad you called," Abby said. Given how out of control things were at all the properties, Max had wanted the property managers to call his office directly if there was a problem. "What seems to be the issue?"

She jotted down all the information Chuck gave her. For some reason the toilets on the fourth floor weren't working and nothing he'd done so far had been able to fix them. They were going to need to call a plumber.

As she was hanging up the phone, the elevator dinged. Abby saw two women from their sales department exit. They were deep in conversation and didn't even bother to look her way as they hurried down the hall in the opposite direction.

Shaking her head, she focused on the task at hand. She needed to call a plumber and get them over to Chuck so the toilets could be fixed. What she didn't need, which was exactly what she'd been doing since she got there, was to keep an eye out for Trent. He said he'd have the proposal to Max by Friday. He never said he'd be dropping it off personally. For all she knew he would be sending it via courier or having his office manager, Trinity, drop it off. She had to admit she was curious about Trinity, even though she knew she had no right to be.

Ever since he'd dropped Abby off in the parking lot, he hadn't been far from her thoughts. None of the Daniels family had. Growing up, she'd spent more time with them than she had her own father. They were her lifeline—what she'd clung to when her world had been flipped upside down.

How were they? Were any of his brothers married? Paul had been engaged to Melissa when Abby had gone off to college. Did they get married? Were they still together? She thought she'd read somewhere in the sports pages that Gage had recently gotten hitched—in Vegas if she remembered correctly. It was hard to think of Gage, the baby of the family, all grown up with a wife.

She blew out a breath and started searching the Internet for a plumber, but it didn't keep her mind from wandering. Trent didn't wear a ring, and he hadn't mentioned a wife, so she was pretty sure he wasn't married. Then again, maybe he was. He was thirty-one years old, one year younger than her, and one of the best guys she'd ever met. Surely he'd found someone he wanted to share his life with by now.

Then there was Chris. She'd tried not to think about him at all, but seeing Trent had brought everything rushing back. As much as she hated to admit it, she was curious. What had happened to him? Had his life turned out how he wanted it to?

What about Marilyn and Mike? They'd been surrogate parents to her, taking care of her when her father couldn't be there.

Thinking of her dad left a deep ache in her chest. It had been ten years and she still missed him as though it were yesterday. He'd been a good dad. He'd done his best as a single parent after her mom died. She still remembered how they'd go to the range and shoot for hours on his days off. It was their time together and she'd cherished it.

A shadow fell across her desk and she glanced up, blinking the moisture from her eyes. Her pulse raced as Trent stared down at her, looking more handsome than she'd ever seen him. Gone were the casual work clothes he'd worn the last time she'd seen him. Today he wore a dark gray suit and tie. His hair was slicked back, tamed into submission, all except one strand that seemed to want to rebel. It brushed against his forehead, begging to be tucked back into place.

Where had that thought come from?

"Are you okay?" he asked when she continued to stare at him.

She swallowed. "Yeah. Fine. You just—you startled me, that's all."

He smiled and her stomach fluttered against her will.

"Looks as if Max is keeping you busy." Trent nodded to the stack of papers she'd been going through.

She had to get her head on straight and fast. "You could say that. It's another parting gift from Mr. Collins' former assistant. I don't think she had an ounce of organizational skill."

He peered over her shoulder. "Confetti?"

Abby followed his gaze to the receipt directly on top of the pile. Sure enough, it was for confetti, streamers, and several other party items. Given the date, Abby was guessing the supplies were for Mr. Collins' birthday. That was only a guess since there was no notation whatsoever saying what the stuff was used for. "Confetti. And just about anything she ordered for the last two years."

Trent opened his mouth to say something, but they were interrupted when Max came out of his office. "Abby, can you call—"

He stopped in his tracks when he saw Trent.

"Mr. Daniels. I didn't realize you'd be stopping by today." To her horror, Max moved to stand a few feet in front of Trent and folded his arms across his chest. There was an air of protectiveness about his stance that Abby didn't miss.

Apparently, Trent didn't miss it either. His eyes narrowed a bit as if he was analyzing the new information. That was different. The Trent she remembered would have been too laid back to care. He would have brushed off the posturing and either walked away or continued on, pretending not to notice.

"I told Abby I'd have the proposal ready for you today. I came by to drop it off." Trent handed the envelope to Max, neither of them adjusting their posture. "You can look it over and let me know if you want to move forward."

Max opened the envelope. He scanned the information, flipping through the pages.

Trent stood there waiting, seeming completely unaffected by whatever it was Max was playing at. Then again, not even she knew what her boss and friend was doing. He'd always been somewhat protective of her, but this was a little much, even for him.

A few minutes later, Max placed the packet of papers on the corner of her desk, reached for a pen, and swiftly signed his name. He handed the packet back to Trent. "How soon can you get started?"

Trent tucked the papers back inside the envelope. "We can begin on Monday."

Max held Trent's gaze and nodded. Then, out of the blue, Max turned his attention to her. "When you're finished here, I need you to call Phil in accounting and let him know I need to see him in my office ASAP."

"Sure."

With a final look in Trent's direction, Max headed back to his office and shut the door.

Trent raised one eyebrow. "I thought you said you were just friends."

"We are." Abby had to admit that Max's actions had irritated her. They were going to have to have a talk about that. Trent hadn't done anything to warrant Max's attitude. "I honestly don't know what's gotten into him."

"Maybe he wants to be more than friends. You're a beautiful woman."

She felt her cheeks heat. "I don't think of him in that way."

"Are you sure *he* knows that?" The teasing glint in Trent's eyes eased some of the tension that had been building in her chest.

Abby grinned up at him. "Positive."

Their gazes held for a long moment before he cleared his throat. "I should get back to the office. Trinity has some paperwork she needs me to go over."

Abby tried not to analyze why the mention of his office manager irked her.

"I should probably call accounting," she said, pushing away the feeling.

He grinned and backed toward the elevator. "I'll see you around."

She waited until Trent had stepped into the elevator and the doors closed before marching into Max's office. They needed to talk.

She didn't bother knocking. He was on the phone. From the sound of it, he was most likely talking to one of his partners back in New York. She leaned against the doorframe and waited.

Max knew she was there. He said goodbye to Eli and hung up the phone before addressing her. "Were you able to reach Phil?"

"I haven't called him yet." She was trying to hold on to her temper. For whatever reason, she couldn't seem to shake her agitation.

"Could you do that, please? I really need—"

Abby stepped farther into the room and closed the door behind her.

He looked up from his work and his brow furrowed. "Is something wrong?"

"Yes." She placed her hands on her hips and took a breath that did nothing to calm her. "You mind telling me what the hell that was all about out there?"

He picked up a paper from his desk, avoiding her gaze. "I don't know what you're referring to."

Abby rolled her eyes. "You know exactly what I'm talking about. Why were you acting like a caveman in front of Trent?"

"I—"

"If you say you don't know what I'm talking about, I swear I'll throw something at your head."

A sly smile tugged at his lips. He leaned back in his chair and folded his hands in front of him on his desk. "Okay, fine. I might have been a little over the top."

"A little?" Her voice rose in pitch.

Max sighed. "I don't want to see you hurt again, Abby. I was there, remember?"

"Trent didn't do anything."

"No, but his brother did."

No matter how many times she'd tried to explain that none of what had happened was Chris' fault, Max had always blamed him. "You know that's not true."

Max shrugged.

She sighed. "Can you please be nice? If I have to work with him I'd prefer not to have to spend half the time trying to explain why you're acting all territorial."

He was quiet for a long moment. "I'll try."

"Thank you."

Abby turned to go. She was halfway to the door when he spoke again. "Be careful, Abby."

She didn't bother looking back.

* * *

Trent made a pit stop at his house to change out of his suit before heading to the office. He made it a point to dress up when meeting with new clients. It made a better impression. Granted, this wasn't his first meeting with Maxwell Collins and given the recommendation he'd received from Mr. and Mrs. Baxter, he didn't think he was in any danger of losing the account. If he was being honest, however, donning a suit for the second time in a week didn't have anything to do with his newest client and had everything to do with Abby. Seeing her again had brought all his old feelings to the surface. He thought he'd moved on—buried the hope of her ever viewing him as more than Chris' little brother—but being near her still did crazy things to his insides.

Trinity was digging something out of a filing cabinet when he walked into the office. She pulled a file out of the metal box and bumped the drawer shut with her hip.

"Holding down the fort?" he asked.

"You know it." She glanced at him, and then went back to reading whatever was in the folder. "How'd it go?"

"He approved the plan. We start on Monday." Trent strolled over to her desk and sat on the edge, facing her. "I need you to double the order of sod and mulch for the next couple of weeks. We're going to be blowing through what we have until we can get these properties up to par."

She nodded, not looking up from her reading. "Who do you want me to reassign?"

"Alan and Craig. They work fast and will make sure things are done right."

She tossed the file on her desk before walking over to the coffeemaker they had set up in the corner. "That's going to push back the Harris job by a day or two."

"I know." Trinity had a bowl of candy on her desk and he helped himself to a peppermint. "I trust you to smooth things over."

"Let's just hope Mrs. Harris is willing to be charmed." She chuckled as she took a seat behind her desk.

He leaned in closer to her and lowered his voice as if he were confessing some big secret. "You could sweet talk the pants off anyone, Trinity. Even little old ladies."

"I know." She sighed dramatically. "You're quite lucky to have me."

"Quite." Trent grinned. He and Trinity had always had an easygoing relationship. It made work, even the parts he detested, less dreadful. "So what is it that you needed me to look over?"

For the next two hours, they went over the inventory reports from the previous month. Something wasn't adding up and Trinity wasn't able to find the problem. They'd gone over it together—twice. He'd even gone out to the sheds and done some recounting of his own. The figures didn't match. Granted, it wasn't by much, but it still bugged him. His guys were required to log what they removed from the sheds in the yard every morning and what they returned with every night. It could be as simple as something getting marked down wrong. They were all usually very good at keeping track since he was a stickler for such things, but no one was perfect.

"I'll talk to the guys when they come in . . . remind them to make sure they take an accurate count of what they take and put back."

Trent nodded. "If you find something, call me. Otherwise, I'll see you on Monday."

"Have a good weekend."

He hopped into his truck and drove into the yard where they kept all their supplies. It took about fifteen minutes to load everything he needed into the back and log it on the inventory sheet. He'd told his dad that he'd help replace a tree in their backyard that hadn't made it. Mike Daniels loved to work in the yard, but he didn't have the best luck when it came to plants.

On his way to his parents' house, Trent decided to take a little detour. Okay, maybe it wasn't so little, but he felt compelled to drive by their old house.

The first thing that struck him when he turned down the street he'd grown up on was that it hadn't changed all that much. One of the houses had new siding and another had put up a fence. Other than that, it was exactly like he remembered.

He pulled along the curb and put his truck in park, leaving the engine running. As he sat there, he could almost see him, Chris, and Abby chasing each other on the front lawn. Gage was sitting close to the porch playing with one of his toys and Paul was working on his bike with their dad.

Trent shifted his attention to the house Abby had lived in with her father. The memory of her racing down the sidewalk to greet her dad when he'd come home from work filled his vision.

His buddy . . . his friend. That's how he'd thought of her until he was fourteen.

It had been a long, boring summer. Abby had gone away to some camp. Chris had gotten his driver's license. And Trent had been left to his own devices for the first time.

He remembered the day she'd returned as if it were yesterday. She'd climbed out of her father's car when she'd seen him and run down the street to greet him.

Trent had known right then that something was different. He'd reacted to her in a way that he hadn't before. She'd changed over the summer and his young male body had taken notice.

But he was young and he hadn't understood what it was exactly that he was feeling. He'd made some excuse that he needed to go help his mom in the house and had left her standing on the front porch looking confused. Trent had felt horrible about how he'd treated her, but he didn't know what to do.

Before he could figure it all out, Chris had made his move. Trent had been heartbroken when he'd heard his older brother had asked her to go to the movies with him—on a date. There was no way he could compete. Chris was sixteen and could drive. Trent was only fourteen. Of course Abby would choose Chris.

As much as it had pained him, Trent had stepped aside and let his older brother get the girl.

A woman peered out her front door to stare at him. It was Mrs. Webley. He smiled and waved, not wanting her to think he was some criminal trying to case the neighborhood or anything.

It took her a second to recognize him, but when she did, his old neighbor grinned back at him.

Trent figured he should probably get out of there before someone who didn't know him called the cops. People weren't as carefree as they used to be about strange vehicles hanging around.

"I thought you'd changed your mind," his dad said when Trent pulled into his parents' driveway about thirty minutes later.

"Got tied up at work." It wasn't exactly a lie.

Mike Daniels nodded and headed into the backyard.

After grabbing his work gloves and a shovel from the bed of his truck, Trent followed his dad around back. They had work to do.

It took them over an hour, but they finally pried the sapling out of the ground. Trent was covered in sweat and dirt, surrounded by nature. It felt great.

"Going to tell me what's on your mind?" his dad asked.

Trent wiped the moisture from his brow and jammed the head of his shovel in the ground beside him. "I was thinking I could bring a silver maple over tomorrow. Since the hole is already here, it shouldn't take us too long."

"That sounds fine. But that wasn't what I was talking about." His dad snagged a lawn chair and sat down. He folded his arms over his stomach and raised his eyebrows.

Why was it that at thirty-one years old his dad could still make him feel like he was five, getting in trouble for fighting with his brothers?

Trent decided it was better to get it over with. Drawing it out would only make his dad think there was more to it than there was. "I ran into Abby this week."

"Abby Hoffman?"

He nodded. "Her boss is the nephew of one of my biggest clients and my company was recommended to do some work for them."

His dad pursed his lips. "Been a while since she's been home."

Trent didn't comment.

"You know . . . your mom and I went to her dad's funeral. She was there. Haven't seen her since."

He remembered that day. If he hadn't had a final, he would have been there as well.

"She's a personal assistant to a lawyer named Maxwell Collins."

His dad smiled. "Abby always was a smart girl."

Trent turned and began gathering up the debris scattered around the area where they'd been working. "Yep."

After a few minutes, his dad pushed himself out of the chair and helped Trent carry the dead tree to his truck. While they could have cut it up and left it on the curb, it was easier for Trent to dispose of it. He could run it through the wood chipper in a matter of minutes.

With the tree secured in the bed of his truck, they went inside for some much needed refreshment. He could smell his mother's cooking as soon as he stepped through the door. It always put a smile on his face.

Marilyn Daniels was at the stove putting the finishing touches on dinner when they walked in. "Go clean yourselves up. Dinner will be ready in a few minutes."

His dad ducked into the small bathroom down the hall, so Trent headed upstairs.

When he reentered the kitchen his mother was taking something out of the oven. Trent took a deep breath and recognized the distinct smell of his mom's eggplant parmesan. "Smells good, Ma."

She didn't miss a beat. "There's water and lemonade in the refrigerator. Help yourselves."

Trent opened the cabinet and removed two glasses. He filled them both with ice and water, and then handed one to his dad before downing his and refilling it.

His mother smiled. "Did you get everything done?"

Mike sidled up to his wife and kissed her cheek. Trent averted his eyes. Even after all these years, his parents were still very affectionate. It never mattered if their children were around or not.

"We did," his dad said as he took the large pot of spaghetti his wife handed him. "Trent's going to bring a replacement tree over tomorrow."

Marilyn brought a plate full of eggplant to the table and his dad followed with the pasta. Trent grabbed the warm bread his mom had removed from the oven moments before and took his seat. Even though all her children had left the nest many years ago, his mom still cooked as if she had four hungry boys to feed. Considering he'd skipped lunch, Trent's mouth was watering with anticipation.

He managed to get a few bites in before his father brought up the one subject he didn't want to talk about. "Trent ran into Abby."

His mother set her fork down on her plate and straightened her shoulders. "Really? Where? We haven't seen her in ages. How is she?"

Trent opened his mouth to speak, but his father cut him off. "He's doing some work for her boss."

"Does that mean you're going to see her again?" his mom asked, her eyes full of hope. He knew she missed Abby. With all boys, having Abby around had given his mom the opportunity to share girlie things with another female.

"Probably. It's a big project." Considering she was his point of contact, he'd most likely be talking to her on a weekly basis. He wasn't sure he wanted to share that with his parents, though. For whatever reason, Trent got the feeling Abby wasn't thrilled she had to deal with him at all.

The look on his mom's face should have prepared him. He should have known what was coming. Should've, but didn't.

"Oh, Trent, you have to invite her to Sunday dinner."

CHAPTER 4

ABBY SPENT the weekend cleaning and unpacking the rest of her things. With the exception of her furniture, she'd brought almost everything else with her to Ohio. Max wouldn't leave until he was satisfied things were as they should be, so she was expecting to be here for at least three months. If she was going to be here for that long, she wanted to be comfortable.

Earlier in the week, she'd gone to the store and bought some cheap bookshelves. They weren't anything like the ones she had at her apartment in New York, but they would keep her books and craft supplies organized. It was better than digging through boxes every time she needed something.

As she sorted through her craft supplies, Abby admired her collection of beads. One of the other admins in the New York office got her hooked on making bracelets and necklaces. Something about threading each individual bead relaxed her.

Sighing, she put the plastic bin containing her supplies on the shelf. So far, since she'd been in Ohio, she hadn't had time to work on any of her projects. Hopefully, once they got through the initial craziness, she'd be able to get back to them.

The next box took her longer. It was a mixture of things, including some outfits she hadn't worn in a while. Abby sorted through the clothes, putting the ones that would need ironing in a separate pile and hanging up the rest.

She reached into the box for the next item and her fingers brushed against something that wasn't clothes. Nudging an old shirt out of the way, Abby removed the green shoebox. Her fingers traced over the edges as if it would impart some great wisdom if she could only find the correct rhythm.

Moisture filled her eyes, clouding her vision. She wiped the tears from her lashes and stood to put the box in her closet. The memories seemed closer to the surface today than they had in a long time and she knew why. Being back here in Ohio—being back home around the people who'd once meant so much to her—was making it feel fresh again.

Before she could begin crying in earnest, Abby grabbed the book she'd started reading a few days before and headed into the living room. The rest of the boxes could wait. She needed a break from reality for a while.

By Monday morning, Abby was feeling more like herself again. She walked into the office ready to tackle whatever challenge might come her way, her armor securely in place.

In New York her job was to answer the phone, schedule appointments for Max, and make sure he kept to his schedule. Here she found herself organizing invoices, dealing with frustrated employees, and trying to be there for Max as best she could without having much of a clue as to what she was doing.

Her thoughts were interrupted by her cell phone ringing. It was Max. "Hello?"

"Where are you?"

"Getting into the elevator. What do you need?"

"There's some sort of emergency over in Wedgewood and I'm stuck at the hospital with my parents." He sounded frustrated. Max was a bit of a control freak. He didn't like there to be problems he couldn't fix.

She stopped the elevator doors from closing and stepped out. "What do you need me to do?"

"Just fix it. I trust your judgment. I didn't even get the whole story from the property manager, but something about water going everywhere. I don't know."

"Okay, okay. Just take a deep breath. I'm on it."

Max exhaled loudly. "Thanks, Abby. I really don't know what I'd do without you."

"Oh, you'd just find another woman to order around." She hoped her response would break some of his tension.

It worked. She heard a deep rumble of laughter through the phone.

"Why don't you take the day off and spend time with your folks?" she said as she made her way back to her car. "I can handle things here."

"That's okay. I—"

"That wasn't a suggestion, mister."

"I should fire you," he said with absolutely no malice.

"You couldn't do this without me."

"True."

"Go take care of your parents. I've got this." Even as she said it, she was sliding behind the wheel of her car.

He relented. "I'll call you later."

After disconnecting the call with Max, Abby scrolled through her contacts until she found the receptionist's number. "Collins and Baxter Property Management. How may I direct your call?"

"Janice, it's Abby, Mr. Collins' assistant." They were all still getting to know each other, so she wasn't sure the woman would know who she was if she'd only said Abby.

"Oh, hi, Abby. What can I do for you?" Janice asked.

"Mr. Collins is going to be out of the office today and I need to head out to take care of a situation at one of the properties."

"You need me to handle the phones?"

Abby smiled even though Janice couldn't see her. "You read my mind."

"No problem. I'll take messages and have one of the mail clerks run them up to your desk later."

"Thanks."

"Anytime."

With the phones taken care of, Abby drove to Wedgewood. She had no idea what she'd find once she got there. When she'd been introduced to the manager a little over a week ago, she hadn't been impressed. Max hadn't been either, but he was trying to give everyone the benefit of the doubt, no matter how incompetent they seemed. The last thing he wanted to do was fire everyone and start from scratch.

When Abby pulled up to the front of the office building, she couldn't miss the fountains of water spraying in all different directions. She had no idea what was going on.

Stepping out of her car, she spotted the manager. "Marty, what's going on?"

"I don't know. The sprinklers turned on this morning and they just started going everywhere."

She willed herself not to roll her eyes. The man's clothes weren't even wet. Had he even attempted to shut off the water? "Did you try turning them off?"

"The only water shutoff I can find is the main one. There are at least a hundred people in this building. I can't just turn off all the water." He looked at her as if she'd lost every brain cell in her head.

"There isn't a separate shutoff for the outside sprinklers?" Trent's comment about things being worse than he'd thought ran through her head. Was this another thing the previous landscapers hadn't done correctly?

"If there is, then I haven't found it." He acted irritated that he'd had to repeat himself.

"Show me."

"Show you what?" he asked.

She gritted her teeth and plastered a smile on her face. "I'd like to see the controls for the sprinkler system. I need to know what we're dealing with."

He huffed. "Fine. But it ain't gonna do no good."

Somehow, Abby managed to follow him through the maze of sprinklers without getting soaked. She thought they'd be going to the basement, but Marty led her to the side of the building. There was a control panel hidden behind a row of bushes. She could see it, but they weren't able to get close without getting caught by the spray.

"See. I told you," he said with pride. "No shutoff."

"And you're sure there's nothing inside?"

"Do I look like this is my first day on the job?"

Abby wanted to give this man an earful, but she bit her tongue. Yelling at him wouldn't solve the problem and for now she needed him. Marty knew the building better than she did.

She took in the situation around her and knew what she had to do.

She dug out her cell and scrolled until she found Trent's number. Abby hesitated for a moment before dialing. He'd crossed her mind more than once over the weekend, for reasons that were completely unrelated to work.

"Daniels Landscape Design."

"Hi, Trent. It's Abby."

His tone changed to one of familiarity. "Abby. What can I do for you on this lovely morning?"

She tried not to think about her body's reaction to the change in his voice. "I'm having a bit of a crisis over at Wedgewood that I'm hoping you can help me out with." Marty lingered close by, but she ignored him. "There's something wrong with the sprinkler system and we can't seem to shut it off without interrupting the water to the building."

There was the sound of a door opening and then closing. "Are you there now?"

"Yes."

"I'm not far away. I'll be there in five." The phone went silent.

Abby closed her eyes and gripped her phone a little tighter as her heart rate picked up. Five minutes.

Taking a steadying breath, she tucked her phone back into her pocket and turned to face Marty. "Someone from the new landscaping company will be here in a few minutes. Hopefully he'll be able to come up with a solution."

Marty shrugged, but otherwise didn't comment.

Abby decided to try a different tactic. "Do you happen to have some coffee around here? I ran out of the office before I was able to get my morning fix."

"Sure. Follow me."

They retraced their steps through the maze of water to the front of the building. Instead of heading inside, he turned toward his van. Marty opened the door and reached inside. He reemerged with a thermos in one hand and a Styrofoam cup in the other. He held them both out for her to take.

She hesitated before taking the offering. "Thanks."

"You're welcome," he said, seeming overly pleased with himself. "I'm going to run inside and check on some things. You gonna be okay for a few minutes?"

Abby resisted the urge to roll her eyes. "Sure. You go ahead."

He walked away and she was grateful for the few minutes alone. She was anxious about seeing Trent again and she needed to get her head on straight. There was no reason why she couldn't work with him. Not really.

If she was being honest with herself, she'd missed him. Leaving Trent behind had been one of the hardest parts about moving to New York. She'd sent him a few letters the first two years . . . up until she went to Fort Lauderdale for spring break. After that, she hadn't been able to write to him anymore. She'd been too afraid of what she might say, or of what Chris might have told him. It had been easier to close the door on that part of her life.

The thermos remained in her hand, untouched, as did the cup. What would he think of her if he knew the truth? What would they all think of her?

Her thoughts were cut short when she saw Trent's pickup truck pull into the parking lot. He was here and she had a job to do.

* * *

Trent had been surprised to hear from Abby so soon. He'd planned to check in with her at the end of the week, but he hadn't considered the possibility that she'd reach out to him first.

As soon as he turned into the parking lot at Wedgewood, he understood why she'd called him. There were at least ten sprinklers set up at strategic locations around the building. All of them were on and looked like they'd been that way for a while. There were puddles of water pooling near the sidewalks.

He parked his truck next to Abby's vehicle and hopped out. She was about twenty feet away, leaning against a white van. Her hair was pulled back in some sort of twist. He had the urge to remove the clip and run his fingers through it.

Trent was so focused on her, he almost missed the man who was striding toward her. He chuckled to himself. No woman had ever been able to distract him like Abby had. Maybe that was why he'd never settled down and gotten married. No one had ever called to him like she had.

She glanced in his direction and smiled. There was a nervous edge to it. "Hi."

"Hi." He kept his eyes on her and ignored the other man. Something was bothering her and he didn't like not knowing what it was.

Abby straightened her shoulders. "Thank you for coming so fast."

"Not a problem." No, coming to her rescue wasn't a problem for Trent.

She swallowed hard and motioned to the building. "As you can see, we're having a bit of a problem with the sprinklers."

Trent glanced over his shoulder at the fountains of water, looking for a control panel. "Where's the shutoff?"

That was when the man he didn't know spoke up. "There isn't one. Not that I can find, anyway. The only shutoff is the main one inside and we can't leave the whole building without water."

Who installed a sprinkler system without a shutoff?

"Trent, this is Marty, the property manager," Abby said, gesturing to the grumpy-looking man to her left.

"Is there a control panel at least?" Trent directed his question to Marty.

"Yeah." Marty frowned and started walking around the side of the building.

Trent turned to Abby before following the guy. "I'll be back."

He was able to dodge the streams of water until they got close to the control panel. There was no way to tell for sure what he was dealing with unless he got a closer look. That meant he was going to have to get wet.

The cold water felt like little knives poking at his skin. It was a good thing it was the middle of summer.

By the time he crawled behind the bush where the control panel was, he was pretty much drenched. Trent tried to ignore the water pelting him from behind as he searched for a shutoff. The setup was fairly basic. He pressed and held what should have been the reset button, but nothing happened.

"There's not a valve on the other side of this wall that can be closed?" Trent asked.

"If there is, then it's behind drywall."

Trent got up and ran out of the line of fire. He raked a hand through his hair to get some of the water off him. "There's a finished wall on the other side of this?"

"Yep. Bathroom."

Shaking his head, Trent headed back toward Abby. When he'd been out to take a look at the property the week before, he'd made a note to upgrade the control panel for the sprinkler system. He had no idea why it was outside to begin with.

Abby's eyes widened as he neared her. He knew he was probably a mess. Not only was he wet, he'd been crawling around in mulch behind bushes. His khakis were covered in mud.

Luckily, he always kept a towel in his truck. This wasn't the first time he'd gotten an unexpected shower on the job.

He dried off the best he could, and then walked over to where Abby was standing in front of her vehicle. She still had that wide-eyed look and he wondered what was going through her mind. If they'd been alone, he would have asked her.

Trent cleared his throat.

Abby met his gaze and blushed. It made him even more curious as to the direction of her thoughts.

"So what do you think?" Marty asked. "Can you fix it?"

Trent turned away from Abby. There would be time to find out what had caused that blush later. "It will take some doing, but yeah, I can fix it. Unfortunately, we're going to have to turn off the water inside the building. I'll try to keep it to under an hour, but I can't guarantee that."

Marty shook his head. "They ain't going to be happy."

The man was beginning to get on Trent's nerves. "There's no way to redo the system with the water free flowing like it is now."

The other man nodded reluctantly.

"When can you get it done?" Abby asked, breaking her silence.

Trent noticed that the blush had faded. He had to admit he was a little disappointed. Still, he was there to do a job, not flirt with Abby. "I'll need to head back to the office and pick up some supplies. Shouldn't take me more than an hour to get everything together and get back here." Then he looked to Marty. "Think you can spread the word inside the building that they're going to be without water in about an hour or so?"

"I'll take care of it," Abby said a little too quickly. It made him wonder what was going through that head of hers. "Trent, you need to get out of those wet clothes, and Marty, you should probably change into something you don't mind getting dirty, in case Trent needs your assistance."

Marty didn't look all that happy that Abby had volunteered him. Trent doubted he'd need the other man's help, but considering he would be on his own with this one, he wasn't going to turn down the extra pair of hands.

"Sounds like a plan to me," Trent said as he gave the back of his neck another swipe with the towel.

Abby headed into the building, careful to avoid the sprinklers that were positioned to cover the walkway. It reminded Trent a little of playing hopscotch.

Marty didn't wait for Abby to get inside the building before he got into his van and drove away. Trent shook his head. He wasn't sure if Marty was in a bad mood because of the sprinklers or if that was his normal demeanor. Either way, his short responses to Abby weren't likely to gain him any points with his new boss.

Not wanting to follow that train of thought, Trent drove to his house to change and get another set of clean clothes. Chances were good that he'd get this set wet or muddy, or both, before the day was over. He still couldn't figure out why someone would install a sprinkler system without an emergency shutoff. It made no sense.

He threw the extra set of clothes in the cab of his truck and slid behind the wheel. As he backed out of his driveway and headed to the office, his thoughts returned to Abby. Was it too much to hope that her blush had been triggered by seeing him standing there with his clothes plastered to his body from the water?

Trent knew a good deal of women found him attractive. He'd used it to his advantage more than once and he wasn't ashamed of it. But with Abby it was different. It always was.

He'd sat on the sidelines back when they were teenagers. Chris had asked her to be his girlfriend and she'd said yes. As much as he hated it, he'd respected her choice and settled for being her friend. Trent wasn't willing to do that this time. Not when there was a chance she felt something for him.

His phone rang as he pulled up in front of his office. Figuring it was Trinity checking in with him, Trent let it go to voice mail. Before he could turn the engine off, his cell was ringing again. He unbuckled his seat belt and removed his phone from his pocket.

Gage's name was on the caller ID. He hit accept and held the phone up to his ear. "Hey, little brother, what's up?"

"Rebecca went into labor last night. I'm a dad."

Trent could hear the pure joy in Gage's voice. "That's great! Congratulations."

"We named her Madison Elaine." The pride in his brother's voice resonated through the phone.

Trent was happy for Gage. He'd come a long way since Rebecca steamrolled into his life, which made it that much more fun to poke at him. "Your wife won that one, huh?"

"You know, I can be in Cincinnati in less than four hours."

Trent chuckled as he imagined the look on his brother's face. "I think I'm safe."

"For now."

Trent shifted the phone so it rested between his ear and his shoulder, leaving his hands free to grab the paperwork he had piled on the other side of the truck. "How is Rebecca doing?"

"Good, but exhausted. She was in labor for about sixteen hours." Gage paused. "I had no idea it would be like that."

"Did something happen with Rebecca? The baby?" Trent asked, concerned.

"No. Nothing like that." Gage paused. "Madison showed up a couple weeks early, but she's healthy. That's what's important. I've just . . . I've never felt so helpless in my life. Rebecca was in so much pain and there wasn't anything I could do."

"Can't say I know what that's like," Trent said as he leaned against his truck.

"You will one of these days."

Trent's thoughts immediately turned to Abby, but he shook them off. "That would require me to have a lady in my life. Which I don't."

"Things happen. Sometimes love knocks you on your ass when you least expect it."

He was quiet for a long moment before he responded to his brother. "Maybe."

CHAPTER 5

It felt like hours had passed since Trent left to go get whatever he needed to repair the sprinkler system. She'd let the building's occupants know what was going on so they could prepare, and then returned to her car to wait. It would have been easy to go back to the office and leave Marty and Trent to handle everything. She could call Marty later and get a rundown of all they'd done. It would be easy.

The problem was she didn't really want to leave. Being around Trent brought with it a lot of mixed emotions. At one point in her life, he'd been her safe place to fall. She still felt that, but there was other stuff in there as well, including how she'd reacted to seeing his wet clothes plastered to his body. It was confusing and frustrating—and that didn't even factor in the complicated history she had with his brother.

Abby closed her eyes. Nothing could change the past. Her life hadn't turned out the way she'd planned, but that was all right. She'd come to terms with it.

A knock on her car window made her jump.

She opened her eyes to find Trent smiling at her. His eyes sparkled with mischief and Abby felt a tiny fluttering in the pit of her stomach.

After opening the door, she stepped out of the vehicle and plastered a smile on her face.

The sparkle in his eyes dimmed as he looked her over. "What's wrong?"

"Not a thing."

"Abby, I know you well enough to know that's not true."

"You haven't known me for twelve years. You know nothing about me anymore," she snapped.

Trent was quiet for a long moment. He seemed to be weighing his options. "Fair enough. But that doesn't mean I can't tell that something's bothering you. I was always your friend, Abby. I'd like to be again."

"That's not all you want." She had no idea why she was reacting this way. His concern appeared to be genuine. Why was she getting so irritated?

Again, he took his time answering and when he did his voice was lower and softer. "You're right. It's not."

The air around them seemed to change. She had the urge to run away, but for whatever reason her feet didn't want to move.

Abby took a deep breath and tried to push all the conflicting emotions away. Trent had done nothing to deserve her wrath. "I'm sorry. I shouldn't have snapped at you."

He shrugged and gave her that signature grin of his. "I can take it."

She breathed a sigh of relief and smiled back at him. "Still, I'm sorry."

"Apology accepted."

He held her gaze until she felt that fluttering start up again, then turned his attention to something behind her. "I need to see about getting this sprinkler problem fixed. Are you sticking around?"

When he looked at her again, the light in his eyes was back.

"Yeah. I told Max I'd report back to him when it was fixed."

Abby followed Trent up the walkway and they made their way into the building. Marty stood there waiting for them. He'd changed into jeans and a T-shirt that said Collins & Baxter Properties on it, and he looked as if he'd rather be anywhere but where he was.

For the next hour, Abby stood off to the side while the two men tore apart the old system and replaced it with the one Trent had brought with him. This new one looked a lot more complicated than the original, but it did have a shutoff valve and it was in the boiler room where the rest of the mechanics were located.

"Thanks for your help," Trent said to Marty as they walked out of the building toward the parking lot.

Marty released a grunt of assent before heading to his van.

She and Trent watched as Marty drove off.

"Interesting fellow," Trent said.

"Yeah. Interesting."

Trent loaded some tools he'd brought with him into the back of his truck. "I'm starving. You want to join me for lunch?"

Abby hesitated. "I don't know. I should probably get back to the office."

He took a step forward. There was still at least two feet between them, but she suddenly felt crowded. "I think they can manage for another hour or two without you."

It was a warm day, but it felt as if the temperature had gone up about ten degrees in the last few minutes. "This isn't a good idea."

"What isn't? Going to lunch? We both have to eat." The look on his face was pure innocence but his eyes told a different story. He was flirting with her and that wasn't good. She couldn't go there.

"You know that's not what I mean."

Trent took another step forward. He was close enough that she could reach out and touch him if she wanted.

"You don't think it's a good idea for us to spend time together?" That soft seductive voice was back.

Abby shook her head. She needed to stay strong.

"I disagree." He tucked a strand of hair behind her ear. "I think us spending time together is an excellent idea."

She grabbed on to the only thing she could think of at the moment —the only thing she thought might put some much needed distance between them. "What about Chris? I don't want to cause problems between you and your brother."

"Chris is happily married. Why would he care if we spent time together?" The tips of his fingers trailed along her neck. "We were friends once."

Abby released a shuddering breath. "Trent."

"It's just lunch." His voice was like a caress against her skin.

He made it sound so simple.

She opened her mouth, ready to give some excuse as to why she couldn't go, but instead she heard herself say, "All right."

Trent's answering smile had Abby's pulse racing. What was he doing? What was she doing?

He dropped his hand and went to open the passenger side door of his truck for her.

"Shall we?"

Abby nodded and climbed inside.

In the time it took him to walk around his vehicle and get behind the wheel, her sanity began to return. This wasn't a good idea. The look in Trent's eyes when he'd touched her wasn't one of innocent friendship. It was full of heat and promise. She couldn't go there with him.

But even as Abby was sitting there counting the reasons why going to lunch with him would be a bad idea, she made no move to get out of the truck. Maybe this was part of her punishment. Maybe Trent coming back into her life and turning his charm on her was the universe telling her she hadn't suffered enough all those years ago.

She snuck a peek at Trent as he drove. He had been cute as a teenager, but as a man, he'd grown into his long limbs and broad shoulders. She had no doubt that Trent Daniels had to chase the females away.

"How long have you owned your own business?" That's something an old friend would ask.

Trent glanced over at her before returning his attention to the road. "About eight years."

He was only thirty-one. That would mean he had to have been twenty-two or twenty-three. "Not many people would open a business like that right out of college."

"I did an internship with a landscape designer my senior year, and then I spent a year working as a landscaper. I wanted to get a feel for everything before I ventured out on my own. I knew I wanted to do more than just design the spaces and then subcontract everything out." He talked like it wasn't a big deal, but she knew it was.

"You seem to have done very well for yourself. Lillian Baxter doesn't recommend just anyone."

"Thanks. I've worked hard to get where I am. Ma and Dad always told us to go after what we wanted in life, so that's what I did. It paid off." He smiled at her and she felt her stomach flip-flop again. So much for keeping it friendly.

She looked out the window, trying to regain her equilibrium.

Trent cleared his throat as he pulled into the parking lot of a restaurant that had a big rooster on its sign. "Speaking of my parents . . . Ma wanted me to invite you to Sunday dinner."

All notion of being hungry disappeared. "Come to dinner?"

He found a parking spot and maneuvered the truck into it. "They would love to see you."

Abby twisted her hands in her lap, unsure of what to say. If she refused, it would most likely hurt Marilyn's feelings. That was the last thing she wanted. Abby could never repay Mr. and Mrs. Daniels for all they'd done for her growing up.

But how could she say yes? How could she face them knowing what she'd done?

* * *

Trent walked behind Abby as they made their way inside the restaurant. They were shown to a table along the wall and he took a seat across from her. She hadn't uttered a word since he'd extended the invitation to join his family for dinner. Given her comment about Chris earlier, Trent wondered if she was nervous about seeing him again. No one in the family really knew why the two had broken up.

"You gonna tell me what's wrong?"

Before she could answer him, they were interrupted by their

server. Once they'd placed their order, he waited for her to answer his question but she didn't.

"Abby?"

She took a sip of her water and looked anywhere but at him. "I don't know if it's such a good idea for me to come to dinner with your family."

"Why wouldn't it be a good idea? My family loves you. They always have." It was true. When she'd stopped writing him, it had stung. She might not have been born into their family, but she was still part of it. She always would be.

"I know." Abby picked up her napkin and began folding over the corners. She still wouldn't meet his gaze.

"I don't understand. Is it Chris? Are you worried about seeing him again?" He wasn't sure how he would feel if her answer was yes. If she cared that much about Chris' feelings then maybe she wasn't completely over him.

"It's complicated."

"I'm listening." He winked, hoping to put her at ease. His stomach was in knots waiting to see what she'd say, but he didn't want her to know that.

She continued to play with her napkin for several minutes. He was beginning to think she wasn't going to answer, but then she looked up at him through her lashes. "Chris and I . . . we sort of left things unfinished, I guess you could say. I don't know how he'd feel about me showing up unannounced like that."

"What do you mean by *unfinished*?"

"Trent I don't—"

Their server walked up to the table with a plate of wings and placed it in front of them. "Can I get you anything else right now?"

"I think we're good." The last thing Trent wanted was for Abby to find some reason not to continue. He needed to know what this unfinished business was with his brother. Trent needed to know if he had any type of a chance with her.

Alone once more, Trent picked up a wing and motioned for her to do the same. She grabbed one and twirled it between her fingers before taking a bite.

"I'm sorry if I'm being pushy. I don't mean to be."

"It's okay." She looked sad and he didn't want that.

He wiped the sauce from his fingers and reached across the table to place his hand over hers. "You've known me for a long time."

She nodded, but the melancholy look didn't leave her features. He needed to chase it away.

"You know when I want something, I tend to go after it. Even if it's not the smartest thing to do."

The side of Abby's mouth tipped up a little. "Like that frog."

Trent chuckled. It had been years since he'd thought about that. They'd been about ten. He'd caught sight of a huge frog and decided he had to catch it and bring it home. It had taken him over two hours and he'd ended up covered in mud up to his waist, but he'd done it. "Exactly like that."

A full smile bloomed on her face. He loved seeing her happy. He always had.

"I need to tell you something." It was time to put his cards on the table.

She swallowed. "Okay."

"Back in high school, I had a huge crush on you."

She glanced down, a blush staining her cheeks.

"I didn't act on it back then because . . . well, because I was young and stupid. And then Chris made his move and you seemed happy with him, so I stepped aside."

"Very noble of you," she mumbled so low he almost didn't hear her.

He ignored it and continued on. "If you tell me you still have feelings for my brother or someone else, I'll back off, but I still feel that same pull toward you now that I did back then. The difference is that I'm not a confused kid anymore."

There was no way she could mistake his meaning. He turned her hand over and began tracing circles on the inside of her wrist.

Abby stared back at him for what felt like forever. "I don't still have feelings for Chris. I haven't for a long time."

A feeling of relief washed over Trent. "Good."

She pulled her hand back. He could have forced the issue, but decided to let her go.

"Am I coming on too strong?" he asked.

Abby shook her head. "It's not that."

"Then why did you pull away? Do you not see me in that way? Am I still like a little brother in your eyes?"

"I never saw you like that," she said. "Not really. You were my best friend in high school."

He grinned and went back to eating his lunch. It was progress and he'd take it. While he still wanted to know what had happened between her and Chris, he was willing to let it go for now.

"I still don't know if you and I getting involved is a good idea."

He stopped mid bite. "Why?"

"What happens when I move back to New York?" she asked.

"Is that happening soon?" Given what he knew, Trent didn't think it was.

Abby took a drink before answering. "No. I think we're going to be here a while. Max isn't going to want to leave as long as his family needs him."

"So why are you worrying about something that could be in the distant future?"

She ate in silence for several minutes. "I've always been a planner. You know that. It's just how I am."

"Let's make a deal, all right? No worrying about what the future may hold. No worrying about my brother or even my family. All I want is to spend time with you—get to know the woman you are today."

Abby raised a single eyebrow.

"You doubt me?"

Trent made sure to inject enough astonished disbelief into his voice that Abby laughed.

"You don't give up, do you?"

"Nope. So you should just give in now and agree." He flashed her a smile that in the past had served him well when it came to the opposite sex.

"I'm not sure what I'm agreeing to."

"To spending time with me, of course."

He waggled his eyebrows back and forth, making her giggle.

"Fine. We can spend some time together."

"Outside of work," he clarified.

Abby rolled her eyes. "Okay. We can spend time outside of work, if that will make you happy."

"It will. It does."

With that settled, they went back to eating their lunch. It was comfortable and he enjoyed the simplicity of it.

It wasn't until their server had cleared their plates that Trent brought up dinner at his parents' again. "What about Sunday dinner? Will you come with me?"

"Come with you, or *with you?*"

He shrugged as if the distinction didn't matter. As far as he was concerned, it didn't. He just wanted her there.

She leveled a pointed stare in his direction. "That doesn't answer the question."

Trent slid out of the booth and offered her his hand. She took it but he didn't miss the look she gave him either.

Taking Abby home as his date would be a clear message to his family, including Chris, that he was serious about her. Then again, it would also get his parents' hopes up. At one point in time, they were sure Abby would be an official member of the family. "Why don't we play it by ear? I mean we haven't even gone on a first date yet."

"A date?" She looked nervous again.

Trent placed a hand on her lower back as they walked out into the parking lot. "Did you miss that whole conversation we had back at the restaurant? I want us to spend time together."

"Yes, but I didn't realize you meant you wanted us to go out on a date."

He opened the passenger door and waited for her to get inside. "What did you think I meant?"

"I don't know." She looked a bit lost.

Trent reached for her hand again and brought it up to his lips. He waited until she met his gaze. She seemed so unsure of herself, which wasn't like the Abby he used to know. "Go out with me on Friday night. Let me show you a good time?"

"What if it doesn't go well?" she asked.

"Are you questioning my ability to show you a good time?"

She grinned. "No."

"So is that a yes?" he asked as he rubbed his thumb along the inside of her wrist. Trent knew he was playing dirty, but he'd waited so long for his chance with her.

Abby closed her eyes and nodded.

His day might not have started under the best of circumstances, but his week was definitely looking up.

CHAPTER 6

ABBY HAD no idea what she'd been thinking, agreeing to go on a date with Trent. The two of them getting close again wasn't a good idea. Yet she hadn't been able to say no. That, apparently, hadn't changed either. Even as kids, he'd been able to talk her into doing things she wouldn't normally do.

She'd picked up her phone at least a dozen times since he'd dropped her off at her car on Monday, ready to tell him she'd changed her mind. But every time she started to dial the number, something would stop her. She had to be a glutton for punishment.

So instead of calling him like she knew she should, Abby did her best to ignore the pending date on her calendar. She went about her day, taking care of things for Max and trying to get through the boxes of paperwork that never seemed to end.

Her efforts at avoidance were going well until Thursday morning rolled around. She pulled up to the office, parked her car, and began walking toward the building. A man was shoveling mulch into a wheelbarrow not far from the walkway. She didn't think much of it until he turned to the side and she got a glimpse of his face. It was Trent.

Abby thought maybe she'd be able to sneak by without him seeing her, but luck wasn't on her side. He looked up right as she passed. Their gazes met and she seemed unable to move. His hair was in complete disarray from the work he was doing and his shirt was already clinging to his body from the heat of the day. It was one of the sexiest sights she'd ever seen.

A slow smile lit up his face. He knew she was checking him out.

Before she could do something to embarrass herself, Abby forced herself to look away and raced inside. Her face heated as she hurried toward the elevators. She could only imagine what was going through his head after she'd stood there ogling him.

It was useless to try and deny that she was attracted to him. On some level, she'd always been. When they were younger, they'd had a special connection. If she was honest with herself, Abby knew that if Trent had asked her out back when they were teenagers, she would have said yes.

But as he'd pointed out, he wasn't a kid anymore and the feelings he was evoking within her were anything but childlike.

Like the coward she was, Abby had lunch delivered in case Trent was still working out front. She sat in Max's office, catching up on what was happening with his dad. Hearing that the doctors were suggesting the family talk to a hospice helped to cool her libido. Max might live six hundred miles away from his parents, but they were still close. It was one of the reasons it had hurt Max so much to find out about his dad's illness. Now he had to face the reality that his father would most likely die in the not-too-distant future.

What Max was dealing with made her problems seem small and insignificant. She almost felt guilty for fretting so much about Trent and his family when Max had so much on his plate.

On her drive home that night, Abby decided to take a detour. With all the talk of family, she was missing her dad. He'd been gone for over ten years, but there were times when she could still feel him with her.

Abby turned down the familiar street and followed it for several miles until she saw the blue and black sign of the shooting range her father used to take her to. She found a parking spot and went inside. The place felt familiar, even after all this time.

She walked up to the counter, already scanning the guns in the case. Since she lived in New York City, she didn't own a firearm anymore. Gun laws there were beyond strict and she'd had no desire to jump through all the hoops one had to go through in order to purchase a firearm, so she'd have to rent one.

"How can I help you?" the man behind the counter asked.

"I'd like to rent a 9mm and some range time."

"Sure." He reached behind him, and then placed a form in front of her. "Fill this out, and I'll need a valid driver's license. You said a 9mm?"

"Yes, please." It used to be her favorite to shoot.

The man nodded and left her to complete the paperwork.

Twenty minutes later, Abby was standing in front of a paper target. The gun felt good in her hands as she clicked the magazine in place and racked the slide. She took aim and fired the first shot, then another. As the bullets hit the target, Abby felt some of the tension leave her body. This was exactly what she'd needed.

Abby went home that evening feeling a lot more relaxed. Unfortunately, when she woke up the next morning all her anxiety had returned. It was Friday, which meant her date with Trent was only hours away.

When she arrived at work that morning, she did her best to keep busy. Max was working on something with accounting, so at least she didn't have to explain to him why she was so jittery.

She was shutting down her computer at the end of the day when Max called her into his office. Abby grabbed her notebook in case he needed her to write something down, and made her way into his office.

Max motioned for her to take a seat. "I wanted to talk to you."

"I gathered that." She smirked as she lowered herself into the chair. Max intimidated a lot of people, but she knew him too well. He was a teddy bear under that tough exterior.

He grinned. "We've been so busy this week, I feel like we haven't talked about anything except for work and my family."

"Both of which are important."

"Yes, but I dragged you halfway across the country. Away from your life. And I've pretty much abandoned you."

"I'm a big girl, Max. I don't need a babysitter."

"I know. I didn't mean to suggest that." He ran a hand through his hair in apparent frustration. "I just wanted to know how you're adjusting. Are you getting settled into your apartment? Do you need anything?"

"I'm fine. Really. You have enough to worry about."

He swallowed and she knew something was coming. "What about Daniels? I know you spent a lot of time with him on Monday. And I saw him working out front yesterday."

The last thing Abby wanted to do was talk to Max about Trent.

Max sighed, pushed back from his desk, and stood. "We haven't spent any time together outside of work since we've been here. What do you say we go grab a pizza and talk about anything other than work?"

"I can't. I have plans."

"What kind of plans?" he demanded.

Abby stood and shot him a look.

When he realized what he'd done, he tucked his head down sheepishly. "Sorry. I didn't mean it to sound like that."

She knew he'd been under a lot of stress lately. "It's okay. I forgive you."

Abby moved toward the door, and Max followed. He placed his hand on her arm before she could step out into the hallway. "Promise me you'll be careful with Trent Daniels, okay?"

Shock crossed her face. "How did y—"

"If you had plans with anyone else, you would have told me." His tone was one of resignation.

Max's parting comment stayed with her on her drive home. He was right. If it had been anyone but Trent, she would have told him. Max was her best friend. She told him everything.

The problem was Max knew what had happened with Chris. He knew how much it had messed her up and he was afraid she'd get hurt again even though what had happened wasn't Chris' fault. That didn't seem to matter to Max and he was transferring his irritation onto Trent. Abby understood. She was as nervous about whatever was going on with Trent as Max was. But making Trent pay for something he had no part in wasn't fair either.

After parking her car in front of her apartment, she pressed her hand to her stomach. It was flat now. The baby that had been inside still haunted her dreams when she least expected it.

She took a cleansing breath and made her way inside. Dwelling on the past wouldn't do her any good—especially tonight. She had to get ready for her date.

Two hours later, there was a knock on her door. Abby crossed her small living room and went to answer it. She placed her hand on the knob and steadied herself. *You can do this.*

Seeing him standing there in dark jeans and a short-sleeve button-down shirt, Abby almost forgot to breathe. He'd left the top two buttons open and she could see the movement of his throat as he swallowed. Was he nervous, too?

"Wow. You look amazing, Abby."

She'd tried to keep it simple with a yellow sundress. It wasn't anything special, but it was far removed from what she wore to work. Living and working in New York, she had to present herself as professional and confident at all times. Looking feminine wasn't always an advantage. Tonight she looked like a woman. She wasn't hiding behind layers of fabric. It was just her—take it or leave it.

The look in Trent's eyes said he liked what he saw, which gave her some confidence.

"Thank you. You don't look half bad yourself."

Trent took a step forward, his eyes dark and full of heat.

She felt a little lightheaded as he stared down at her. In that moment, everything else faded away. He parted his lips and her gaze was drawn to them.

Trent leaned down and covered her mouth with his.

His lips were so soft. They moved gently over hers, and before Abby could contemplate the consequences, she reached for him. It felt like a lifetime ago since she'd felt desire like this racing through her veins.

Abby tangled her fingers in his hair, needing to get closer. He responded by wrapping his arms around her waist and pulling her flush against his chest. She could feel his heat radiating through his clothing and hers.

Trent rested his forehead against hers, his breathing labored. He hadn't let her go and to be honest, she didn't want him to. Being in his arms felt right.

She looked into his eyes. They were even darker than before and full of emotion. It made her throat tighten and her chest clench. She knew that look. Even still, she couldn't bring herself to back away.

"I've wanted to do that since you came home after spending the summer away at camp," Trent whispered.

She remembered that day. "Why didn't you?"

He ran his hands up and down her back before resting them on her hips. It put some space between them and she wasn't sure she liked that. He placed a single kiss on her lips, and then guided her over to his truck.

Opening the passenger side door, he waited until she was situated inside before he answered her question. "I was young and scared." He cupped the side of her face with his hand and she couldn't help but lean into it. "I'm not a kid anymore . . . and I know what I want."

Abby was still trying to come to terms with what he'd said as he pulled out onto the highway. There'd been no need for him to finish his thought. The implication was clear. He was going to go after what he wanted, and what he wanted was her.

* * *

Trent probably shouldn't have kissed her. He knew that. It had been pure instinct. He saw her standing there all pretty and perfect, and he couldn't resist.

On his way to her apartment, he kept reminding himself that he needed to take things slow. Abby had been reluctant to agree to the date in the first place. He didn't want to scare her off.

Plus, he had no idea what had transpired between her and Chris. He got the feeling there was a lot more to the story than he and the rest of the family knew. It wouldn't be wise to rush into anything.

His brain, however, hadn't relayed that message to the rest of his body. The urge to pull the truck to the side of the road and kiss her again was strong, but he resisted. He had to spend the entire drive to the boat calming himself down. Otherwise, he'd be giving the rest of the boat's passengers an eyeful.

By the time they arrived at the marina, Trent was more in control. That was good given her reaction once she realized where they were. Abby grabbed hold of his arm and looked at him with wide eyes. "We're going on a boat?"

Trent nodded. "A dinner cruise."

She glanced at the paddleboat about fifty feet away. "I've never been on a cruise." He wasn't sure if she was talking to him or to herself.

"First time for everything," Trent said as he pocketed the keys and got out.

Abby was already standing beside the truck by the time he reached the passenger side. She hadn't waited for him to open the door for her. Trent tried not to let it bother him. He'd been taught to open doors for women, especially women he dated.

He could still hear his dad's voice in his head. *"It's a sign of respect. And if you don't respect the woman you're with then you shouldn't be with them."*

"Shall we?" he asked, offering her his hand.

She hesitated for a moment, and then linked her fingers with his.

They walked across the parking lot and joined several other couples who were waiting in line to board. "That fancy job in New York doesn't send you on business trips?"

Abby shrugged. "Sometimes. But I usually don't see much outside of the airport and whatever we pass in the car getting to our hotel and the office building."

"Sounds rather boring."

"Oh, really?" Abby gave him a look that made him chuckle. She hadn't lost her sense of humor.

"Yeah, really. I mean there should be some perks to being stuck in an office all day." Trent squeezed her hand and winked.

"What about you, big shot? Have you ever been on a cruise before?"

They moved forward in the line and Trent dug out their tickets. "No. But then again, I'm a simple guy."

Abby snorted and bumped him with her shoulder. "Yeah, right."

He grinned and handed their tickets to the man standing beside the ramp leading to the boat. The man punched their tickets and gave them back to Trent. "Enjoy your evening."

The cruise wasn't scheduled to begin for another twenty minutes, but by the looks of it, most everyone was on board already. There were a few kids about, but most of the other cruise-goers appeared to be couples. Since his brothers had all gotten married, Trent often felt like the fifth wheel. Not tonight. Tonight he had Abby beside him.

She leaned her back against the railing, the wind blowing her hair, and looked up at Trent. "You're thinking really hard about something."

Trent chuckled and rested his forearms on the railing beside her. "I was thinking how nice it feels having you with me tonight."

"Oh." She turned her head toward the back of the boat.

He'd made her uncomfortable again and he knew he needed to fix it. "You remember Gage, right?"

"Of course," Abby said, looking at him again.

"He and his wife just had their first child." She shifted to face him, so he went on. "A little girl."

"Wow. It's hard to picture Gage all grown up with a family."

Trent raised one eyebrow. "You do know that Gage is one of the best quarterbacks in the country, right?"

"I know he plays football." She blushed. "I-I saw him on the cover of a magazine once, posing in his uniform."

Apparently, Abby wasn't immune to his baby brother's charms any more than the rest of the female population seemed to be. Even though he was now happily married to Rebecca, Gage still had to fend off female fans from time to time.

Abby looked down, playing with the strap of her purse. "What about Paul and Melissa? Are they still together? They used to be inseparable."

"No. She . . ." Trent cleared his throat. "She died in a car accident about five years ago."

"Oh, I'm so sorry. I didn't realize—"

"It's okay. You had no way of knowing." He moved a little closer to her, their arms barely touching. She didn't move away, so he counted that as a positive sign. "Paul had some rough years, but he's much better now. He recently got remarried." Trent grinned. "To Gage's wife's sister."

Abby's mouth dropped open. "You're kidding."

Trent's chest vibrated in amusement. "Nope. It's a long story, but Megan was exactly what he needed."

It took her a few moments to digest all the information.

For several minutes, they peered out at the water. Eventually, though, Trent had to address the elephant in the room. "You're not going to ask about Chris?"

She didn't answer right away and he wasn't sure what to make of it. "I wasn't sure you'd want to talk about him, considering . . ."

"Considering your history?"

"Yeah." She glanced over at Trent and held his gaze.

He stepped closer and she turned her body to welcome him. Did she even realize that?

"I'm a big boy. I can handle it. I was there, remember?" Trent slid the tips of his fingers down the side of her arm, making her shiver. "Cold?"

"No," she whispered.

The look in her eyes drew him in. Trent had no idea what it was about Abby, but there'd always been something that had called to him. He tried to remember what they'd been talking about before.

Oh, right. Chris.

"My brother is married to a wonderful woman named Elizabeth. They live about an hour from here."

Abby blinked as if awaking from some sort of trance. She licked her lips, and it took everything in him not to kiss her. Luckily, the captain's voice came over the intercom, announcing that they would be getting underway in a few minutes.

"Are you hungry?" he asked.

"Yes. That sounds good." She pushed away from the railing and began walking to the front of the boat where dinner was being served.

Trent caught her arm before she could get too far. She stared up at him, a wary look on her face.

Splaying his hand along her lower back, he held her as the other guests abandoned the back of the boat in favor of food. He waited until they were relatively alone, and then leaned down to brush his mouth against hers. "I don't care about Chris or your history with him, okay? Tonight is about you and me. *This* is about you and me."

Her eyes fluttered open. He could see her mulling over what he'd said.

"Do you like me, Abby?"

She swallowed hard. "Yes."

"Good," he said as he went in for another kiss.

CHAPTER 7

Abby felt slightly drunk even though she hadn't had a drop of alcohol. Her lips were still tingling and her heart was beating a little faster than normal. All of it was Trent's fault. Although the kiss outside her apartment had been pretty spectacular, the one he'd given her moments before as they stood with the gentle breeze blowing off the water had her forgetting the people around them. It was a good thing he'd retained his sanity and ended the kiss, because she was moments away from embarrassing herself.

Thinking about how her body reacted to him had her blushing again.

"I love it when you blush. I imagine you're thinking dirty thoughts," Trent whispered in her ear.

Of course that only made the color on her cheeks darken.

He chuckled and pressed his lips to her temple.

They got in line and filled their plates with the wide array of food. Everything seemed to have a tropical theme, down to the little umbrellas in the drinks. A DJ was playing music that transported Abby to a faraway beach somewhere, away from work and life and all the worries that came with it. She closed her eyes and sighed.

"That's a good sigh, I hope."

"This all makes me want to be whisked away to a tropical island." She smiled and speared a bite of fish. "It's been a long time since I've taken a real vacation. Max doesn't take much time off."

"He's a slave driver, huh?" Abby noticed Trent sobered a little when she mentioned Max.

"He can be." She concentrated on her food for a few minutes while she tried to gather her thoughts. "You don't like it when I talk about Max."

Trent took a sip of his drink. "If I'm being honest? No, I don't."

At least he hadn't denied it. "Why?"

He looked out at the water, and then at her. "I know you said you're just friends, but it's hard to wrap my head around."

"What? You don't have any female friends?" she asked.

"Not really. I mean I guess you could say Trinity and I are friends, but we don't have much interaction outside of work."

Abby remembered the feeling of unease she'd gotten when he'd taken that call from Trinity. She wondered if he was experiencing something similar when it came to her interactions with Max.

"He seemed rather possessive when I delivered the proposal last Friday," Trent said, pulling her out of her thoughts.

She shrugged. Abby didn't want to get into the reasons why Max was so protective of her, but she knew Trent deserved some sort of answer. "It's not you. Some things happened back in college and he was there for me. I'm sure if you had a sister, you'd be the same way with her."

Trent raised both eyebrows. "So you're saying he thinks of you as a little sister."

"Yeah."

"Is he gay?"

She would have laughed if he hadn't asked with such a straight face. "No. Max is most certainly not gay."

"Are you sure?"

"Pretty sure. I walked in on him once when I forgot a file at the office. Lucky for me they were still covered from the waist down."

Trent mulled that over. "I don't get it."

"What don't you get?"

He put his fork down and scooted closer to her. She could smell his cologne as he took her hand and brought it to his lips, waiting until she met his gaze. "You're gorgeous, Abby. I have a hard time believing that a red-blooded heterosexual male wouldn't be trying to get in your pants."

"And is that what you're trying to do, Trent Daniels?" she asked.

He turned her hand over and ran his lips along the inside of her wrist. "Most definitely."

There was a twinkle in his eye as he lowered her hand to her lap and went back to his food.

She rolled her eyes. "Nice."

"Just being honest," he said. "I wouldn't want you to mistake my intentions."

"And your intention is to sleep with me." She really couldn't believe they were having this conversation amid a boat full of people.

"Among other things." Where they were didn't seem to be having any effect on him.

"What other things?"

He wiped his mouth and leaned forward in his chair. His eyes were sparkling. She could see flecks of gold mixed in the soulful brown depths. "You'll have to wait and see."

"Trent—"

Before she could finish that sentence, he stood and held out his hand. "Dance with me?"

She glanced down at the food on her plate.

"The buffet's open until nine. I promise I won't let you starve."

When she looked up at him again, heat pooled in the pit of her stomach. Without stopping to think, she placed her hand in his and let him lead her onto the small dance floor. Trent circled his arms around her waist and held her close.

As they swayed back and forth to the gentle island music, Abby realized this was the first time in years she'd been so relaxed on a date. Most of the time she ended up being bored out of her mind or things became awkward. This didn't feel like either of those. Trent held her just right. She felt safe, protected, and loved.

That last part brought her up short.

"What's wrong?" he whispered in her ear as he twirled them around.

Abby thought about denying it, but when she felt his arms tighten around her, she knew she couldn't. "Where is this going, Trent?"

"Well, since we're on a boat, probably not far. Not unless you're in the mood for a swim."

That made her laugh. "You know what I mean."

"I do."

He continued to dance, so she waited. Abby needed to know what he expected to come from this.

However, he surprised her by asking a question of his own. "Where do you want it to go?"

That was a loaded question. If he were anyone else besides Chris' brother, she wouldn't even think twice about them spending time together. But he was Chris' brother and no amount of wishing would change that. "I don't know."

He took her hand and led her from the dance floor. They weaved through several groups of people until they were once again at the back of the boat. The sun was beginning to set, sending a soft glow over the deck. It was beautiful and heartbreakingly romantic.

She tried not to think about that as he guided them to the railing. Abby looked out over the water as if it held some great wisdom.

Trent moved to stand behind her. He wrapped his arms around her waist, pulling her against him once more. She was surrounded . . . trapped. She should want to get away, put some distance between them, but instead all she wanted to do was burrow deeper in his embrace. Abby hadn't felt this content since before she'd left for college.

Thinking of that time in her life brought Chris once again to the forefront of her mind. She tensed and, of course, Trent noticed. "Talk to me."

"I can't." She wanted to, though, and that was perhaps the scariest part of all.

"Is it about my brother?"

She nodded.

Trent hesitated for a long moment, which wasn't like him at all. He seemed to be debating whether or not to voice his thoughts. "Are you still in love with him?"

Abby turned around to face him. She probably shouldn't have been surprised at his assumption. "No. I haven't felt that way about him for a long time."

He placed his hands on her face, caressing her cheeks with his thumbs. Her eyes drifted closed as she sank into the feeling his fingers evoked when he touched her. "Then what's the problem?"

She shook her head. "I can't—"

Trent pressed his mouth against hers and a quiet moan bubbled up from her throat. He gathered her close as he licked and sucked at her lips with a sweet seduction. It felt surreal. As if this was happening to someone else and not to her. Every argument, every rational reason why being with Trent was a bad idea fled from her mind.

"You make it easy to forget where we are," he murmured.

She opened her eyes to find him looking down at her in such a way that did nothing to cool the fire in her belly. "You're the one that keeps kissing me."

He hummed. "I do, don't I?"

Abby grinned. Things should be complicated with him, but instead they felt so easy. Natural. The way they always had.

* * *

Trent couldn't remember the last time he was this happy. After watching the sunset with Abby, they'd gotten themselves a little more food and enjoyed the remainder of the cruise. They'd talked more about her life in New York. She had him laughing as she told him how she'd missed her stop on the subway and somehow ended up in Chinatown.

It was the best date he'd had in . . . well, ever.

His euphoria began to fade when he parked in front of her apartment complex. He wasn't ready to say goodbye to her yet.

Following her up the sidewalk, Trent waited while she dug her keys out of her purse.

She shifted her weight and looked up at him with hesitant eyes. "Do you want to come in?"

"If I come in, you know what will happen. I don't think you're ready for that." Maybe that made him sound arrogant, but given their kisses earlier, he didn't think it would take much for them to end up in her bed.

She didn't dispute his assertion. At least that told him he hadn't been misreading her. She was feeling it, too.

They stood there for several moments. The longer they stood there, the more he wanted to forget his good sense. "You need to go inside, Abby, or I'm going to forget that I'm a gentleman."

The fear he saw flash across her face reaffirmed that she wasn't ready. "Good night, Trent."

"Good night, Abby."

He waited until she closed the door behind her and flipped the lock before heading back to his truck. Resting his forehead against the steering wheel, he tried to remind himself why leaving her at her door was a good idea. It was a hard argument.

Trent sat in the cab until he saw her turn on her upstairs light, then he started the vehicle and drove home. He'd bought the three-bedroom ranch a few years ago and he loved it. Usually. Tonight as he ambled through his house, it felt as if something was missing.

They'd only been on one date and he was already thinking of her in his home. Would she like it? She'd always had a knack for design. What would she think of his hand-me-down furniture and bare walls?

He grinned. She'd want to change it, of course. She'd want to spruce it up with knickknacks and all sorts of other girlie things. And he would let her, because it was Abby.

After stripping out of his clothes, he strolled into his bathroom and hopped into the shower. The water pelting down on him did nothing to dispel his thoughts of Abby. The sight of her standing there with her back to the sun, her hair blowing in the wind, would be etched into his memory forever. He knew he'd be counting down the hours until he was able to see her again.

As much as he would have enjoyed seeing the look on Abby's face on Saturday morning if he showed up on her doorstep, he had work to do. The sprinkler issue on Monday had taken him off another job, and he was already stretched thin due to the addition of the Collins properties.

It was good, though. It got him focused on something other than Abby for a while. Or at least it gave him an outlet to work off some of that sexual frustration he'd been feeling the night before. Abby had been the only girl—woman—who'd always been able to make him feel slightly off balance and yet centered at the same time. It was unnerving, but that didn't matter. He hadn't been able to walk away when he was a teenager and her pull hadn't lessened over the years.

When he finished with the mulching he'd abandoned earlier in the week, Trent swung by his house to clean up, and then made his way over to his parents'. It was sort of an unspoken rule that he came over on Saturdays after work to help with whatever needed to be done. He was single and he lived the closest. Plus, it always meant that he got to enjoy his mom's cooking. A definite plus.

He pulled into the driveway and noticed Chris' truck. Trent hoped nothing was wrong.

Trent was getting out of his vehicle when he saw his brother marching toward him, a huge smile on his face. "Hey."

"Hey," Trent said. "I didn't know you'd be here tonight."

Chris shrugged. "Elizabeth wanted to hit some of the flea markets, so we decided to stay down here tonight instead of driving home and then back again tomorrow."

"Makes sense."

They walked around the house and into the backyard where their mom, dad, and Chris' wife, Elizabeth, were sitting on the deck, sipping iced tea. His dad had the grill going and Trent could smell meat cooking. It made his mouth water. Lunch had been hours ago.

"About time you joined us, son. I thought we might have to eat without you." Their dad pushed himself out of his chair and went to check on the meat.

"No such luck." Trent took a seat beside his sister-in-law. "How's my brother treating you? If he's slacking, let me know. I'm always willing to step in."

Elizabeth laughed and rolled her eyes. "I'm sure you are."

Chris, on the other hand, gave him a hard shove, pushing Trent out of his chair and onto the deck.

"Hey!"

His brother lowered himself into the seat Trent had just been unceremoniously removed from. "Back off, little brother. Get your own woman. This one's mine."

Trent stood and brushed himself off, not bothered in the slightest by Chris' caveman behavior.

Elizabeth snuggled up to her husband and whispered something in his ear. A pang of jealousy hit Trent. Not because he wanted Elizabeth for himself. No, this was more along the lines of him wanting the type of relationship that his brother had. There was a level of intimacy there. He'd seen it plenty of times over the years with his parents, and one by one he'd seen it with his brothers and their wives.

The vision of Abby on the boat came to mind and he had an intense longing to see her. They hadn't made plans again, mainly because he didn't want to rush her. Something had happened between her and Chris, beyond what Trent and the rest of the family knew. That much was obvious.

His mom handed him a plate. "Did you see Abby again this week? Is she coming tomorrow?"

"You saw Abby?" Chris asked. He still had his arms wrapped around Elizabeth, but his attention had shifted, awaiting Trent's answer.

Elizabeth looked bewildered. "Who's Abby?"

"We grew up together." Chris paused and glanced at his wife. "And she was my girlfriend in high school."

"Oh."

Trent wondered if Chris and Elizabeth had ever talked about Abby. Judging by the look on Elizabeth's face, Trent was guessing they hadn't. Then again, none of them thought they'd ever see her again.

"Well?" his mother prompted.

Ignoring what was going on between his brother and sister-in-law, he answered his mom. "Yes, I saw her. And I don't know if she's coming. She said she needed to think about it."

His mother frowned. "But why? I don't understand."

Mike Daniels put an arm around his wife's shoulders, comforting her. "I'm sure she has her reasons, honey."

A look of guilt crossed Chris' face. Trent hadn't wanted to push Abby, but that didn't mean he couldn't get answers from his brother.

After they finished dinner, Chris ran upstairs to get something. When he emerged from the spare bedroom, Trent was waiting for him in the hall.

"Oh," Chris said, after nearly running directly into Trent. "I-Is something wrong?"

Trent leaned back against the wall and crossed his arms. "I was hoping you'd tell me."

His brother looked confused.

"What happened between you and Abby?"

Chris tilted his head back until it hit the wall with a thud. "It's a long story."

"I'll wait." Trent wasn't leaving here tonight until he got some answers.

His brother seemed to be weighing his options. "I don't . . ." Chris blew out a breath. "Look, I'm not proud of what I did, okay? I was young and stupid, and it should have never happened."

Trent waited.

"You know she and I broke things off when I went off to college."

They all knew that.

Chris glanced down the hall toward the stairs. Trent wasn't sure if it was because he didn't want to look at him or if Chris was making sure they were still alone. "It was my junior year and I went down to Fort Lauderdale for spring break with a group of my friends."

"I remember. Ma wasn't thrilled you weren't coming home."

"Yeah. Well. Abby was there." Chris swallowed and closed his eyes. "We hooked up. We were both drunk and not thinking clearly. But that's not an excuse. It never should have happened."

"And then what?" Trent knew there had to be more. Two exes hooking up on spring break couldn't be the whole story. It didn't explain Abby's hesitation.

"When we both woke up the next morning, reality set in. We'd made a huge mistake and we both knew it. Although, I probably should have handled it better. I ended up saying something about forgetting it ever happened. I left shortly after that, leaving her alone in the hotel room." Chris ran a hand over his face. "Ma would kill me if she knew."

Trent couldn't disagree with that. Their mom excused a lot of things when it came to her boys. Being disrespectful to a member of the opposite sex wasn't one of them. And their dad would have been right beside her to help deliver the fatal blow.

"Is that all?" For some reason, what Chris had told him still didn't mesh with the vibe he'd gotten from Abby. Or Max, for that matter. Friends, no matter how protective, didn't tend to act like that just because someone had a drunken hookup with an ex-boyfriend.

"What do you mean?" Chris asked, looking at Trent for the first time since he began his tale.

Trent sighed, a little frustrated. "I mean, did anything else happen?"

Chris shook his head. "No. Not that I know of. The last time I saw her was when I walked out of the hotel room. Why?"

Trent pushed off the wall. If something else had happened, Chris wasn't aware of it. "No reason. Just trying to put the pieces together. I knew there had to be something. You looked too guilty out there."

His brother cringed. "I'm going to have to tell Elizabeth."

Trent clapped his brother's shoulder and moved toward the stairs. "Yeah. Better you than me."

Instead of heading out to the backyard when he reached the bottom of the stairs, Trent turned toward the front of the house. He paused briefly to look at a picture his mom had on the wall of all of them playing out in the backyard as kids. He was around nine at the time. Abby was there, right in the thick of things, with a huge smile on her face.

Before he could think better of it, Trent walked out the front door. He needed to talk to Abby—needed to hear her voice. His family would have to wait because right now, she was at the forefront of his mind and he needed to know she was okay.

Even though he knew it was just another day, that what had happened with Chris was years ago, for him it was fresh. The only thing that was going to make him feel better was talking to her. At least, he was hoping that was enough, because what he wanted more than anything was to take her in his arms and comfort her.

Trent dialed her number and waited patiently as Abby's phone rang four times before going to voice mail.

He debated whether or not to leave a message. Would it seem stalkerish if he hung up without saying anything? Probably.

"Abby, it's Trent. Call me later if you can." Direct and to the point.

He hated talking to machines. Worse, it hadn't even been Abby's voice on the recording. It was some generic 'the person you're trying to reach is unavailable' type thing.

Disappointed, Trent made his way back into the house. Normally he loved spending time with his family, but tonight his heart wasn't in it. He was too distracted by his thoughts of Abby.

CHAPTER 8

ON SATURDAY MORNING, Abby did some therapy shopping—anything to get her mind off Trent. After he'd dropped her off, she'd gotten herself ready for bed and tried to sleep. *Tried* being the operative word. No matter what she did, the memory of his arms . . . his lips . . . his body . . . assaulted her. She could still smell the scent of his cologne when she closed her eyes.

She finally gave up on sleep around four o'clock and pulled out her beads. If she wasn't going to sleep, she might as well do something productive.

Around noon, Abby exited one of her favorite stores with two new additions to her wardrobe. Buying something pretty for herself usually brightened her mood. Today it barely scratched the surface.

Throwing the bags in the trunk of her car, Abby considered her options. She could go home and continue to dwell on what was or wasn't happening with Trent, she could do some more shopping— even though it wasn't really helping—or she could visit Max and his family. They were the only people she knew here anymore besides the Danielses, and going there wasn't an option.

Katherine Collins, Max's mother, greeted Abby before she'd even had a chance to knock on the door. "I was wondering if we'd see you today. Max said you had a date last night."

It didn't surprise Abby that Max had mentioned her date to his mother. Given her position as Max's assistant, Abby spoke to Katherine often. They had a good relationship. And while Abby had never bonded to Max's mother like she had Marilyn Daniels, Abby still cared deeply for the woman. Knowing what she was going through with Max's father broke Abby's heart.

Abby hung her purse on the coat hanger to the left of the door and followed Katherine down the hall to the sitting room. "Yes, I went out with an old friend."

There was a time when Katherine had entertained the notion that Max had romantic feelings for Abby. That wasn't going to happen and eventually she grew to accept it.

Katherine halted outside the room and placed a gentle hand on Abby's arm. "I hope you don't take this the wrong way, but I want you to know that I'm here if you ever need another woman's perspective. I know you have Max, but, well . . . he's a man and there are just some things men don't understand."

"Thank you," Abby said. "I appreciate that."

With a warm smile, Katherine dropped her hand and continued into the sitting room where Max and his father were waiting. When Max saw her, he met her gaze for a long moment before nodding. She knew he'd been worried about her, but it wasn't as if Trent would do anything to intentionally hurt her. Then again, Max didn't know Trent like Abby did.

Shaking off her own personal issues, Abby focused on Max's father, Jacob. "How are you feeling today?"

He grinned at her, but it was weak. "Ready to get up and dance a jig. You willing to be my partner?"

Max snorted.

Abby chuckled. "Whenever you need me."

For the rest of the afternoon, the four of them enjoyed the sun shining in from the large windows of the sitting room. They talked about everything except his dad's illness. They didn't need to. The stark reminder was there in the paleness of his skin and the fragileness of his features. The first time Abby had met Jacob Collins, he'd been an imposing figure. With the cancer eating his insides, he looked as if the slightest gust of wind could blow him away.

Patsy, a middle-aged woman the Collinses had hired to help around the house, strolled into the room at four thirty to let them know dinner was ready. Katherine stood and wheeled her husband toward the dining room.

Abby started to follow, but Max stopped her. When she met his gaze, she saw unease. He was nervous about something. Was it his dad? Had something happened she didn't know about? "What?"

"How was your date?"

Oh.

"You really want to talk about this? Here? Now?"

He shrugged and gave her a sly grin, sinking back into the more confident Max she knew. "Why not? I've been biting my tongue for the last hour as it is. The suspense is killing me."

Abby rolled her eyes.

"Well?"

"You're a pain in my ass, you know that?"

He brought his arm up to rest on her shoulder and they began walking toward the dining room. "Ah, but you love me anyway."

She leaned into him. It wasn't like the feeling she had when Trent's arms were wrapped around her, but it was comfort just the same. "I do."

When she didn't say anything more, Max took her silence the wrong way. "Do I need to pay him a visit?"

"No." Abby glanced up at him. "It was good. We had a nice time."

He stopped. "Did you two . . . I mean did he . . ."

"Are you trying to ask if he spent the night?" Abby didn't know if she was more annoyed or amused. Even if she had slept with Trent, Max had no reason to make a big deal out of it considering how many women he'd slept with over the years they'd known each other.

"I know it's none of my business."

She narrowed her eyes a little and gave him a pointed stare. "You're right. It's not."

He nodded and dropped his arm. Max looked as if she'd just kicked his puppy or something. Men and their egos.

Abby sighed, letting go of her annoyance. "No. I didn't sleep with him. Happy?"

Max countered by asking a question of his own. "Are you?"

"I don't know. I like him. A lot. And he makes me feel things . . . things I haven't felt in years." She never would have admitted it to anyone other than Max.

"But?"

"But what about when he finds out what happened with his brother?" She paused, and her voice took on a grave tone. "And the baby. I don't know if I can risk it."

"But you want to," Max said. "I can see it in your eyes."

Abby didn't bother to deny it.

Max opened his arms and she went willingly into his strong embrace.

"I'll be here no matter what you decide, Abby. You know that." He kissed the top of her head. "And I'm always willing to kick his ass if need be."

She laughed and pushed him away. "Come on. I'm starving. And your parents are going to think we got lost."

Once dinner was over, they all moved outside. As they sat next to the large pool, Max's father told stories of his childhood. While she enjoyed hearing about him as a little boy, it also broke Abby's heart. It was as if he was trying to share as much as he could with his family because he knew he didn't have a lot of time left.

The first time Abby had met Jacob Collins he'd been larger than life, standing beside his wife in a white dress shirt and slacks. It was Max's college graduation and they were beaming with pride. Knowing what he was like then, compared to now, had her fighting tears she knew Max's father wouldn't appreciate. He'd accepted his fate. The people who cared about him had to as well.

At seven thirty, Jacob was worn out. Katherine hugged Abby and gave her son a kiss on the cheek before wheeling Jacob inside.

"I should probably get going, too," Abby said.

Max nodded. "I'll walk you out."

He waited until they were at her car before reaching into his pocket and pulling out a flash drive. "My mother found this in my father's briefcase. Can you take a look?"

"Sure." Abby took the flash drive and dropped it into her purse. "Any idea what's on it?"

He shoved his hands in his front pockets. "I plugged it in long enough to see it's a bunch of spreadsheets, but I didn't have time to dig any further."

"I'll let you know what I find." She started to get into her car, but something about his stance made her pause. "Anything else you want to tell me?"

"I have a conference call with New York tomorrow morning, so if you try to call me I might not answer right away."

Abby narrowed her eyes as if she were trying to find some sort of hidden meaning behind his words. "Okay."

She climbed into her car and reached for the door to close it.

"No plans with Daniels this weekend?"

"No."

"Oh. I figured since you said your date went well—"

"He invited me to dinner with his family tomorrow."

Max seemed to sense her *but*. "You're not going to be able to avoid his family forever. Not if you keep seeing him."

"I know. That's what worries me. Trent I'm fine with." Better than fine, if she was being honest with herself. "The rest of them? I don't know."

"I'd offer to go with you—"

Abby snorted. "Yeah. I don't see that ending well."

"What? You don't think I can control myself?" Max asked with a twinkle in his eye.

"Not one bit."

He clutched his chest in mock hurt.

She shook her head. "Joke all you want. I know how you are. Especially when it comes to Chris."

Max sobered. "He hurt you."

"I don't think he did it on purpose. We were young and stupid and it never should have happened."

"Doesn't matter."

Abby closed the car door and started the engine. "Good night, Max."

"Call me if you need me."

While she wanted to roll her eyes and tell him she was a big girl and could take care of herself, she just nodded.

An hour later, she'd downed several glasses of wine and her head was about ready to explode from staring at her computer screen. There had to be fifty files on the flash drive Max had given her—each one a spreadsheet full of numbers. It would take her weeks to make sense of it all, and that was assuming she could match up the numbers with actual accounts. It looked as if Emily had struck again, and Abby was left to clean up her mess.

At some point in her search through the seemingly endless spreadsheets, her phone rang. Figuring it must be Max, she ignored it. She didn't want to talk about her personal life any more tonight.

Draining the rest of her wineglass, Abby stood and made her way into the kitchen. Her phone sat on the small kitchen table where she'd left it when she came home. As she rinsed her glass, it occurred to her that the call she'd chosen to let go to voice mail could have been from Trent.

She tapped her fingers on the counter as she stared at the phone.

A second later her feet were moving. She picked up the phone and logged into her voice mail. Trent's voice came through the line and she felt a pang of longing in her chest. He didn't say much, but before she realized what she was doing, Abby was calling him back.

* * *

Trent had hoped Abby would return his call, but by nine o'clock he'd all but given up hope. He'd said goodbye to his family and headed home.

As he was walking through the door, his phone rang. He didn't bother looking at the caller ID before answering. "Hello?"

"Hi." Abby's voice was timid, unsure. "I'm sorry I called so late. I didn't realize what time it was."

Trent strolled into the living room and sat down. "Don't worry about it. I just got home."

"Okay."

The silence stretched out between them.

"Is everything all right?" he asked.

"Yeah, I'm fine."

"Are you sure? I can come over if you need me to." There was a part of him that wanted her to say yes, even though logically he knew it probably wasn't a good idea.

"I'm good. I promise." She paused. "I've been thinking."

"About?" Fear raced through him waiting for her answer.

"You and me. Us."

"I should probably come clean about something." Trent figured this was as good a time as any to bring up his conversation with his brother. "I spoke to Chris tonight. He told me what happened between the two of you in Fort Lauderdale."

"You asked him?"

"Did you really expect me not to?"

Abby hesitated. "I guess not."

"He owes you an apology. What he did . . ." Trent could feel the anger bubbling up inside him again.

"It was a long time ago."

"Doesn't matter."

"You sound like Max. Both of you need to relax. I'm not such a fragile flower."

"I know that, but it doesn't excuse my brother's actions." The words came out a bit harsher than he'd wanted them to.

Abby grew quiet again.

"Sorry. I didn't mean—"

"It's fine."

Why did he get the impression that it wasn't? "Did Chris not tell me the whole story? Did something else happen?"

All his protective instincts surfaced when he heard what sounded like a sniffle.

"Abby?"

She cleared her throat. "I should let you get to bed. I'm sure you have a busy day tomorrow."

In that moment, Trent didn't care if it was a good idea or not. He needed to see her. Hold her. To know for himself that she really was all right. "I'm coming over. I'll see you in ten minutes."

Trent grabbed his keys and darted out the door.

When he pulled up to her apartment he half expected the lights to be off and her not to answer the door when he knocked. After all, he'd kind of acted like a caveman on the phone. Neither of those happened to be the case. She'd left her light on for him and she opened the door as he approached.

As soon as he saw her, he couldn't stop himself from taking her in his arms. She molded her body against his, only solidifying that racing over to her apartment had been the right thing. Abby clung to him.

He guided her over to the couch and tugged her down onto his lap. For several minutes, he sat there holding her, comforting her from whatever past wrong his brother had caused her. With every passing second, the desire to punch his brother grew.

"Don't be upset with Chris," she murmured against his neck, as if she could read his mind. "It wasn't all his fault. I was there, too, remember."

"He left you there. Alone."

She blew out a harsh breath. "Can we talk about something else?"

Trent gritted his teeth and decided not to push his luck. "Sure. What do you want to talk about?"

"Tell me what you've been up to since the last time I saw you. Besides starting your business, I mean."

Shifting them both into a slightly more comfortable position,

Trent tried to relax and enjoy the fact that he was with the woman he'd spent countless nights fantasizing about. "Let's see. Well, first I finished high school."

Abby reached between them and pinched him.

"Ouch," Trent said, feigning injury.

She met his gaze. "You deserved it."

Unable to resist, he bent down and brushed his lips against hers.

"I've missed you, Abby."

She closed her eyes and tucked her head into the crook of his neck, making herself comfortable. This was how it was supposed to be. Her cuddled up in his arms.

He rested his cheek on the top of her head and continued with his story. "I ended up going to the University of Cincinnati. During the summers I got a job doing some landscaping with a company outside of Springfield. Chris knew the owner and he was glad to have the extra help in the busy season. Other than that, I helped Ma and Dad around the house, and saved up to buy my own place."

Abby ran a hand down the front of his shirt and his anatomy stood up and took notice. He did his best to ignore it. That wasn't what this was about. That wasn't why he'd come over.

He picked up her hand and repositioned it higher on his chest. "What about you? What happened after you left for college?"

She stiffened.

"You don't have to tell me if you don't want to."

"It's okay."

He was patient as she gathered her thoughts. The few times she'd written to him those first two years of college had mostly been about her classes. Even before she stopped sending him letters, he'd felt the growing distance between them.

"You know I went to NYU. During my first week there, I was trying to find one of my classes and ended up literally running into Max. He was a junior and gladly pointed me in the right direction."

"And you became fast friends?" Trent tried to insert some humor into what felt like a rather serious conversation.

"Not exactly. We saw each other around campus a few more times before he joined me one day in the cafeteria for lunch. We talked about our classes and bonded over both being from Ohio." Abby was quiet for a long moment. "Then he asked me out."

Trent knew it. There was no way Max, if he was indeed straight, hadn't made a move on her.

"I told him no."

"Why?"

Abby sat up and he immediately wanted her warmth back.

"Lots of reasons." She twisted her fingers in her lap. "But mainly because I wanted to concentrate on my studies. Even though it had only been a few weeks, I was having to study harder than I ever had to in high school. The last thing I wanted to do was fail."

"And he accepted that?" With what little he knew of Max, he couldn't see the man giving up after one no.

She grinned. "No. He kept coming around. Eating lunch with me. Walking me to class. That sort of thing."

It pained Trent to ask, but he needed to know. "So did you two ever?"

"No. That spring another girl in my dorm caught his eye and he asked me for help in getting her attention." Abby smiled. "At first I said I wouldn't help him, but Max can be very persuasive when he wants something bad enough. I think he was hoping to make me jealous or something."

Trent frowned.

She took his face in her hands and brushed her lips against his. "You have no reason to be jealous of Max. By the end of the year, he realized that he didn't want to jeopardize our friendship with a romantic entanglement. He's been my best friend ever since."

It did make him feel a little better to know that she and Max had never dated.

He was so lost in his thoughts that he hadn't realized Abby had shifted her weight so that she was sitting astride him. It was the feel of her lips against his neck that brought him back to his senses. He gripped her hips with both his hands and groaned.

"I don't want to talk about Max anymore." She kissed the spot right beneath his ear. "I don't want to talk about Chris either. Or your family." She trailed her mouth up until it was a breath away from his. "Or mi—"

Trent didn't let her finish that sentence before he tangled his fingers into her hair and crushed her lips to his.

CHAPTER 9

Abby had lost all her common sense. She had to have because she didn't know what she'd been thinking when she decided to straddle Trent and begin teasing him.

Okay, she'd known what she was doing. Kind of. Her goal had been to distract him from any more talk of Max or college or anything else that might potentially lead her to spilling her guts. She should have known better.

Whenever Trent kissed her, she lost all capacity for thought and reason. This time was no different. As his mouth moved against hers and his fingers pressed against her scalp, holding her head exactly where he wanted it, the only thing she could concentrate on was how she wanted to melt into him.

Trent ran his hand down her back until he reached the edge of her shirt. He toyed with the hem briefly before snaking his hand beneath the thin material. The calluses on his palms sent shivers down her spine and a rush of heat to the spot between her legs. She couldn't remember the last time she'd reacted this way to a man, especially this quickly. It seemed that all Trent had to do was touch her and she was like a live wire.

He lifted her and twisted, changing their position. Before she knew it, she was beneath him, the lower half of his body pressed against her. The feel of his erection straining in his jeans left little doubt as to how much he wanted her. She lifted her hips, begging him for more friction as he continued to kiss her with a passion that left her dizzy.

His hand slid up her side to cup her breast. She couldn't stop the deep moan that escaped. It felt so good having his hands on her.

The more he touched her, the more she wanted. They were still fully clothed and that was a problem. Abby wanted to touch him, to caress the muscles she could feel beneath. She reached for the bottom of his shirt and began working it upward.

His shirt was bunched up beneath his underarms when he stopped kissing her and buried his face in her neck. "Why is it that when I'm with you it's so easy to forget myself?"

Abby felt him shiver as she ran her hands along the skin of his back. It thrilled her to know she wasn't the only one so affected by what was happening between them. "For me, too."

Trent lifted his head and looked her in the eye. He seemed to be searching for something. "I want you, Abby."

His whispered confession moved her in a way she didn't want to overanalyze. Trent had always been special to her, but it was more than that. Her heart felt as if it might burst as she stared into his eyes.

Abby pulled his mouth back down to hers.

He kissed her back, the previous moment's indecision gone.

She cupped the bulge at the front of his jeans, reveling in the feel of him in her palm. With each stroke the fire in her belly grew stronger, hotter.

Fingers gripped her wrist, pulling her hand away from his erection, and she groaned in frustration.

Trent chuckled and brought her arms up over her head, pinning them above her.

"Not funny," she gasped as he kissed his way down her neck.

Releasing her arms, he nudged the cup of her bra aside with one hand and rolled her nipple between his fingers. Abby arched her back, begging him for more. Whatever she'd been about to say was forgotten as she gave in to the sensation.

They lay there on her couch for what felt like forever, kissing and touching. She'd explored his shoulders, his back, his chest—anywhere her hands could reach. Trent had an amazing body, forged by physical labor, and she took pleasure in becoming acquainted with it as they made out in her living room.

"Trent?"

"Mmm?" He was nibbling on her ear and driving her crazy. It had been too long since she'd been intimate with a man and the desire to feel his skin against hers was almost unbearable.

"We're wearing too many clothes."

He grazed his lips along the line of her jaw, placed an all too chaste kiss on her lips, and then rested his forehead against hers. The look in his eyes told her that he was just as turned on as she was. "Our clothes are the only thing keeping me in check."

"What if I don't want you in check?"

Trent groaned and buried his head in her neck. Even then, she could feel the moment dissipating. She didn't want this connection between them to end, even though she knew eventually it would.

"What's wrong?" she asked. "I thought . . ."

He pushed himself up and away from her. Cool air washed over her body as he moved to sit on the other end of the couch. The look on his face was serious.

Abby sat up, tucking her legs beneath her, and straightened her clothes. She waited for him to speak. He obviously had something he needed to say and whatever it was, she owed it to him to hear him out.

As she gave him time to gather his thoughts, her gaze zeroed in on the still prominent bulge in his pants. She wondered if it was as impressive as it felt.

"You really need to stop looking at me like that."

She snapped her head up to meet his gaze. He'd caught her staring at his crotch. Heat rushed into her cheeks.

"That's not helping either." His voice sounded strained, as if he was barely holding on to his control.

Abby grinned.

He extended his hand, silently asking for her to come closer. She glided her fingers over his palm and followed willingly as he pulled her in.

Trent tucked her against his side. "I'm trying to be a gentleman here and do the right thing. You aren't ready for us to make love."

She wanted to argue with him, but she knew he was right. This wasn't some random guy. This was Trent and it would mean something if they slept together. A big something.

He sighed and brushed his lips against her hair. "How about some TV?"

They spent the next hour watching a documentary on ancient Egyptian artifacts. She wouldn't have pegged him as being interested in such a thing, but Abby was finding that there was a lot about Trent she didn't know.

Spending time with him was nice. Every so often he would give her a kiss or brush his fingers along her arm, but it was all very innocent. Trent knew she was keeping something from him. She was pretty sure he thought it had to do with Max since he kept bringing up her friendship with him. Abby wished that were the case.

"Are you sure you're going to be okay?" Trent asked as he stood at the door ready to leave nearly two hours after he'd arrived.

She wanted him to stay, but he was right. She wasn't ready. And even if she was, sleeping with him while harboring such a huge secret —one that would affect his entire family—wasn't something she was willing to do. She cared too much about him. "I'm fine. I promise."

He still looked unsure. She never should have allowed herself to break down in front of him.

Abby went up on her tiptoes and kissed him. "Thank you for coming over."

"Anytime. You know that." He splayed his hand on her lower back and returned the kiss. It left her ready to throw away all her good intentions and lead him to her bedroom.

"Good night, Abby," he whispered, backing away. "Sweet dreams."

"Good night."

She closed the door and leaned back against it. Her life had gotten a lot more complicated than it had been a few weeks ago, and she had no idea what she was going to do about it.

That night Abby tossed and turned more than she had in years. Her mind kept jumping back and forth between her time with Trent and those last months of her pregnancy when she'd been afraid and confused. If she continued to see Trent, she was going to have to face her past and Chris.

When she woke up on Sunday morning, Marilyn Daniels' invitation weighed heavily on her mind. She thought about calling Max and asking his opinion, but he'd either talk her out of going or insist on going with her. That wouldn't help the situation. If anything, it would make it worse.

As noon approached, Abby knew she couldn't put it off any longer. She was either in or she was out.

Abby stood in the center of her apartment, clasping the pendant dangling at the end of her necklace. Her gaze zeroed in on the couch where she and Trent had made out the night before. As wrong as she knew it was, she wanted to do it again . . . and again . . . and again. And being with Trent, even temporarily, would mean dealing with his family. She was surprised his mom hadn't shown up on her doorstep already.

Before Abby could talk herself out of it, she went to her bedroom to get ready.

It took her longer than normal to find something to wear. She didn't want to appear as if she was going out of her way to impress, but she needed as much confidence as possible if she was going to be in the same room as her ex-boyfriend, his wife, and the man she was beginning to have more feelings for than was probably smart.

Abby gave herself a pep talk as she took a final look at her appearance in the bathroom mirror. Everything was going to be fine. She was going to go, eat dinner, and socialize. Heaven knew she did that often enough at dinner parties Max hosted in New York.

Unfortunately, those people didn't know her like the Daniels family did. She also didn't care about the movers and shakers in the city like she did Trent's family. At one time they'd meant as much to her as her own father.

Taking a deep breath, she squared her shoulders and marched toward the door. It was showtime.

* * *

Trent pulled up in front of his parents' house and parked behind Paul's car. Chris and Elizabeth's truck was still in the driveway where it had been the night before. They'd been doing these family dinners for as long as Trent could remember. As kids, everyone always knew they had to be home on Sunday afternoons. It was family time.

As they got older, college and jobs got mixed up in there and they all couldn't always make it, but they all tried. Paul drove the two and a half hours from Indianapolis every week unless he was working. Chris was the same. The only one of his brothers who didn't come often was Gage. That was mainly because his job as a professional football player had him living in Nashville these days. It wasn't feasible for him to make the five-hour drive every week. Even still, they all made the effort to get home whenever possible.

Trent sat in the cab of his truck, staring at the front door. He knew he needed to go inside before someone spotted him, but his thoughts kept drifting back to Abby. It wasn't until this moment that he realized how much he wanted her there with him. Inside, his family was waiting—all of them with significant others to share their lives with. He was the only one now without someone special in his life.

Over the years, he'd dated more than his share of women. He'd liked most of them well enough, but he'd never seen himself settling down with any of them. There'd always been something missing he couldn't quite put his finger on. Now he knew what it was. He'd never gotten over Abby. Even during all the years she'd been away, she'd had a hold on his heart.

After he'd left her the night before, he'd replayed his conversation with Chris in his mind, and then Abby's reaction to what his brother had said. She'd downplayed it. Trent didn't know if that was because it really wasn't a big deal to her, or if it was and it was her way of avoiding an uncomfortable subject.

Abby insisted she wasn't still in love with Chris, yet she was reluctant to accept his mother's invitation to join them today—something she'd done nearly every Sunday when she'd lived down the street from them. He was missing something. Something vital. Trent just wished she'd talk to him about it. Surely it wasn't as bad as she thought it was.

After locking up his truck, he headed inside. He was almost to the door when he heard a vehicle pull up. When he turned to see who it was, he was startled by the sight of Abby's car pulling up to the curb.

His heart skipped a beat and he had to stop himself from racing across the lawn to get to her. She'd come. The last thing he wanted to do was scare her off before she made it out of her car.

Trent strolled back toward the road, watching Abby the whole time. She turned off the engine but made no effort to exit.

When he reached her car, Trent opened her door.

Abby looked up at him as if she was waking from a daze. "Thanks."

As she stepped out of the vehicle, she looked more nervous than he'd ever seen her. He wanted to comfort her. After last night, he hoped she'd welcome his touch.

Trent pulled her into his arms and tucked her head under his chin. She didn't hesitate to wrap her arms around his waist.

"I'm glad you came," he whispered.

Her only response was to squeeze him tighter.

"You don't have to go inside if you won't want to. No one's forcing you." Trent needed this to be her decision. It didn't matter that he didn't understand her reaction. Abby was scared, that much was clear.

Abby let her arms drop down to her side and gazed up at him. He saw a spark of determination in her eyes. "We should go in before I lose my nerve."

Trent looked at her for a long moment before reaching for her hand.

"Trent—"

He cut off her protest with a kiss.

She sighed when he pulled back, her eyelids fluttering open.

"Ready?" he asked.

She nodded.

Trent held her hand as they made their way toward the house. He wondered if she'd try to put some space between them, but if anything, she tightened her grip.

The house was buzzing with activity when they went inside. Voices trailed in from the kitchen, filling the house with life. It was one of the things he'd always liked about coming home.

Abby froze. "Maybe this wasn't such a good idea."

"We'll turn around and go, if that's what you want."

"You'd miss your family dinner for me?" She seemed a little dismayed by the idea.

"In a heartbeat." There wasn't much he wouldn't do for Abby. It had been the truth when they were growing up and it was even more so now.

Before she could respond, the decision was taken out of their hands. Megan came around the corner with Chloe. "Oh. Hey, Trent."

Megan's gaze fell on Abby, and Trent figured introductions were in order. "Abby, this is Megan and Chloe, Paul's wife and daughter." To Megan he said, "Abby grew up with us."

"Nice to meet you," Megan said.

She extended her hand, but was sidetracked by Chloe. "Can we find my surprise now?"

Megan brushed the hair away from Chloe's face. "Just a sec, okay?"

Chloe nodded, but her lower lip jutted out in a pout.

"Grandma told Chloe there's a surprise upstairs and we were on our way to get it," Megan explained.

"We wouldn't want to keep you from your surprise, now would we?" Trent knelt down and tickled his niece.

Chloe squealed and hid behind Megan's legs.

They all laughed.

"I'd better get her upstairs so we can be back down in time. It was nice meeting you, Abby."

Trent grinned as Megan followed Chloe upstairs. Those two were joined at the hip these days. It was hard to believe that they hadn't even known Megan a year ago.

When he turned back to Abby, his happiness faded a little. "What's wrong?"

She shook her head and gave him a halfhearted smile. "Nothing. I was . . . I was just wondering how old Chloe is."

"She's five."

Abby nodded and dropped her hand from his.

He opened his mouth to question her, but then his dad nearly tripped over them coming inside the door they'd just entered. "Oops. I didn't see you two standing there." Then he noticed who it was. "Abby Hoffman? Is that really you?"

For the first time since she pulled up in front of his parents' house, Abby cracked a smile. "It's me."

Mike Daniels didn't hesitate. He pulled Abby into a bone-crushing hug, and then held her at arm's length as if to get a good look at her. "It's good to see you, young lady. You've grown up."

She chuckled but Trent could still hear a bit of uncertainty behind it. "Thanks."

Not letting her go, Mike threw his arm around her shoulders and ushered her through the living room toward the voices they'd heard earlier. Trent was two steps behind them, but before he crossed the threshold into the kitchen, he heard his mom squeal, "Abby!"

Within seconds, the meal was forgotten. His mom greeted Abby with even more enthusiasm than his father had. Tears were streaming down his mother's cheeks as she embraced Abby. It wasn't until Trent saw his mom's reaction that he realized how much Abby never coming back to visit must have hurt his mother.

"I'm so glad you came," his mother gushed as she dragged Abby over to the stove.

While his mother fussed over Abby, he helped his dad finish setting the table. Paul was chopping vegetables for a salad, but he turned when Megan and Chloe walked back into the room. His brother's lips tilted up slightly as his bride came into the room. After years of mourning, his oldest brother had finally found happiness again.

Of course, thinking about Paul and Megan had his gaze drifting back to Abby. She was engrossed in conversation with his mom, who was fawning over her. Her fingers were laced together in front of her and she kept sending glances his way. He tried to offer her an encouraging smile.

Something was pressed against his stomach, drawing his attention away from her. He looked down to find his dad shoving a bowl at him.

"Put that over there on the end of the table." His dad shot Trent a knowing look as he went to grab something else from the counter.

Trent did as he was told. It was obvious his dad had noticed his interaction with Abby.

The patio door slid open and Elizabeth walked in carrying a tray of meat that smelled heavenly. A second later, Chris followed, closing the door behind him. When she saw Trent, Elizabeth smiled and brought the food over to the table.

Chris placed the dirty grilling utensils he'd been carrying into the sink, then joined Elizabeth at the table. They both took their seats. The exchange was almost too calm and Trent wondered if his brother had told Elizabeth about Abby last night after he'd left.

It was in that moment Chris spotted Abby across the room. Elizabeth seemed to sense her husband's attention had shifted and followed his gaze.

It took a few moments for everyone in the room to realize the atmosphere had changed. Trent saw Abby stiffen.

Without thinking it through, Trent crossed the room to stand by Abby's side. He wanted to be there if she needed him. The ball was in Chris' court and they all waited with bated breath to see what would happen next.

CHAPTER 10

ABBY FELT Trent come up next to her and she appreciated his support.

Chris watched her for a long moment, stood, and walked over to stand in front of her. "It's good to see you, Abby."

"You, too." She hated how unsteady her voice sounded.

He glanced at his brother, and then back to her. "Trent didn't mention you were coming today."

"It was a last minute thing."

Abby had been so focused on Chris that she didn't notice the woman behind him until she held out her hand. "Hello. I'm Elizabeth. Chris' wife."

Elizabeth's demeanor was friendly enough, but there was also an edge to it. Chris' wife was staking her claim, which meant she knew Abby and Chris' history—at least some of it. Abby couldn't say she blamed the woman for being a bit territorial.

"Nice to meet you," Abby said, shaking her hand.

"Daddy, I'm hungry." Chloe's voice broke through the awkwardness.

Marilyn whirled around, a casserole dish in her hands. "Then you're in luck. Dinner's ready."

Chloe beamed and ran to take a seat at the table.

"Chris, would you grab the lemonade out of the refrigerator, please? I forgot." Marilyn acted as if the exchange between Abby and Chris was completely normal.

"Sure."

Elizabeth grinned and returned to her seat, and Marilyn pulled yet another dish out of the oven. It brought back memories of Abby's teenage years. Marilyn always made so much food, and yet there were rarely any leftovers. One of the hazards of having four boys, she used to say. By the looks of it, getting older hadn't done anything to diminish their appetites.

Trent brushed the back of his hand down her arm, sending tingles in its wake. It reminded her of the night before when his hands had been in lots of other places on her body. "You doin' all right?"

"Yeah, I'm okay." Abby wanted to lean into him, but she settled for a smile instead. "I'm glad you're here with me."

"Dinner's ready," Marilyn announced.

"After you?" Trent said, gesturing toward the table.

Abby nodded.

She chose the seat across from Paul's wife, Megan. Trent lowered himself into the chair beside her. Chris and Elizabeth were at the other end of the table.

Food was passed around as everyone filled their plates. It felt very familiar. The years hadn't changed this tradition.

Once everyone's plate was full, they all began eating. The food was delicious and she found herself smiling as she ate.

"Trent said you grew up around here," Megan said about halfway through the meal.

Abby didn't miss how Elizabeth paused, waiting to hear Abby's response. "Yeah, I think I spent more time at the Danielses' old house than I did my own."

"We loved having you. You know that. You helped to balance out some of the testosterone." Marilyn winked at her before going back to her food.

Everyone laughed—even Elizabeth chuckled a little. Maybe this wouldn't be so bad. She couldn't avoid Chris entirely, but as long as she was careful and didn't make his wife feel threatened, then Abby thought she'd be okay.

Elizabeth had nothing to worry about, though. Chris was still as handsome as ever, but Abby didn't feel anything remotely romantic for him anymore. Whether that had to do with what had happened between them or not, Abby had no idea. It didn't matter.

"So tell me," Megan said, "what were these guys like as kids? Did they get into trouble a lot?"

Abby felt Trent's hand on her thigh and she laced her fingers with his. "They all had their moments, but I think Gage was the worst. Then again, maybe that was just because he was the youngest and he was always trying to show up his older brothers."

"Oh, I don't know," Marilyn said, a huge grin on her face. "They all got into a fair amount of mischief growing up."

The conversation swiftly turned to each brother sharing embarrassing stories about the others. She recalled most of the things they brought up, including when Trent and Chris decided it would be a good idea to build an underground fort. Marilyn and Mike had come home to find a hole three foot deep in the backyard—the entrance to the fort. Abby had been right there with them, helping to carry buckets of dirt away from the construction site.

They all continued to reminisce long after they were finished eating. Chloe had run off to the living room as soon as she was done to start reading the new book her grandmother had gotten her. It was all very normal. She couldn't remember the last time she'd laughed so hard she'd cried.

Eventually, Marilyn announced it was time to get things cleaned up and they all stood to help. Abby had always been impressed with was how everyone pitched in. Paul, Chris, Trent, and Gage had chores growing up. In fact, she remembered coming over one day and feeling left out because they all had stuff to do and she didn't. Marilyn picked up on it, of course, and had asked if she'd like some chores to do, too.

Looking back, Abby couldn't believe she had actually asked for work to do, but she'd wanted to feel included more than anything else. It had made her feel like she was part of their family. She loved her dad like crazy, but it had only been the two of them and he worked a lot trying to support them. Abby didn't know what she would have done with herself if the Daniels family hadn't embraced her like they did.

With eight adults working together, it didn't take long to get things cleaned up and put away. Abby, Trent, and Elizabeth worked to put the small amount of leftover food in the containers Marilyn had fished out of the cabinets, while Megan found a spot for them in the refrigerator.

Mike filled the sink with water and Paul dug a couple of dishtowels out of the drawer for him and Chris. It was quite a sight to see, really. Everything was in sync. They all knew their jobs and got them done.

The guys were about halfway through washing the dishes when Marilyn guided the women outside. "We'll let the boys finish up."

Marilyn, Abby, Megan, and Elizabeth headed out to the deck that ran almost the entire width of the house. Considering the size of the yard, which was smaller than the one they'd had before, the wooden structure should have felt overwhelming. Instead, it complemented the space and framed the landscape. Abby wondered if it was one of Trent's designs.

Abby sat in one of the lounge chairs and took a sip of her lemonade. It was warm out, but there was a nice breeze. She closed her eyes and tried to enjoy the moment.

She should have known it was too good to last.

"Trent seems awfully protective of you. Is there something going on between you two?" At Megan's question, Abby opened her eyes. The reprieve was apparently over.

She glanced at Marilyn, but there was nothing on her face but curiosity. "Um."

Abby was saved from having to answer when the sliding door was pushed open and a woman she didn't know walked out, cradling a baby in her arms. The child only looked to be a few days old.

Marilyn hopped up from her chair and rushed over to the woman. Everyone turned their attention to the new arrival, so they didn't notice the change in Abby. A cold chill shivered down her spine and took up residence in the pit of her stomach as realization set in. Given the other women's reaction and the news Trent had shared with her on their date Friday night, Abby had to assume this was Rebecca, Gage's wife, and their new baby.

"I want to hold my niece," Megan said, already taking the baby from the woman's arms. Rebecca and Megan were sisters, if Abby remembered correctly.

Megan cradled the child as if it were the most precious thing in the world. She placed her finger in the girl's tiny hands and stared down in awe.

"Pull up a chair, Rebecca," Elizabeth said, moving another seat next to hers.

Rebecca released a contented sigh as she relaxed into the lounge chair. "I never realized how much longer that drive would seem with a baby."

"Why didn't you tell us you were coming?" Marilyn asked.

"It was a last minute decision. The team has a bye week and since we didn't know when we'd get the chance to get up here to visit next, we thought we'd better take advantage."

Megan, Marilyn, and Elizabeth gushed over the baby. It brought back memories of Kaylee. Little Madison had the same head full of dark hair and strong jawline all the Danielses had—including Kaylee.

Abby felt the emotions bubbling up inside her. Flashes of her child filled her vision and made it difficult to concentrate on the conversation happening right in front of her.

"Abby?"

She blinked several times before refocusing on Marilyn. "Sorry. I missed what you said."

"Are you feeling all right?" Marilyn looked concerned.

"I'm fine. I just . . ." Abby did her best to smile through the pain she was feeling. "Excuse me for a moment."

Not giving any of them time to ask any more questions, Abby disappeared into the house and made a beeline for the bathroom she'd passed on her way in. She felt the tears threatening and she didn't want to start crying in front of them.

Abby closed the door behind her and sank down onto the floor. Moisture filled her eyes and she let the tears fall down her cheeks as grief overtook her. Seeing Chloe had been bad enough, but Gage's daughter looked too much like Kaylee had, the one and only time Abby had gotten to hold her. Kaylee who, instead of making happy gurgling sounds like Madison, had been silent . . . lifeless.

It had been years since she'd felt the loss of her daughter so acutely, but seeing Madison had hit home like nothing else could. Abby wrapped her hand around the pendant dangling from her neck —her constant reminder that her daughter had existed.

* * *

Once the women headed outside to the deck, leaving the men alone in the kitchen, the questions began.

Chris held a cup in one hand and a dishtowel in the other. "What's going on between you and Abby?"

"I don't know what you mean," Trent said as he finished drying a plate.

Paul snorted. "Denial, man. It won't get you anywhere. Believe me."

"They were holding hands when I came in the house," his dad chimed in with a smirk on his face.

Trent couldn't believe his father had just thrown him under the bus.

Chris placed the cup down on the counter and narrowed his eyes at his younger brother. "So there is something going on."

"No slacking, boys. You can work and grill your brother at the same time." Mike Daniels thrust another glass in Chris' direction.

He took it, but didn't relax his stance as he glared at Trent.

At the sound of the front door opening, they all stopped. Trent didn't miss how Paul's right hand slipped into his pocket. His brother was no doubt carrying. Being a cop, Paul didn't go very many places without being armed. He said it was safer that way. There was always a chance of running into someone he'd arrested.

A heartbeat later, Chloe let out an excited squeal. "Uncle Gage! Aunt Becca!"

The dishes were momentarily forgotten as the new arrivals made their way into the kitchen.

"I didn't know you guys were coming," Paul said, walking over to take a peek at the newest addition to the family.

"The team's got a bye week, so we thought we'd come and let you all meet Madison."

The five men formed a small circle around the tiny baby sleeping in her carrier. Madison was only a week old. Her head was covered in dark hair and she was sucking on one of her fists.

"Where's Ma?" Gage asked.

Mike Daniels looked up at his son. "The ladies are relaxing out on the porch."

"Why don't you hang out in here with the boys and I'll take Madison to see your mom?" Rebecca said.

Gage set the carrier on the table so Rebecca could pick Madison up and take her outside.

"How's it feel to be a dad?" Paul asked once the door had closed behind Rebecca.

"It's great. I don't even mind when she wakes up crying in the middle of the night."

Paul chuckled. "Give it a month."

They all laughed.

Chris tossed a clean towel in Gage's direction and they got back to work on the dishes. Luckily for Trent, the subject of his relationship with Abby didn't come up again. Everyone was too caught up in Gage, Rebecca, and Madison.

That was until Abby came rushing into the house like something was hot on her heels. She didn't even glance in his direction before ducking into the bathroom down the hall.

"Is she okay?" Paul asked to no one in particular.

"I don't know." Trent threw his towel down on the counter and marched toward the bathroom.

The door was closed by the time he reached it. He debated whether to knock, but something didn't seem right about the way she'd run past. Something was wrong. "Abby? Are you okay?"

She didn't answer.

"Abby . . ." Trent rested his forehead against the door, considering his options. That's when he heard what sounded like crying coming from inside.

Not thinking about anything but getting to her, he reached for the doorknob. It wasn't locked. He cracked the door open. "Abby, I'm coming in."

What he saw when he opened the door broke his heart. Abby was sitting on the floor along the back wall with tears streaming down her face.

Stepping inside the cramped space, Trent closed the door and knelt down in front of her. "What happened?"

"I'm okay," she hiccupped. "I just need . . . I just need a minute. That's all. I'm—"

"Do *not* tell me you're fine. You're clearly not fine, Abby."

She looked up at him, her eyes bloodshot.

Trent didn't care that there was barely any room, he sat down and reached for her.

Abby didn't fight him. She crawled into his lap and buried her face in the crook of his neck.

He had no idea how long they stayed in that position—long enough for his legs to protest. No one came to check on them. Trent was positive his father was to thank for that.

"I should go," she whispered against his neck.

"All right. I'll follow you home."

"You don't have to do that."

He placed a finger under her chin, turning her so that he could place a chaste kiss on her lips. "Take a few minutes in here while I tell everyone we're leaving, and then we can go."

Abby held his gaze for a long moment and then nodded. She climbed off his lap and stood, brushing the moisture from her cheeks.

Trent gave her another brief kiss, and went to find his family. They were all huddled together in the kitchen with worried looks on their faces.

His mother was on him the moment he entered the room. "Is she all right?"

"She's fine. I'm going to follow her home."

"I don't understand," Elizabeth said. "One minute we were all talking and then the next minute she was taking off."

"No one said anything to her?" Trent didn't think they would, but he felt as if he had to ask considering he'd found Abby alone and crying in the bathroom.

Megan shook her head. "No. We were all focused on Madison."

An uneasy feeling settled over Trent. He tried to shake it off, but it wouldn't go away.

Trent leaned down and gave his mom a kiss on the cheek. "I'll call you later."

Abby stood in the doorway to the bathroom when he returned. "You ready to go?"

She took a deep breath that seemed to take a huge amount of effort on her part. "You don't have to leave. I didn't mean—"

He closed the gap between them, pulled her into his arms, and kissed her protest from her lips. "Let's get you home."

When he started moving them toward the front door, Abby didn't object.

He walked her to her car and opened the door for her. "I'll be right behind you."

Questions swirled through his mind as he followed her home. Something had to have happened to cause Abby's reaction. She'd been fine at dinner.

Trent parked his truck in the visitors' area and then jogged over to where Abby waited for him by her car. He had no idea if she wanted him to leave or not, but he had to make sure she was going to be okay.

All he knew was that he didn't want her to spend the rest of the night holed up in her apartment, alone, crying.

He was still weighing his options when she asked, "Do you want to come in?"

"Do you want me to?"

She pressed her lips together and nodded.

Once they were inside her apartment, Abby kicked her shoes off and dropped her purse on the coffee table. "Do you want something to drink? I don't have any beer, but I have wine."

"I'll take some water." Trent thought it was best if he kept a clear head.

He walked over to the bookcase along the wall while Abby was in the kitchen. It was full of pictures. There was one of Abby and her father at her high school graduation. And another one of her at maybe four or five years old with both her parents.

Abby also had a picture of her and Max. They were both wearing NYU sweatshirts.

Even now, knowing that Abby didn't think of Max as more than a friend, Trent couldn't completely push away the jealousy.

A few minutes later, Abby returned with a glass of water for him and a full glass of wine for herself. He took the water and placed it on the coffee table before reaching for her. She came willingly.

"Thank you for following me home."

He kissed her forehead and met her gaze. "I'll be your knight in shining armor anytime you want. Just say the word."

She giggled and took a sip of her wine.

The pain in his chest eased a little. "Do you want to talk about it?"

"Not really."

"Okay." Trent wanted her to confide in him, but he wouldn't push.

She backed away from him and reached out her hand. "Come with me."

Linking their fingers together, he let her lead him down the hall to her bedroom. Once in the room, she released his hand and strolled over to her closet. Abby removed a shoebox and walked to the bed.

She took a huge gulp of wine, placed the glass on the nightstand, and sat down.

Trent stood by the door until she patted the mattress beside her. He crossed the short distance and lowered himself down onto the bed.

Abby held the box in her lap for the longest time. He had no idea what was inside, but whatever it was, it had to be important to her.

Her hands were shaking when she opened the lid. He wanted to reach out, but something told him he shouldn't. This was uncharted territory and he didn't know what to do.

She extracted something from the box and handed it to him. It was a picture. An ultrasound picture, to be exact.

"What's this?" he asked.

Abby swallowed hard, but her gaze never left the picture he held in his hands. Tears welled up in her eyes once more.

"Abby?"

She looked up at him, her eyes full of sadness. "It's a picture of my baby. My daughter."

CHAPTER 11

ABBY HELD HER BREATH, waiting to see how he'd react.

He blinked several times, and then lowered his gaze to her stomach. "You're pregnant?"

The sides of her mouth pulled up slightly in a half smile, despite the seriousness of the conversation. At twenty, she'd been so conflicted about having a baby. Now she'd give just about anything to be able to hold her little girl again.

"No. It was . . . a long time ago."

Trent handed the picture to her and she reverently placed it back in the box. After another long look at the grainy black and white picture, Abby stood and returned the box to the closet.

When she sat down beside him once more, Trent appeared to be deep in thought. Her insides clenched waiting for his reaction. Would he put the pieces together on his own?

"Where . . ." Trent cleared his throat. "Is she back in New York?"

"Yes."

He took a deep breath and nodded. "With her father?"

This was it. Abby couldn't skirt around the issue anymore. It was time to take that leap and jump off the proverbial cliff. "No. She's not with her father."

Trent stared at her, confusion etched into his features.

"Kaylee was stillborn. The doctors tried, but they weren't able to revive her." It was impossible to keep the tears at bay.

He wrapped his arms around her shoulders and tucked her against his side, trying to console her. She latched on tight, knowing this could be the last bit of comfort she received from him. Once he knew the truth, would he push her away?

"I'm so sorry," he murmured against her hair.

Abby enjoyed the warmth of his embrace for several minutes, soaking it up while she could. "I need to tell you something else."

Trent looked a little disappointed when she sat back up, putting distance between them, but he let her go.

Abby folded her hands in her lap and laced her fingers together, as if that would somehow keep her grounded as she spilled her secrets.

He placed his hand on top of hers and gave it a comforting squeeze. "Whatever it is, we'll get through it."

Abby shot him a wary look before taking a deep breath and plunging ahead into unknown territory. "It's about Kaylee's father."

When she didn't continue, he asked, "What about him?"

It was now or never. "I never told him about her. I was scared, so I kept putting it off and putting it off. Then I went into labor and . . ."

A lump formed in her throat. It felt as if every emotion she'd experienced over the years was rushing to the surface all at the same time. Max had paid for her to go to therapy after Kaylee's funeral, but talking about losing her daughter never got easier.

"And you never told him?" Trent asked.

"No." She would have given just about anything to know what he was thinking.

Trent didn't respond for several minutes and when he did, it wasn't what she'd expected. "Did you love him?"

"I did once, yes." She inhaled and ripped the Band-Aid off. "It was Chris."

He let his hand drop, but he didn't say anything.

When Abby glanced over at him, he was staring straight ahead with an unreadable expression on his face. She couldn't tell if he was angry or in shock.

A long time passed with neither of them saying anything. With every passing minute, she drew closer and closer to the edge. It had been years since she'd felt anything even close to what she felt when she was with Trent. The last thing she wanted was to lose him over a mistake she made twelve years ago.

"Please, say something." Even her whisper sounded loud in the room.

"What am I supposed to say?" He didn't look at her, and Abby couldn't blame him. She wouldn't want to look at her either.

"Do you hate me?" she asked.

He turned his head in her direction and she could see all the conflicting emotions in his eyes. "I don't know what I'm feeling right now, Abby. But no, I don't hate you. I don't think I could ever hate you."

She released a breath she hadn't realized she'd been holding, and the weight pressing down on her chest eased up a bit.

That was until he uttered his next words. "But you need to tell Chris. You have to. He deserves to know."

Over the years, she'd come close to picking up the phone and calling Chris at least a dozen times, but something always held her back. "I don't know how to tell him."

Trent shook his head. "I can't help you there. It's something you're going to have to figure out and soon. I can't—"

"I know." She'd never heard Trent so serious in all the years she'd known him.

He dug his cell phone from his pocket and held it out to her.

She stared at it as if it were a snake ready to strike. "Now?"

"No time like the present. His number is in my contacts." He nudged the phone in her direction again, encouraging her to take it.

With the enthusiasm of someone about to jump into the ocean without a life jacket, Abby closed her fingers around his phone and rested it in her lap. She stared at it, unable to drum up the courage to scroll through the list of names to find Chris'.

"Do you want some privacy?" Trent asked.

"No!" She grabbed onto his arm, as if somehow that would prevent him from leaving.

He looked at her long and hard, then nodded.

When she still didn't make a move, Trent inclined his head toward the phone. "It's not going to get any easier the longer you wait."

Abby knew he was right. She'd been putting off this call for twelve years.

Squaring her shoulders, she scrolled through his contacts until she found Chris' name. She pushed the call button before she could chicken out, and held the phone to her ear.

A part of her was praying it would go to voice mail, but no such luck. After two rings, Chris answered. "Hey, I was about to call you. How's Abby?"

It was that right there that made the Daniels family so easy to love. Even though she and Chris hadn't been together in over a decade, he was still concerned about her wellbeing.

"Chris, it's me. Abby."

It took him a moment to respond. "Are you all right?"

"Yeah. I'm . . . I'm fine." She opened her mouth to say the words she knew she needed to, but swiftly closed it again. This wasn't something he should have to hear over the phone. If she was going to do this, then he deserved to hear it from her in person. "I was wondering if maybe I could talk to you."

"Of course you can. You know that." He almost sounded offended that she would think otherwise.

"Do you think you could stop by my apartment? Are you still at your parents' house?"

He hesitated for a moment, as if her request threw him off. "Yeah. I mean, we were about to head out, but we can swing by your place. What's your address? I'll put it in my GPS."

Abby rattled off her address for him, amazed that she was able to get it out at all, considering how nervous she was.

"We'll be there in about twenty minutes." He paused. "Trent's there with you?"

"Yes." She wondered what he thought about that.

"All right. We'll see you in a few." She knew by *we* Chris meant him and his wife. Of course Elizabeth would come with him to see his ex-girlfriend.

Chris hung up and she let her hand fall to her lap. Abby looked at Trent who was still sitting next to her. "He and Elizabeth will be here in about twenty minutes."

Trent pried the phone from her grasp and stuffed it in his pocket.

As fear gripped her, Abby stood abruptly. "I need some more wine."

Before he could comment, she swiped her empty wineglass from the nightstand and hightailed it to the kitchen. Abby desperately needed to steady her nerves. Telling Trent had been hard enough. She had less than twenty minutes to find the resolve she needed to reveal her dark secret to Chris and his wife.

She was polishing off her newly refilled glass when Trent strolled into the kitchen. He leaned against the doorjamb and crossed his arms over his chest. His eyes seemed to bore into her soul and she wanted to crawl into a hole and hide.

When she went to set her glass on the counter, Abby miscalculated the distance and it went tumbling onto the floor. She jumped as broken glass flew in all directions.

Trent hurried forward. He pulled her clear and moved her to stand in the doorway. "Stay there."

He carefully made his way through the glass, opening several of her cabinets until he found the trash can under the sink. Next, he located her broom and dustpan. He gathered the smaller shards into a pile, scooped them up, and dumped them into the trash.

The entire time he worked, she stood there staring at him. Abby knew she should help him, but she couldn't seem to get her limbs to move.

Trent was putting the trash can back into place when the doorbell rang. It startled her so much she let out a squeak.

Trent approached her and rubbed his hands up and down her arms. "Ready?"

"Not even a little."

He stepped toward the living room and held out his hand for her. Abby looked at it, and then at him, before taking a deep breath and linking their hands. It was time to face the music.

* * *

Of all the things Trent could have dreamed of Abby telling him, finding out she had borne his brother's child hadn't even been on his list of possibilities. He'd told her he didn't know what he was feeling, but that wasn't entirely true. His feelings ran the gamut from anger on his brother's behalf to a fierce protectiveness at seeing Abby so obviously upset. One moment he wanted to take her into his arms and whisper that it would be okay. The next he wanted to yell and ask her how she could have kept such a thing to herself. Which is why he'd chosen to keep his own counsel for now.

He stood off to the side as Abby went to open the door. She glanced back at him with her hand on the doorknob. Trent didn't envy her. Chris would be upset, and rightly so.

The doorbell sounded again, and Abby shivered. He resisted the impulse to go to her. This was something she needed to do on her own. He'd be there, but he couldn't take the burden from her.

She seemed to brace herself before twisting the knob and pulling the door open.

"Chris. Elizabeth." Despite how nervous she was, her voice was steady as she invited them inside.

His brother saw him standing against the wall when he and Elizabeth stepped into the apartment. Trent did his best to keep his expression neutral.

Elizabeth stayed close to her husband, plainly curious as to whatever was about to take place. She looked around, taking in her surroundings. Trent felt bad for her, too. This would affect her and Chris both.

Chris took a good look at Abby and frowned. "You've been crying."

"It's been a long day." She rubbed her palms down her sides in a nervous gesture. "Do you want to have a seat?"

Chris seemed reluctant to move, but Elizabeth took his hand and guided him over to the couch. Abby closed the door and trailed after them. She sat down in the high-backed chair a couple of feet away.

Trent remained lounging against the wall, watching the awkwardness of the situation. He debated asking Elizabeth to join him in the kitchen to give Chris and Abby some privacy, but decided against it. Abby looked as if she was barely holding herself together, and he doubted Elizabeth would be all that eager to leave her husband's side.

"Tell me what's going on," Chris demanded, derailing Trent's thoughts.

"I need to tell you something and I thought it was better if I did it in person." Her voice trembled and Trent knew his brother heard it.

Chris' hand twitched in Abby's direction before he pressed it firmly against his thigh. "I'm here. You can tell me. Whatever it is."

Abby's shoulders slouched a little. She clasped her hands in her lap and met Chris' gaze. "That night we . . . we hooked up in Fort Lauderdale."

His brother stiffened and opened his mouth to speak—probably to offer an apology—but Abby cut him off.

"Something happened that I need you to know about." She took a deep breath but it didn't appear to help calm her in the slightest. "I don't know if we were too drunk to use a condom or if one broke, but . . . about eight weeks after I got home, I found out I was pregnant."

Chris clenched his fists and his breathing picked up. "What are you saying?"

Elizabeth's eyes were wide with shock. Trent could relate. He was still a bit stunned himself.

Abby hurried to try and explain. "I'm sorry I didn't tell you. I was scared and I didn't know what to do, so I did nothing. I kept making excuses not to call and tell you. Then . . . then I went into labor."

The color drained from Chris' face as the tone of Abby's voice changed. He knew something was coming.

Elizabeth placed her hand over her husband's, but he didn't seem to notice.

"During delivery the umbilical cord got tangled around her neck somehow. By the time the doctor got her free, she was blue." Abby's voice grew softer. "They couldn't save her."

Even though he couldn't see her face, he knew Abby was crying again. Trent forced himself to stay put. It was one of the hardest things he'd ever done in his life.

"She?" Chris swallowed.

Abby nodded. "Yes."

His brother stared at nothing in particular and then asked, "What did she . . . I mean . . . do you have a picture of her?"

"In my room." Abby stood. "I'll go get it."

Before any of them could respond, she was down the hall and out of sight.

Chris' gaze settled on Trent. "You knew?"

"She told me about five minutes before she called you."

"I don't understand," Chris said.

Trent opened his mouth, but quickly closed it again when Abby reappeared. She crossed the room and held two pictures out in front of her. One he recognized as the ultrasound photo she'd shown him earlier. The other was new.

Chris ran the tips of his fingers over the two pictures. "Where—"

Emotion left the words lodged in his throat, but Abby seemed to understand what he was asking anyway. "She's buried in New York."

Chris released a shaky breath, handed her back the photos, and stood. "We need to go."

"Chris, I'm sorry. I know I should have told you. I just . . ."

His brother took Elizabeth's hand and led her toward the door. He didn't stop until he was halfway outside. His brother glared back at Abby, his eyes full of emotion. "Yes. You should have."

Abby wrapped her arms around her waist. She looked utterly defeated. "I'm sorry."

Chris blew out a breath and shook his head. "I need some time."

She nodded, but Trent doubted his brother saw it. Chris hurried down the sidewalk, leaving Trent and Abby alone.

Trent walked across the room and shut the door. When he turned back around, he found Abby crumpled into a heap on the floor. He gathered her into his arms and held her as she let go.

They sat there until shadows began to fill the room. Trent helped her up, and then scooped her back into his arms. He carried her down the short hallway to her bedroom. The whole time, Abby kept her eyes closed. He had no idea if she knew where he was taking her or not.

Trent got his answer when he laid her down on the mattress and went to remove her shoes. Abby opened her eyes and blinked several times, as if even the little bit of light coming in through the windows hurt her eyes. When he went to pull the blanket over her, she reached for him. "Don't leave me."

Without giving it a second thought, he kicked off his shoes and climbed onto her bed. She snuggled against him. Trent placed a kiss on her palm and folded her hand against his chest.

They didn't speak and that was fine with Trent. Elizabeth would take care of Chris, and Trent would see to Abby. He could do that. And on some level, he needed to do it.

Eventually Abby's breathing evened out and he knew she'd fallen asleep. He ran a hand over her head and down her back. A lot had happened today and he didn't know what it would mean for them— for the relationship they were trying to build. He was upset, sure, but it didn't change how he felt about her.

If she'd kept the baby from Chris out of spite or something, Trent was sure he'd feel differently. But that wasn't what happened. He believed her when she said that she'd been scared. There was no way at twenty he would have felt ready to have a child.

But, if it had happened, he would have stepped up and done the right thing. He knew Chris would have as well. Had she told his brother back then, Chris would most likely have married Abby. Surely she would have known that.

Maybe that was another reason she'd kept it to herself. Abby knew Chris. Knew he would do the responsible thing.

Trent closed his eyes and pressed his lips against her forehead. The anger on his brother's behalf was fading and it was being replaced by sympathy. He ached for the young woman who'd found out she was pregnant after a one-night stand with her ex. He ached for that same young woman who was told her baby didn't survive.

Eventually his eyelids began to feel heavy and he let sleep claim him. His dreams that night were full of Abby, Chris, and Elizabeth. It was all a jumbled mess that didn't make any sense and was immediately forgotten when he felt the mattress shift, waking him.

He opened his eyes to find Abby on the edge of the bed. Her back was to him, but he could feel the sadness rolling off her.

Sitting up, Trent scooted across the bed until he was behind her. He circled his arms around her waist and rested his chin on her shoulder. Despite the circumstances, it felt good to be here with her like this.

Abby leaned into him. "Thank you for staying."

Trent kissed her neck in response, sensing she needed the reassurance.

They sat on the edge of her bed, watching the sunlight slowly fill the room. There was so much that needed to be said, but neither seemed to be in a hurry to revisit the subject that was weighing on both their minds.

When it couldn't be put off any longer, Abby turned her head to the side and met his gaze. "I'm gonna make some coffee. You want some?"

"Sure."

She got up and made her way out of the room.

Trent scrubbed a rough hand over his face and walked the short distance to the bathroom. After taking care of business, he went to find Abby.

She was standing in front of the large glass door that led to a small backyard behind her apartment. The smell of coffee brewing filled the air. As appealing as the caffeinated beverage was, Trent was drawn to Abby more. He crossed the room and wrapped his arms around her.

This time she didn't seem to welcome his touch. She stiffened and moved several feet away, turning her back to him.

"What's wrong?"

"Why are you still here?" she asked in barely more than a whisper.

"Do you want me to go?"

Abby met his gaze. "No. I don't want you to go. I should. It would be easier if you did . . . easier if you and I avoided each other . . . kept it professional."

She paused and he waited.

"What must you think of me?" Abby looked at him with wide eyes full of unshed tears.

That protective instinct hit him again. "I'm not going to lie and say I don't care that you kept something this big from my brother, because I do. I can't imagine what he's going through right now. But I know you, Abby. I know that you aren't a vindictive person. I know that you had to have been scared when you found out you were pregnant."

When he didn't go on, she prompted him. "But?"

"But I don't understand why you didn't come to us. We were like family to you growing up. How could you think we would have abandoned you, or hated you, or . . . how could you think we would have been anything but supportive?" Maybe he shouldn't have been so blunt about it, but he was feeling rather raw this morning.

She looked out the large glass door again, as if she were putting up a wall between them. He didn't like it. "That isn't why I didn't say anything."

"Then why?"

Abby wrapped her arms around her middle again, hugging herself. "Because I know your family. I know Chris. And I knew that once he found out, he'd expect me to marry him."

CHAPTER 12

BEFORE TRENT COULD DECIDE how to respond, his phone rang. He wanted to ignore it, but he figured whatever it was had to be important if the person was calling at six thirty in the morning.

"Daniels."

"Trent, it's Brian." There was an edge to his voice that got Trent's attention. "Sorry to call so early, but you need to get here ASAP. It looks like the lock on the gate has been busted."

Trent looked at Abby, who'd turned her back on him again. He didn't want to leave her—leave things like this. The thought crossed his mind to call Trinity and let her deal with it, but he dismissed the notion. He was the boss. Like it or not, it was his problem to deal with. "I'll be there in twenty minutes. Keep everyone in the parking lot."

"You got it."

Trent disconnected the call and returned his cell to his pocket. Abby was standing in front of the coffeemaker, still not looking at him.

He started toward her, and then hesitated. The set of her shoulders said she wouldn't welcome his touch at the moment. "I need to go."

She nodded and reached into a nearby cabinet. "I'll get you some coffee to take with you."

"Abby—"

"Can we not talk about this right now? I'm really tired of crying," she said.

Even though he didn't want to, Trent agreed. "Sure."

She relaxed her shoulders and continued to get his coffee for him. He had the urge to comfort her, but he resisted.

Abby turned, one of those travel mugs in her hand. She held it out for him and he took it. Their eyes met for the briefest moment before she looked away.

He gritted his teeth and forced himself to move toward the door. "I'll call you later."

Trent didn't wait for her reaction. She'd probably tell him he didn't have to or something along those lines. He didn't want to hear it.

His worry over Abby was cut short when he turned into the parking lot in front of his office. The entrance to the yard where all their equipment was kept was at the far end. Brian and five other guys were waiting for him.

"Sorry, Trent," Brian said as he approached. "I figured you'd want to know."

Trent took a look at the damage and understood why Brian had called him. The lock was cut and even from outside he could tell some stuff was missing. He pulled out his phone and called Trinity.

"A little early isn't it, Boss?" At least she sounded like he hadn't woken her up.

"I know, but I need you to get here as soon as you can. There's been a break-in."

"What?" she practically screamed into the phone.

"I'm going to be busy dealing with the cops, so I need you here."

"I'll be out the door in five minutes." He could already hear her moving.

When he hung up with Trinity, he motioned to Brian who was standing in a huddle with the other guys about ten feet away. "None of the guys have been inside the yard?"

Brian shook his head. "No. I was the first one here. As soon as I saw the lock was broken, I called you."

Trent glanced up at the security camera he had positioned near the entrance. It looked as if the angle had been changed. Who knew if they would get any useful footage from it, but he'd cross that bridge later.

At the moment, he had to get his guys moving. Just because their yard was now a crime scene didn't mean the work stopped. They were going to have to improvise. "Put together a list of what everyone is going to need for the day. We can rent any machinery and you can go to the store and pick up the rest. I'll take care of the police report, but we can't just sit on our asses while we wait for them to do their thing."

Brian nodded and strolled back over to the group of guys. He'd been with Trent almost from the beginning. He'd make sure to get everyone moving in the right direction.

While his crews figured out what they would need to get the day's work done, Trent called to report the break-in. With all the drama going on in his personal life, he didn't need to be dealing with this, too. Unfortunately, he was the boss. He didn't get to choose.

It took almost two hours for the police to arrive. There wasn't any imminent danger, so in their book there was no need to rush.

The detective showed up a little after ten. He was bald and looked to be in his late fifties. Trent walked through the yard with him as he asked about security and Trent's employees. With his brother being a cop, Trent knew the routine. He also knew that he and his employees would be prime suspects until proven otherwise.

None of the large equipment was stolen—that was a plus—but a good portion of his hand tools were missing. At first glance, he would estimate over five thousand dollars in shovels, picks, and drills were taken. There was also mulch and some small bags of gravel missing. Whoever it was had chosen items that could be picked up and moved without too much trouble.

When they went inside to look at the security footage, Trent wasn't surprised to find it was worthless.

"How many people have access to the gated area?" Detective Travers asked.

"My four crew leaders all have keys, as well as the office staff."

Detective Travers scribbled something down in his notebook. "How many is that?"

"Three. Trinity is my office manager. Joss helps with scheduling and he's in charge of deliveries. And Kevin handles our accounting."

"I'm assuming you have a key as well." The detective made more notes.

"Of course."

"Can you account for your whereabouts last night, Mr. Daniels?"

Trent had known the question was coming. "Yes. I was with a friend."

The detective raised an eyebrow.

"A female friend," Trent clarified.

"Her name?"

"Abigail Hoffman."

Detective Travers nodded.

Several more moments went by before he tucked his notebook in his pocket and met Trent's gaze. "I don't know how well you know your staff, Mr. Daniels, but this feels like an inside job to me. Someone knew where that camera was and how to avoid it. They also appear to have known exactly what they were going for."

Trent's first reaction was to get defensive, but then he remembered the missing mulch from two weeks ago. Besides, it wouldn't help his case if he ticked off the detective. "Most of them have been with me for at least a few years. I trust them."

Detective Travers didn't seem surprised by Trent's answer. "We'll run the fingerprints, but I wouldn't hold your breath. Chances are they'll all match those of your employees."

The detective was probably right.

"I'll be in touch," Detective Travers said as he moved toward the door. "I might also suggest that you put some security cameras inside the yard. And if I were you, I would keep the fact that they're there to yourself."

"Thanks."

Detective Travers gave Trent a curt nod before he showed himself out.

Sighing, Trent lowered himself into his chair. He was having trouble wrapping his head around the idea that one of his employees would steal from him. But if it wasn't someone who worked for him, then how did they know exactly where the security camera was positioned and how to avoid it? He felt nauseous just thinking about it.

A knock sounded at his door. "Come in."

The door opened and Trinity walked into his office. She set a cup of coffee down on his desk. "I thought about bringing you something a little stronger, but I figured that wouldn't be a great example in front of the employees."

He took the offering and brought it to his lips. "Thanks."

Trinity had shut the door behind her, so for all intents and purposes they were alone. "Do they have any leads?"

"No. Not yet." Trent shook his head and took a sip of his coffee. What Detective Travers said kept ringing in his ears. It didn't sit well with him that he had to keep this from everyone, including his office manager.

"Well, hopefully they'll have something soon, right?" she asked.

"Hopefully."

Trent decided it was best to change the subject. With all the activity that morning, there was plenty to go over and an inventory had to be made of all their supplies and equipment. The insurance company, as well as Detective Travers, would need an accurate count of what had been taken.

At noon, Trent sent Trinity out to get lunch for the office. It was the least he could do. All four of them would be spending most of the afternoon counting inventory in the hot sun. Not exactly how he'd wanted to spend his day and he was sure they didn't either.

With Trinity picking up lunch, Trent shut himself in his office and dialed Abby. He was worried about her and how they'd left things.

Her phone rang four times, and then went to voice mail. Had she made it to work today?

Trent was still mulling over his options, which included calling Max—as averse as he was to the idea—when Trinity returned with the food. His stomach growled, reminding him that he'd skipped breakfast. Pushing his worry over Abby aside for the time being, Trent joined his employees at the conference table and dug into his lunch.

* * *

Somehow, Abby had managed to drag herself into work this morning when what she really wanted to do was crawl back in bed and pull the sheet over her. She thought she'd been doing pretty good keeping up appearances for the last two hours, but she should have known Max would figure out something was wrong.

He skidded to a halt in front of her desk after exiting the conference room for the second time that morning. "What did he do?"

She thought about lying, but what would be the use? "Trent didn't do anything. I-I told Chris."

Max sucked in a deep breath and moved to her side of the desk. He placed his briefcase on the floor and knelt down beside her. "What happened?"

Tears formed in her eyes again. She would have thought with all the crying she'd done in the past twenty-four hours that she'd be cried out. Apparently not.

Without warning, Max pulled her up out of her chair and practically carried her into his office. He took her over to the couch along the wall, made sure she was comfortable, and then walked back out of the office. He returned a few seconds later, briefcase in hand.

As he moved about the office, there was no doubt that this was his domain. Max intimidated a lot of people and it was easy to see why. He forwarded the phones, locked the door so they wouldn't be interrupted, and joined her on the couch.

"Tell me what happened," he demanded, taking both her hands in his. The gesture was in complete contrast to his tone.

Abby pulled her hands out of his grip and wiped a stray tear from her cheek. "Things with Trent were . . . heating up. I had to tell him. I couldn't let things continue between us and then have it come out later."

"And?"

"He said I needed to tell Chris. That he deserved to know." She leaned forward, burying her face in her hands. "He was right, of course. How many times over the years have I thought about calling Chris and telling him about Kaylee, and then chickening out?"

"How'd he take it?"

She groaned and dropped her hands. "He was upset."

When she didn't go on, Max's eyes narrowed. "What did he say?"

Abby knew if she said the wrong thing he would be out the door in a heartbeat, and be on Chris' doorstep within the hour.

"Not much. He said he needed time to think, and then he left."

Max's jaw stiffened. "And Trent?"

She looked away. "He stayed with me."

"That's what you wanted, right?"

Abby nodded.

"So why do you look as if your world just ended?" Max asked.

She twisted her fingers in her lap. "Trent asked me this morning why I'd never told Chris. He wanted to know what had held me back since I had to know that he and his family would all have supported me and my decision to keep the baby."

Max reached for her hands again, but she stood, pulling away from him. She didn't want his comfort—didn't deserve it.

"I told him the truth. That Chris would have wanted to get married and . . ." She walked over to the large window that framed the back of Max's office.

"And you told him you didn't want to marry his brother."

She nodded again.

"I take it that didn't go over very well?" Max got up and moved to stand beside her.

"I don't know. We didn't get to discuss it. He got a phone call and had to leave."

Max turned toward her, resting his hip on the windowsill. "So what has you more upset? Chris? Or that you don't know what Trent thinks about you saying you didn't want to marry his brother?"

"I'm sorry I upset Chris. I never meant to. Looking back, I know I should have sucked it up and told him. There was nothing that said I had to marry him if I didn't want to." She met Max's gaze. "I am worried about what Chris will do after he has time to think about it, but . . ."

"But you're more worried about Trent's reaction."

She nodded.

"This thing between the two of you, do you see it going anywhere? Are you planning to stay here when I return to New York?"

Abby opened her mouth, but nothing came out.

"I didn't mean to put you on the spot."

"It's okay. I know you're worried."

Max pulled out the chair behind his desk and took a seat. "I am. I think you're falling for this guy and your history with his brother is going to make the two of you being together complicated."

"I know that," she defended.

"I hope so, because things could get ugly. Chris' reaction is just the tip of the iceberg. How do you think his parents are going to feel once they find out? If you're with Trent long term, that's something you're all going to have to deal with."

She blanched. Abby had been so caught up in Chris and Trent that she hadn't thought much about what Mike and Marilyn would say. Or Paul. Or Gage.

He studied her face for a long moment. "I want you to take the day off. Go get a massage or something. Relax. And try not to think about it for a while. Going by all those stories you used to tell me about growing up with the Danielses, I would bet one or both of them are going to show up on your doorstep sooner rather than later. You need to be mentally prepared, and right now you're a mess."

"Thanks." She absentmindedly ran a hand through her hair.

Max grinned at her sarcasm. "Go. Pamper yourself. Forget all about the Daniels family for an afternoon. Clear your head."

"What about—"

"Work will wait. Heaven knows those boxes of invoices you've been working on aren't going anywhere. And if something comes up, I'll take care of it." She saw the determined look on his face. He wasn't going to take no for an answer.

She threw her arms around his neck and gave him a tight squeeze. "Thank you."

It took her less than five minutes to gather her things. The receptionist waved to her as she passed through the lobby. "Going out, Miss Hoffman? Do you need me to cover your phones?"

"Yes, thank you." The fact that she hadn't thought to call the woman and let her know that the phones would be diverted for the rest of the day proved just how out of it Abby was. Maybe Max was right. She needed some 'me time' to get her head on straight before she dealt with any of the Danielses. Of course, that was going to be easier said than done, since as soon as she slid behind the wheel of her car, she wanted to drive over to Trent's work and talk to him.

As strong as that pull was, she resisted. If she went to see him now, Abby knew she'd end up breaking down in tears again. Granted, she couldn't guarantee that wasn't going to happen anyway the next time she saw him.

Using her GPS, she found a full service spa not too far away. Since she didn't have an appointment, she had to take what openings they had. That was okay, though. The soft music helped to ease the tension in her muscles as she changed out of her clothes and into a fluffy robe the spa supplied.

For the next six hours, Abby tried not to think about anything. She got a facial, a manicure and pedicure, a massage, and even got her hair done. On the outside, she looked refreshed, even if she didn't feel that way on the inside.

Back in her own clothes, she handed the woman behind the counter her credit card. "Thanks for fitting me in today."

"Not a problem. You picked a good day. Mondays are usually pretty slow."

Abby made sure to leave a good tip for each of the ladies who'd helped her today. Max had been right. She'd needed this.

Once outside, Abby turned her phone back on. She had a text from Max and one missed call. Abby checked the text first.

You'd better be relaxing or else. – Max

She snorted.

That man needed a woman of his own. As much as she loved his protectiveness, sometimes she wished he had somewhere else to direct it.

See you tomorrow morning. – Abby

Abby chuckled and tucked her phone back in her purse. Let him make of that what he would.

The drive home took a little longer than she would have liked. It was rush hour and traffic was backed up because of an accident. She considered taking a different route, but so much had changed since she used to live here. Knowing her luck, she'd get lost.

Finally, the cars ahead of her began moving and she drove the remaining five miles to her apartment complex. As she turned into the parking lot, she had a moment of panic wondering if Trent or Chris would be waiting for her, but there was no sign of their vehicles.

She pulled into her parking space and turned off the engine. It was then she remembered that she had a missed call. After digging her phone out of her purse, she pulled up her call log. The missed call was from Trent's cell. She doubled-checked her voice mail, but he hadn't left a message. She had no idea what that meant.

Forcing herself to go inside, she locked up her apartment, and headed straight into her bedroom. She fell onto her bed and pulled the pillow Trent had used the night before against her chest. His scent lingered and it calmed her more than all the pampering she'd gotten that day at the spa. She closed her eyes and sighed. Within minutes, she was asleep.

CHAPTER 13

TRENT STEPPED off the ladder that led to the loft area above one of the tool sheds. They didn't keep much up there, but he had to check it anyway to be sure. Everything looked to be there, though, so whoever it was had only taken what was easily accessible.

Sweat was pouring off him. It was ninety degrees today and the humidity was stifling. He felt for his crews on days like this.

Grabbing his bottle of water, he downed the rest of the contents. Thank goodness he was finally done with inventory and he could go home and shower.

He took one last look around the shed before heading toward the dumpster to toss his now empty water bottle. When he walked out from beneath the cover of the shed, Trent noticed his brother marching toward him. Chris looked to be on a mission. Trent was glad he'd sent Trinity, Joss, and Kevin home. Whatever his brother had to say, they didn't need to hear it.

Chris waited for him right inside the gate.

"Hey. I didn't expect see you today." Trent moved past his brother to the yard entrance. He'd been out in the heat for hours. If they were going to have the discussion Trent figured they were going to have, he didn't want to be outside when it happened—especially if there was a better alternative.

Chris' footsteps crunched on the gravel as he followed Trent out. He stood silently while Trent locked the gate with the shiny new lock he'd had to buy.

Without a word, they walked over to the office and went inside.

"Did you want something to drink?" Trent asked. "Water? Coffee? I might even have a pop in the fridge."

"I'm good." Chris' voice was clipped.

Reaching in to get a fresh bottle of water for himself, Trent brought it over to Trinity's desk and sat down. He eyed his brother cautiously as he tipped the bottle up and took a swig.

Instead of saying anything, Chris began pacing.

Trent leaned forward, bracing his water between his hands. "You obviously came down here for a reason. Spit it out already."

Chris stopped and looked at him. "You sound like Paul."

Trent released a short laugh. "Not sure if I should take that as a compliment or not."

One side of his brother's lip twitched. Paul was the quintessential older brother. He was the responsible one and he had an opinion on everything.

"I'm guessing you came to see me about Abby."

Chris ran a rough hand through his hair before plopping down in a chair himself. He looked worn down. "Why didn't she tell me?"

While Trent knew the answer to that thanks to Abby blurting it out that morning, he didn't feel it was his place to tell his brother. "What would you have done if she had?"

"I don't know." Chris shook his head. "I thought about it all night, and then today . . . I couldn't stay focused at work. Finally, Elizabeth suggested I drive down and talk to Abby. But what am I supposed to say? My first instinct is to yell at her for not telling me. But what good will that do? It isn't going to change anything. And it was twelve years ago."

"Might make you feel better," Trent suggested. Even as he said it, his body recoiled. Although he knew his brother would never physically harm Abby, the thought of Chris being aggressive to her in any way brought his hackles up.

"Maybe. I'm not sure about that, though." Chris rested his elbows on his knees. "We were young. And stupid. I remember waking up that morning thinking that I had to get my head on straight because something like that couldn't happen again."

He paused and looked out one of the large windows along the front of the office, seeming to need a minute to gather his thoughts. Trent waited. He knew this couldn't be easy for his brother.

"I've been trying to put myself in her shoes. What would I have done in that situation? And . . ." Chris blew out a breath. "I hope I wouldn't have kept it a secret. That I would have felt comfortable enough to share what was happening. But as Elizabeth pointed out, I can't possibly know what it would have felt like to be a twenty-year-old woman, alone, and pregnant."

Chris took another break. He bowed his head and rubbed the heels of his hands against his eyes. Trent was patient. His brother needed to get it out.

"What keeps nagging me most, though, is wondering if she would have ever told me had she not come back." Chris' voice sounded loud in the otherwise quiet room. "Would I have gone the rest of my life not knowing?"

He met Trent's gaze, as if pleading, hoping he had the answers Chris was seeking.

"I can't answer that. She told me she'd wanted to tell you, but didn't know how." That much was the truth.

"Yeah. And on an intellectual level, I get that. But—"

"But you're still mad at her," Trent finished for him.

Chris looked his brother in the eye. "Wouldn't you be?"

Trent didn't answer right away. "Probably."

They were both quiet for a long while. Trent was trying to give his brother time.

Chris shifted in his chair, drawing Trent's attention.

"Are you and Abby together?" The question hung in the air.

"I'm not sure what we are at the moment."

Chris sat up, straightening his shoulders as if he were preparing himself. "Have you slept with her?"

The memory of Abby underneath him on the couch flashed through his mind. "No."

"But you want to." It wasn't a question. "You always did have a crush on her."

Trent was shocked. He'd thought he'd kept his feelings for Abby to himself back then.

"Don't look so surprised. You hung out with us every chance you got. What sixteen-year-old guy chooses to hang with his brother and his brother's girlfriend instead of going out with his friends, unless he's got stars in his eyes for his brother's girl?"

Trent rolled his eyes.

"Seriously, I wondered back then why you never said anything."

Trent looked at his brother as if he'd lost his mind. "She was your girl."

To some that might not have been enough, but for them it was.

Chris nodded. "We always did have the same taste in women."

"Never gonna let me live down the fact that I went on a date with your wife before you did, are you?"

"Not a chance," Chris muttered.

They both chuckled before falling silent again.

"What are you going to do?" Trent asked after several minutes had passed. His brother knew he was talking about Abby.

"Talk to her, I guess. I still have no idea what I'm going to say, but if you two . . ." Chris waved his hand in the air to fill in the blanks. "We can't ignore the elephant in the room."

Trent knew that was true enough. If he and Abby did manage to make things work, then she and Chris would be seeing each other a lot. His brother and sister-in-law only lived about an hour north of Cincinnati. They came down to visit almost every weekend.

Before Trent could say more, Chris stood. "I should go. I told Elizabeth I'd be back tonight."

Standing, Trent followed his brother to the door. He locked up and they both headed to their vehicles.

He rested a hand on the front of his truck and glanced over at Chris. As much as Trent wanted to see Abby tonight, Chris needed to talk to her more. Before he could say anything, his brother asked, "You want to grab some pizza?"

Trent smirked. "Putting it off isn't going to make it any easier. Why don't you pick up a pizza and take it with you to Abby's?"

Chris sighed. "This emotional stuff isn't my strong suit. But you're right. It's better to get it over with."

"Good luck," Trent said as he walked around to the driver's side of his truck and reached for the door.

"Thanks."

Trent watched as his brother backed out and drove away. Every cell in his body wanted to go to Abby, to stand beside her as she and Chris had this very important conversation. But he knew he couldn't. As much as he wanted to be in Abby's life—to be the one she leaned on—this wasn't something he could help her with.

It hadn't escaped his attention that Chris had come alone. Apparently, Elizabeth felt the same as Trent did because he knew she would do anything for his brother, would stand beside him come hell or high water. No, this was something Chris and Abby had to figure out together.

Slipping the key into the ignition, Trent started the truck and headed home to his empty house. It was going to be a very long evening.

* * *

Abby reluctantly opened her eyes and yawned. The nap had done her good.

She sat up and glanced out the window. It was still light out. According to the glowing numbers of her alarm clock, it was a little after seven. As if in response to the time, her stomach picked that moment to protest. The spa had provided a small lunch, but that was hours ago.

Getting out of bed, Abby made her way into the kitchen. She

opened her refrigerator, contemplating her options. There wasn't much there beyond the basics, but surely she could throw something edible together even if it was nothing more than scrambled eggs.

She was removing the egg carton when the doorbell rang. All the relaxation from before vanished and her heart rate skyrocketed. Trent. Abby needed to talk to him. She needed to know that what had happened hadn't damaged their friendship. Even if they could never have anything more than that, she still wanted him—needed him—as a friend.

In less than ten seconds, she was wrenching the door open. But it wasn't Trent standing on her doorstep. It was Chris.

Abby opened her mouth to say something, but the words wouldn't come.

"Hi," he said, lifting the pizza box he was holding. "I brought dinner. I was hoping we could talk."

She stepped back and motioned him inside. "Sure. Um. Come in."

Chris brushed past her. He was large and imposing physically. All the Daniels men were, even their father, Mike. They were all over six feet tall and had strong, broad shoulders. Abby remembered what it had felt like to have Chris hold her, how his touch used to make her heart skip a beat, but that was long gone. There was someone else who held that power over her now. She only hoped Trent would be able to forgive her for what she'd done to his brother—his family.

Abby led Chris into her small kitchen. "Can I get you something to drink? I don't have any beer, but I have some wine."

Chris set the pizza box on the table and pulled out a chair. "Just water."

She nodded and reached up into the cabinet for some glasses. As much as she could really use a glass of wine, Abby figured he had the right idea. Water was the better option.

Abby placed their drinks on the table and lowered herself into a chair across from him. Neither reached for the pizza. They just sat there, staring at each other.

He cleared his throat. "I figure you know why I'm here."

"Yes."

A long silence followed.

He opened the pizza box so suddenly she jumped.

Chris stilled. "I'd never hit you, Abby."

Heat colored her cheeks. "I know that. Sorry. I guess I'm just a little jumpy."

After a long moment, he nodded and returned his attention to the pizza. It was divided into two halves. One side was covered in onions, mushrooms, peppers, and pepperoni. The other half only had cheese and pepperoni. He'd remembered.

"Thanks," she mumbled as she reached for a slice. "You didn't have to get both. I could have picked off the stuff I don't like."

He shrugged and stuffed a large slice of pizza into his mouth.

After a couple of bites, Abby felt as if she needed to say something. He'd come to her, obviously ready to talk. Now it was up to her.

"When I found out I was pregnant, I picked up the phone to call you at least a dozen times," she said.

"What stopped you?" It was a valid question.

"I didn't want to disappoint your family," she whispered.

Chris' eyes widened. "How would you finding out you were pregnant disappoint my family?"

Abby sighed. There was no way to get around this. She could try to dress it up as much as she wanted, but it wouldn't make a difference. Setting her pizza down, she met his gaze. "Because I knew you'd want to do the right thing. You'd want to marry me, and I didn't feel that way about you anymore."

He slammed his fist against the table and dropped the piece of pizza he'd had in his hand. "So because you didn't want to marry me, you decided it was okay to keep the fact that you were having my baby from me?"

Chris was seething and she couldn't blame him.

"I'm sorry." She could say it a million times over and it still wouldn't seem like enough.

For the longest time he glared at her across the table. "Were you ever going to tell me?"

It would be so easy to lie to him. To tell him that yes, she would have told him. One of these days. "I don't know. If she had lived, yes, I would have told you. But it was . . . easier after she died to justify keeping it to myself. She was gone. There was no point—"

"No point?" She saw his nostrils flare. He clenched his fists and Abby knew he was trying to hold on to his temper. "How could you think there was no point in telling me I had a daughter? Whether she lived or not shouldn't matter."

Abby felt about two inches tall. "I know. I'm sorry."

He blew out a breath. "You said she's in New York."

She nodded. "Yes. She's buried in the children's section of a cemetery in Brooklyn. I didn't like her being in the city, but I wanted her close by so I could go visit her."

Chris scraped his chair across the floor and stood. He paced back and forth several times, stopped, looked at her, and then went back to pacing. When he turned to face her, hands on his hips, the look on his face was almost scary. "I want you to take me to see her. I deserve that much. You owe me that much."

Abby didn't know how she felt about taking Chris to New York to see Kaylee's grave, but he was right. She did owe him. "Okay."

He looked as if he'd been ready to argue his point home, so when she immediately agreed, it took him a few moments to shift gears. "I want to go as soon as possible."

"We can go whenever you want." Max wouldn't be happy about it. Not about her going, but that she was going with Chris. Alone. Max would want to come with them.

"This weekend?" he asked. Although it sounded more like a statement than it did a question.

So soon.

"Sure. I'll call tomorrow and make the flight arrangements," she said.

He didn't move for a long time. "I should get home to Elizabeth. She'll be worried."

When he started for the door, Abby stopped him. "I really am sorry, Chris. I never meant to hurt you. No matter what, you didn't deserve that."

Chris paused long enough to let her say her piece, then marched out the door, leaving his half-eaten slice of pizza sitting on his plate to grow cold.

More than anything, she wished she could go back in time and change things. But she couldn't. What was done was done. All she could do now was try and make it right for him. If Chris needed to go to Kaylee's grave, then she'd give him that.

Abby cleaned up and put the pizza in the refrigerator. She made sure everything was turned off and secured for the night before heading to her bedroom. Absentmindedly, she went to the closet and removed the shoebox that contained the little bits of her daughter she had left.

She reached into the box and removed the tiny stuffed bear Max had brought to the hospital for Kaylee. It was pink and fit in the palm of her hand. She set the box aside and curled up on the bed, tucking the bear under her chin.

CHAPTER 14

Trent had tried to keep himself busy. Hell, he'd even started going through the junk in his garage that had been piling up for the last five years. The good news was that he was making progress. He could see the wall again, at least. The bad news was that it had done nothing to keep his mind off Abby.

He took the box cutter he'd been using and sliced through the tape of another box. As he opened the flaps, his cell vibrated in his pocket. Concerned it might be Abby or Chris, Trent dug the phone out of his pocket. Elizabeth's name lit up his screen.

"How's my favorite sister-in-law?"

She released something that sounded like a mix between a laugh and a sigh. "Ask me that again in an hour or so."

Trent stopped what he was doing. "Everything all right?"

"It will be, I think," she said. "I just got off the phone with Chris. He's on his way home."

"I take it his talk with Abby didn't go well?" Trent reached for a stool nearby and sat down, the box forgotten.

Elizabeth made an unintelligible sound. "I guess that depends on how you look at it."

He waited for her to go on.

"They talked, and at least he seems to have gotten some answers. But . . ."

"But?" he prompted.

"Chris wants to go to New York and see where his daughter is buried. They're making arrangements to fly out this coming weekend."

Trent's mind raced with concern for Abby. For Chris. And even for Elizabeth. People he cared about were hurting and he felt as if his hands were tied.

"I take it you don't want him to go?" Trent asked.

"It's not that. I understand his need to go. I just . . . he wants to do this by himself. Just him and Abby," she said, sounding defeated.

"Elizabeth, Chris would never do anything to hurt you. You know that, right? He would never—"

This time he didn't miss her snort. "I'm not worried about him cheating on me with his ex-girlfriend. What I'm worried about is Chris being in New York falling apart, and me being six hundred miles away, unable to be there for him."

There really wasn't anything Trent could say to that. He knew exactly what Elizabeth was feeling in that respect. "Talk to him when he gets home. Maybe he'll change his mind."

"No, he won't."

Trent could have argued, but he didn't see the point. She was right. The chances of Chris changing his mind were slim. His brother was stubborn once he'd made up his mind.

"Can I ask you something?" Elizabeth asked with cautious edge to her voice.

"You know you can."

"Are you and Abby . . ."

He rubbed the back of his head and looked up at the sky. Trent knew what she was asking. "I don't know."

"But you want to be," she said, filling in the blanks.

"Yes." A simple answer, and an honest one.

"I figured as much." She hesitated. "I don't want to overstep here, but if my short conversation with Chris was any indication, I think Abby is going to need someone tonight."

The urge to go to her had been haunting him all evening. "I don't know if I should. She might need time—"

"Trent. Stop second-guessing yourself. Heaven knows, I did enough of that when I first met your brother. If you want to be with her, then be with her. We all make mistakes in life. That doesn't mean we don't deserve to be happy." His sister-in-law knew what she was talking about. She'd spent five years with a man who knocked her around before she'd finally gotten out.

He decided to be honest. "A part of me feels like I'll be betraying Chris."

She was quiet for a long moment. "If the shoe were on the other foot, what would you want him to do? Would you want him to not go after what he wanted, be with who he wanted to be with, because there was history between you and the woman?"

Trent thought about it. Would he mind if one of his brothers had come to him and wanted to date one of his ex-girlfriends? Granted, Trent had never had a relationship with a woman that had come close to what Chris and Abby once had. Even so, he knew the answer. If she was what Chris or Gage or Paul wanted, he wouldn't begrudge them that.

"Thanks, Elizabeth."

"Anytime." He could almost hear her grinning through the phone.

Trent laughed. "You called me for some support and you end up giving me advice. Some friend I am."

"Friends are there for each other. Plus, I'm not only a friend. I'm family."

He smiled. "Have I told you lately how happy I am that my brother manned up and married you?"

It was her turn to chuckle. "No. Can't say that you have."

"Well, I am. He's one lucky bastard."

When they both finished laughing, she said, "Now, get off the phone and go comfort your woman. I have a feeling she's going to need you."

Trent stood and tucked the stool under the wooden bench that ran the length of one wall. "Call me if you or Chris needs anything."

Before Trent ended the call, he was locking the house up and heading toward his truck. It struck him as he was backing out of his driveway how amazing his sister-in-law really was. She had every reason to hate Abby. Not only was she Chris' ex, but Abby had hurt him. Instead, she'd been sympathetic. But that was Elizabeth.

It didn't take Trent long to reach Abby's apartment. He parked his truck, locked it up, and jogged to her door. All the lights inside were off, but he knew she was home. Chris hadn't left all that long ago and her car was still in the lot.

He rang the doorbell twice, but there was no answer, so he tried knocking. Right as he was about to give up, the door opened, and Abby stood there clutching a tiny stuffed bear to her chest. Her eyes were bloodshot. She'd been crying again.

Without a word, Trent walked into the apartment. He closed the door, turned the lock, and then crushed her against him. "I'm here."

Her sobs broke free. "Why? You should hate me for what I did."

"I told you. I could never hate you. Never in a million years." He glanced around. "Were you in your room?"

She nodded.

"Come on." Without waiting for her response, Trent took her hand and headed down the hall to her bedroom. He led her over to the bed, turned down the covers, and encouraged her to get in. Once she was settled, he sat down on the mattress, facing her.

"How did you know to come?" she asked.

"Chris called Elizabeth on his way home, and she called me."

Abby cringed. "I bet she hates me."

Trent nearly growled. "Would you stop with all this talk of people hating you? No one hates you, Abby."

"Chris does. And he should. He has every right to."

"I highly doubt that," Trent said.

"He's not happy with me," she whispered.

Trent brushed the hair away from her face. As conflicted as he was about everything that was going on, there was one thing he wasn't conflicted about. He wanted to be where Abby was. "He needs some time."

She nodded. "He wants . . . we're going to New York this weekend. To see Kaylee's grave."

"I know. Elizabeth told me."

Abby didn't have a response for that, but her stomach rumbled loud enough for him to hear.

"Did you eat dinner?"

She shrugged. "I had a couple bites of pizza when Chris was here. But then, well, I lost my appetite."

"Is the pizza still here?" Trent asked.

"I put it in the fridge."

He pushed himself up off the bed.

"Where are you going?"

"To warm you up some pizza. You need to eat," he said.

Abby shook her head. "I'm not—"

He leaned down and pressed his lips to hers, cutting off her protest. "I'll be right back. Don't go anywhere."

Trent winked before leaving the room. He wasn't used to all this drama. But in the deepest parts of his soul, he knew she was worth it. She always had been.

* * *

Abby sat with her hands in her lap, playing with the small bear while she waited for Trent to come back. She hadn't expected to see him tonight. The fact that he was here made her feel a hundred times better, which was crazy considering they were just friends.

Okay, that wasn't true, and she knew it. Trent meant more to her than that and considering the time they'd spent together lately, she was pretty sure he saw her as more as well. The kisses they'd shared the other night on her couch sure hadn't felt all that friendly. They'd felt possessive and all-consuming.

But that was before she'd come clean and admitted what had happened. Now she had no idea where that left them.

A few minutes later, Trent reentered the room carrying a single plate piled high with pizza. He sat down in the same spot he'd occupied a few minutes before, and placed the plate in front of her. She looked at it, and then up at him. There must have been ten pieces of pizza on the plate. "There is no way I'm going to be able to eat all that."

He selected a piece and brought it to his mouth. "Half is for me."

Abby continued to stare at him while he chewed.

"Eat," he said before taking another bite. "And don't try to tell me you're not hungry. That pizza in your refrigerator looked as if it had barely been touched."

When she didn't immediately start eating, he raised one eyebrow.

Sighing, Abby picked up a piece and lifted it to her mouth. She took a bite, and was surprised to find that she was hungrier than she'd thought. Before she knew it, Abby was reaching for another piece.

Trent smiled and grabbed another piece for himself.

"Did you skip dinner, too?" she asked.

He shrugged. "I can always eat."

That was true from what she remembered. She had no idea how Marilyn had managed to keep food in the house with four teenage boys roaming around.

Thinking about Marilyn brought her right back to thoughts of Kaylee.

"Hey."

Abby looked up to find Trent appraising her. She grinned, but he wasn't fooled.

"Are you worried about going to New York alone with Chris? If you are, I can move some things around at work and go with you."

She shook her head. "No. It's not that."

He patiently waited for her to go on.

"Can we talk about something else? I'm tired of crying and it feels like that's all I've been doing for the last two days." This time she tried to put a little more effort behind her smile. "Tell me about work. Is everything okay? It didn't sound like that phone call this morning was good news."

Trent hesitated for a moment. She figured he was probably trying to decide if he was going to follow her subject change. "Someone broke into the yard last night and stole a bunch of tools, mulch, gravel, and some irrigation hose."

"Oh, no. Trent, I'm so sorry." She wiped her hands off with the napkin he'd provided and reached for his hand.

"I'm insured, so everything that was stolen can be replaced," he said.

But there was something else in his tone that she didn't understand. "Did something else happen?"

"No." He shook his head and sighed, which wasn't like him at all. "The police think it was an inside job."

She gasped, her pizza completely forgotten. "Why?"

"I have a security camera set up outside the gate. Whoever it was knew exactly where it was and they were able to disable it without it picking up anything but a blurry image of their arm."

"It couldn't be someone else?" she asked.

"It could, but the chances of them knowing exactly where it was and how to adjust it in order to avoid detection means they're probably familiar with the yard. I don't let many people back there that don't work for me. There's no need for them to be." He shifted his weight and it moved him farther away from her. "The only exception is the delivery trucks. But that doesn't make much sense either. Then again, neither does one of my employees stealing from me."

"What are you going to do?"

He rested his hand on her knee and she felt heat zing up her leg. "I took inventory today. Found out everything that was missing. This way the cops and the insurance have what they need for their reports. I also put up some additional cameras in case whoever it was strikes again, but I'm not holding my breath." Trent nodded toward the plate that still sat in her lap. "Are you finished?"

She followed his gaze. There were still three pieces left, but Abby had eaten more than she thought she would. "Yeah."

He stood. "I'll be right back."

After he left the room with the rest of the pizza, Abby decided it would probably be a good idea if she took the time to freshen up. When she walked into the bathroom and got a look at herself in the mirror, she cringed. Her eyes were bloodshot and there were streaks of makeup on her cheeks.

Abby gave her face a good scrub, removing the rest of her makeup, and ran a brush through her hair. When she was done, she almost looked human again.

She ambled back into the bedroom to find Trent already sitting on the edge of her bed. He looked up when she walked in, but she couldn't read his mood. Unsure of what to do, she sat down beside him.

"Do you want to watch a movie or something?" she asked.

"We can, if that's what you want. I'm not picky."

He raised his eyebrows in a suggestive way, making her giggle.

"I love to hear you laugh." He cupped the side of her face, stroking her cheek with the pad of his thumb.

When she stared into his eyes, the mood became serious again. "Where does this leave us?"

"All I know is that I'm exactly where I want to be right now." Trent didn't stop touching her and it was doing crazy things to her insides.

She closed her eyes, hoping that would allow her to focus, but it did the exact opposite. Without her sight, her other senses took over. She could feel the heat of his hand and of his leg as it pressed against hers. The scent of him, a mixture of his soap and sweat, swirled around her, drawing her in.

Without conscious thought, she skimmed her fingers up the length of his chest until she could feel the stubble on his neck and chin. She continued higher, to outline his lips and jaw. He kept still as she explored. The only indication that he wasn't completely unaffected was his breathing.

"Abby?"

There was something in his voice that made her open her eyes. It was only then that she realized she'd closed the distance between them. His lips were only an inch away. The desire to feel his mouth on her again was almost unbearable.

She looked up at him, needing confirmation that he felt it, too. The uncertainty she saw in his eyes had her pulling away.

Trent stopped her by framing her face with both his hands. He grazed his lips against hers and held her gaze. "I know how emotional these last few days have been for you. I don't want you rushing into anything you're not sure about."

He was worried that things were happening too fast for her?

"I know you're attracted to me."

Trent snorted. "I'm not denying that. But I've waited seventeen years for you. I can wait a little longer."

Abby looked into his eyes, hoping to convey all she was feeling in that moment. "What if I don't want to wait?"

He released a shaky breath. "I'm trying to do the right thing here. Give you the space and time—"

She pressed her lips against his, and he groaned before kissing her back. It was one of those kisses that set off all her nerve endings at once.

He eased them down onto the mattress, cradling her in his arms. She threaded her fingers in his hair, needing to be closer.

So much in her world was spinning out of control, but Trent had been her lifeline. Even back in high school when Chris had told her he wanted to break up—that he didn't think with him going off to college that they should still see each other—Trent had been the one she'd wanted to go to. She didn't. She couldn't, of course. Instead she'd holed up in her room and cried until her dad had gotten home from work.

Trent had always been her rock. He'd always been the friend she could turn to when all else failed. Now, however, she needed—she wanted—more from him. She wanted to forget what was going on for a while and relish the feel of his strong arms around her. Strong arms that had always been there to protect her whenever she'd asked.

"If you're not absolutely sure, Abby, all you have to do is say the word. We can go into the living room and turn on a movie or—"

She shook her head, hooked her leg around his waist, and rocked her hips against his erection.

He hissed and dug his fingers into her backside.

Abby pressed her forehead against his, meeting his gaze. "I want you to do me a favor, okay?"

"Anything."

"Stop asking me if I want you to stop, all right?"

Trent grinned. "I think I can do that. Anything else?"

"I want you to make me forget my own name. Think you can do that?" She rocked her hips again.

He took hold of the back of her neck with one hand and kissed her hard. "Deal."

CHAPTER 15

TRENT SUCKED in a ragged breath as he pressed the lower half of his body against her. For years he'd imagined what it would be like to make love to her, and now it was happening.

He ran his right hand down the length of her torso, feeling every curve, then back up to cradle her breast in his hand. She fit perfectly in his palm, and his heart soared when she tilted her head back and moaned when he brushed his thumb over her nipple.

"I love hearing you make that sound," he whispered.

Abby looked up at him with pure desire. "We're both wearing way too many clothes."

He chuckled, pushed her shirt up, and pulled the cup of her bra out of the way, giving him better access to her breast. Then he took her nipple between his lips.

She arched her back and reached for him. Her nails dug into his scalp as she held him to her chest as if she was afraid he'd stop. He had no intention of stopping. He loved the feel of her hands in his hair, the feel of her softness on his tongue.

When she made that noise again, the one he loved, the space in his shorts decreased a little more. It was becoming painful, but he wasn't going to rush. Abby was worth the discomfort.

Eventually, her shirt began to annoy him. He wanted full access to her beautiful breasts and her soft skin. The fabric was hampering his efforts, which was unacceptable.

He released her nipple and pushed up off the bed.

She furrowed her brow. "Where are you going?"

In answer, he lifted his shirt over his head and tossed it to the side.

It took her only a second to get with the program. She removed her shirt and unhooked her bra, leaving her breasts bare.

He was so focused on her chest that he didn't realize what she was doing until she hooked her fingers into the belt loops on his shorts. She tugged him toward her and went to work on the button.

"Impatient?" he asked with a smirk.

She lowered the zipper without missing a beat. "Very."

With a quick tug, she had both his shorts and underwear on the floor, leaving him standing there in nothing but his shoes and socks. He swiftly kicked them off.

"Better?"

"Yes." She licked her lips and leaned forward, taking him into her mouth.

He fisted his hands in her hair, not sure if he wanted to keep her there or push her away. It felt amazing and knowing it was Abby made it even more so. He only hoped he wouldn't embarrass himself. All that fantasizing he'd done during his teenage years paled in comparison to the feel of her lips . . . her tongue.

Trent felt himself getting close and had to push her away. She peered up at him with a look he'd only dreamt about. It had his pulse pounding and his breath caught in his throat as the emotion of the moment overtook him. He wanted her more than he ever had before. This time he wasn't pining after his brother's girl. This time, she was all his.

He bent down and covered her mouth with his once more as he lowered her to the bed. "Now you're the one wearing too many clothes."

Abby grinned as he reached between them and began working her pants over her hips and down her legs. He skimmed his fingers up her legs and over the slight swell of her belly, memorizing every curve and dip.

She kissed and touched, exploring him with the same urgency he felt. Everything he gave her she gave right back with equal intensity. The sensations were overwhelming. His need to join with her was unlike anything he'd ever felt with another woman.

When she cupped his ass and ground her hips against him, he dropped his face into her neck and groaned. "This is going to be over before it starts if you keep that up."

She giggled into his hair. "I think you can handle it."

He snorted and repositioned their bodies so he was nestled between her legs, his erection pressing against her clit.

Her nails dug into his backside.

"Do you like that?"

"Yes." She moved her hips again. "I want you inside me."

"Not yet," he whispered in her ear before taking it between his teeth.

Trent began a rocking motion that gave her some friction while he ran his hands over her body. As his fingers were getting to know every inch of her, he licked and sucked on her neck, relishing the sounds she was making—the way her body responded to him. It was a high he never wanted to come down from.

"Please," she begged. "Please, Trent. I need you."

He raised his head to gaze into her eyes. What she was feeling was right there, staring back at him. She needed this as much as he did.

"I have a condom in my wallet." He gave her a swift peck and began to pull away.

Abby placed a hand on his bicep, halting his movement. "I don't want anything between us."

He shook his head. "Abby . . ."

"I'm on the pill and I haven't been with anyone else for a while." She ran her fingers down the side of his face, adding to her plea.

Trent had never had sex without a condom before and he got tested every year during his annual physical. That part didn't worry him. He only wanted to be sure it was what Abby wanted.

Her gaze never wavered as she stared up at him.

"Okay."

She smiled up at him. "Thank you."

He laughed and rested his weight against her once more. "Somehow I think it's me who should be thanking you."

It was good to see her smile again. She'd been too sad these last couple of days.

Trent kissed her long and slow, letting her feel all the passion he had restrained inside him. She seemed to sense he needed this and followed his lead.

When they finally broke apart, her chest was moving up and down rapidly. Her nipples sent little sparks of electricity through his system every time they brushed against him.

He secured his arm beneath her and moved them a little farther up on the bed. Not that he couldn't work with their current position, but it would be a lot more comfortable if they didn't have to worry about their legs falling off the edge of the mattress.

Once she was where he wanted her, Trent reached between them and positioned himself at her entrance. He held her gaze, allowing her to stop him if she'd changed her mind about him going bareback. She hadn't. Abby lifted her hips to meet him as he slipped inside her for the first time.

He closed his eyes, trying not to lose all control and start pounding into her like a madman.

"You okay?" she asked, caressing the side of his face.

When he met her gaze, he saw the worry in her eyes. He realized he'd been still for too long and gave her a gentle kiss. "I'm much better than okay."

"Me, too."

He pressed his forehead against hers and grinned. "You ready?"

Abby answered by bringing his mouth back down to hers. It was all the encouragement he needed. Trent started to move and she tilted her hips up to meet him. With every thrust, he sank deeper into her. For years, he'd loved her. Now he was finally getting a chance to express that love in the most basic and real way he could. More than anything, he wanted to make it good for her.

Running his hand down her side, he skimmed the outside of her leg until he reached her knee. He hitched it higher on his back, allowing him to go deeper still. The new position caused Abby to lose her rhythm. She threw her head back and dug her fingers into his shoulders. The bite of her nails only spurred him on.

"Trent?" she gasped.

"Yeah, baby? Tell me what you need." He lowered his head and went to work on her neck.

Abby arched her back and turned her head to give him better access. He scraped his teeth along her delicate skin and heard her suck in a breath.

"I'm going to make sure you never forget this night," he whispered. "Never forget how it feels to have me inside you, loving you like I've wanted to for so long."

He thrust his hips harder, driving his point home. Abby held on tight, encouraging him with every moan, every touch. Trent never wanted it to end, but he knew it must. He could feel his orgasm beckoning. As much as he wanted to keep going, it was only a matter of time. He needed to make sure she got there first.

Shifting his weight a little, Trent reached between them. Abby sucked in a breath as he began rubbing slow circles over her swollen flesh. He felt her tense up as he added more pressure. That was all it took for her to fall over the edge. She squeezed him tight as her eyes rolled back into her head and her lips parted.

Feeling her climax around him, Trent let go. With only a few more thrusts, he found his own release. His heart rate began to slow and with it came the realization that he'd never felt more satisfied. Then again, he'd never been in love with any of the women he'd slept with. He'd never been in love with anyone but Abby, and in his heart he knew he never would be. Abby was it for him. All he had to do was show her that no matter what had happened in the past, they were each other's future.

* * *

Trent started to move off her, but Abby stopped him. "Not yet."

He brushed a strand of hair from her cheek with so much gentleness that it left an ache in her chest. "I don't want to crush you."

"You're not. I like your weight on me."

Smirking, he flexed his hips slightly. He was still inside her and, while he was no longer fully aroused, she doubted it would take much for him to be up for another round.

Abby was still considering the possibilities when Trent pulled out and rested his head on her chest. His nose brushed against one of her nipples, causing it to harden again. Her body was still humming from her orgasm.

He brushed his fingers over the curve of her hip and up her side until his hand rested along the side of her breast. "You have the most perfect breasts I've ever seen."

Abby chuckled. "Thank you?"

"I mean it. They fit perfectly in my hands, my mouth. And they look absolutely amazing jiggling up and down when I'm inside you." There was no apology in his tone, no shame or embarrassment. He was being honest.

He ran lazy circles over the edge of her breast while she combed her fingers through his hair. It felt natural to be with him like this . . . peaceful.

"Can I ask you something?"

"At this point, I think it's safe to say you can ask me anything. You know all my secrets," she said.

He propped himself up on one elbow and looked into her eyes. Her hand dropped onto the mattress as she waited to see what he wanted to know.

"Why did you change your major? You always wanted to be an interior designer."

Out of all the things she thought he might ask her, that hadn't even made her top ten. She gave him a half smile. "I guess you could say that Max made me an offer I couldn't refuse."

Trent waited.

"A close friend of his family was a senior partner in a prominent law firm in the city. Max's dad arranged an internship for him there. He pulled a few more strings and got me an entry-level job in the administrative department. It was mostly gofer work—getting coffee and making copies—but the chances to move up and make good money were too good to pass up. I'd learned the hard way how quickly life can change."

Trent pushed himself up so that his face was level with hers. He held her gaze for a long moment, and then placed a soft kiss on her lips.

She brought her hand up to cup the back of his neck. "I feel as if I've been hanging onto the edge of a cliff ever since I came back to Ohio and you're the one who keeps me from falling off."

"Glad to be of service."

Abby grinned and smoothed a hand over the stubble along his jaw. "I know. You've always been my rock."

"I hope you know I want to be much more than that," he said.

She didn't respond. In truth, she didn't know how to. What she felt for him was complicated.

He rolled off her and the cold air hit her skin, making her shiver. She wanted to reach for him, but she didn't.

When he turned on his side, he had a determined look on his face. She had the urge to reach up and smooth the lines from his forehead. He was inches away from her, yet it felt like much more.

After several moments had passed, he trailed his fingers up her arm, leaving a warm, tingly feeling everywhere he touched.

The ache in her chest grew. "What are we doing?"

"We're lying in bed together." He smiled. "And I'm contemplating how long I should wait before I try to jump you again."

Abby snorted, which only made his smile grow bigger.

"I'm serious," she said.

He didn't stop caressing her as he spoke, which had heat pooling in the pit of her stomach despite her very real concerns. "Don't you think we should have had this conversation before we peeled off our clothes and I had my way with you?"

"Had your way with me, huh?"

There was a sparkle in his eye and it was hard not to follow his mood. "Definitely."

He closed the gap between them and glided his lips over hers.

Abby sighed.

Pulling her against his chest, Trent ran his nose along her jawline to the space right below her ear. "Tell me. What has you so worried?"

Abby closed her eyes, trying to concentrate. "You know what."

"My family has absolutely nothing to do with you and me." He grazed his teeth over her earlobe.

She sucked in a shaky breath. "How can you say that?"

"They're not in this bed with us, are they?" he whispered in her ear.

A gentle shove to his shoulders resulted in little more than a soft chuckle from him.

"I'm serious."

"So you said."

He readjusted their positions again so she was on her back. With every kiss, every nip of his teeth, Abby was having trouble remembering her argument. Why did he have to be so good at distracting her?

She tried one more time. "I don't live here."

Trent paused in his downward progression and met her gaze. "You're here now."

Before she could think of a response to that, he sucked her nipple into his mouth and began doing something amazing with his tongue. For some reason, whenever Trent got his mouth on her, or his hands for that matter, she couldn't think straight. It had never been so easy for her to forget everything else but the person she was with.

He released her nipple and scraped his teeth along her side, tickling her. Abby pushed at his shoulders and wiggled, trying to get away, but he held on. In less than a minute, she was laughing so hard she could barely breathe.

"Stop. Please. I can't."

Trent's chest vibrated as he stopped his antics and flipped them over so she was sprawled on top of him.

When she could breathe again, she smacked his chest. This, of course, did nothing but make him laugh harder.

"What was that for?" she asked.

"I needed to do something to get that brain of yours to shut off."

Abby scowled at him.

He shrugged. "Worked, didn't it?"

Without answering, she rested her head on his chest.

Trent ran his hands through her hair and down the length of her back. "Do you remember when we snuck into the kitchen and stole Ma's chocolate chip cookies?"

She grinned at the memory. "Paul distracted your mom while you, me, and Chris stuffed as many cookies as we could hold into our shirts."

"Yeah. Too bad we didn't think about the chocolate getting on our shirts. Hard to deny when you have the evidence right there in front of you."

"What about the time when you and your brothers convinced me to eat a worm?"

"I can't believe you bought it when we told you that it would taste like chicken." Even though she couldn't see his face, Abby knew he was smiling.

"Yeah, well, I trusted you." She shivered at the memory. "One of the worst-tasting things ever."

He kissed the top of her head. "I'd never make you eat a worm now."

"Mmm. I wouldn't be stupid enough to fall for it."

Trent tilted her chin up so he could see her face. "You were never stupid. Just too trusting."

She narrowed her eyes.

His eyes sparkled with amusement. "You got your revenge, though."

"I did." A grin lit up her face. "And you boys deserved it."

He cupped the side of her face. "Yes, we did."

Before she could continue with her next thought, he brought her mouth to meet his. "It's hard to have rational conversations when you're lying naked on top of me."

Trent moved his other hand lower to cup her ass and she felt him harden against her stomach.

Going purely on instinct, she parted her legs and placed her knees on either side of his hips. She wanted him again, and in this position it wouldn't take much for him to slip inside.

Abby had never been one to take the initiative during sex, mainly because she'd never before felt comfortable taking control with her partner. As with so many other things, it was different with Trent. She trusted him completely and didn't fear crossing some invisible line.

Staring down into his eyes, her pulse quickened. She wanted him. Wanted him more than she probably should. But for the moment he was here, with her. He was hers and she was his. That was all she was going to concentrate on for now.

She reached between them and brought his erection in line with her entrance. Abby closed her eyes as she sank down onto him and let the sensations overtake her. There would be time to worry about everything else later.

CHAPTER 16

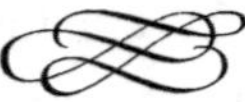

Abby woke up with a smile on her face. Her body felt as if it had been through a good workout the night before, which wasn't far from the truth. The first time they'd made love—and it didn't feel right calling it anything else—there had almost been a desperation to it. As if the world would crumble around them if they didn't come together. She'd needed him as much as he'd needed her.

The second time was slower, even though there'd been very little foreplay. She'd sat atop him for a long time, rocking her hips back and forth as he'd helped her move. There was no rush as they touched and kissed. With every brush of his hand, he'd gotten to know her body, figuring out what she liked.

She lifted her arms above her head and stretched. Her head fell to the side and she glanced at the pillow next to her. It was only then that she realized she was alone.

Sitting up, she surveyed the room and tried to calm the sudden panic flowing through her. He wouldn't have just left. She knew he wouldn't.

Throwing the covers off, she got out of bed and immediately felt the evidence of their previous evening's activities running down the inside of her leg. Abby rushed toward the bathroom to clean herself up.

On her way, she noticed Trent's shirt draped over a chair. Seeing confirmation that he was still there calmed her irrational fears.

When she finished in the bathroom, she headed back into the bedroom to get dressed. She was opening her drawer to get a long shirt and a pair of panties when she got a whiff of bacon. He was cooking?

Abby put the shirt over her head and stepped into a pair of midnight blue panties. No reason not to make a little extra effort this morning. Then she went in search of the source of the delicious smell.

Sure enough, when she strolled into the kitchen she found Trent standing at the stove. His back was to her, so she took a few moments to take him in. He was wearing his khaki shorts from the day before and nothing else. His chest was bare, as were his feet. She leaned against the doorjamb and grinned. This was a view she could get used to.

"Enjoying yourself?" he asked without turning around.

Abby blinked and pushed herself off the wall. She must not have been as stealthy as she'd thought.

"I'm enjoying the view," she replied as she crossed the room.

Trent glanced over his shoulder and sent her a killer smile, one that had her pulse racing again, and then went back to flipping bacon.

She leaned on the counter beside him and nodded at the skillet. "Hungry?"

He had found her largest skillet and filled every inch of it with bacon. Behind it was another slightly smaller skillet with hash browns.

Trent held a large spatula in one hand and reached for her with the other. He pulled her in for a brief but lingering kiss. "I worked up an appetite last night."

Abby sighed when he released her and went back to the food. If there was nothing else going on in their lives, what was happening between them would be pretty close to perfection.

Needing a distraction, she padded over to the refrigerator. "Do you want milk, orange juice, or do you just want to stick to coffee?"

"Orange juice would be great."

She nodded and poured them each a glass of orange juice. Then she went to make some coffee. She needed her caffeine in the mornings.

Ten minutes later, they sat down at her small kitchen table. While she was making the coffee, he'd fried up eggs to go with the hash browns and bacon. It was a breakfast feast, as far as Abby was concerned. She couldn't remember the last time she'd eaten so much to start her day. But, in all honesty, she also couldn't remember the last time she'd burned so many calories in bed. Trent was right. They had both worked up an appetite.

"When do you have to be at work?" Trent asked after reaching for yet another slice of bacon.

Abby looked at the clock above the stove. Until he'd mentioned it, work had been the last thing on her mind. "Most days I try to get there around seven thirty, but as long as I'm there before Max gets in I'm okay."

"And when is that?"

His tone was lighthearted, but she was curious as to why he suddenly wanted to know. "It varies. But he has an offsite meeting this morning, so he won't be in until after nine. Why?"

The smile that crossed his face was downright wicked. "Just wanting to make sure we have enough time."

She swallowed. "Enough time for what?"

He chuckled and went back to his food.

Abby nudged him with her foot. "Enough time for what?"

When he looked up this time, his eyes had that heated look to them that had caused her to melt the night before. "I want to make sure we have enough time to clean ourselves up."

All the moisture left her mouth.

"Finish your breakfast," he encouraged, tucking into his own food with gusto.

"I'm not sure I'm hungry anymore."

"Eat. Trust me. You're going to need your energy." He winked.

Abby shook her head and picked up her fork. "You can't say stuff like that to me and leave me hanging."

He laughed. "Why not?"

Against her will, a small smile pulled at her lips. "You know why not."

Trent placed his hand on her knee and skimmed it up the inside of her leg. A shiver ran through her. "Eat your breakfast, baby, and I promise I'll make it worth your while."

Right before he reached the edge of her panties, he removed his hand from her leg and reached for his orange juice. Was it his goal to drive her mad? Well, two could play at that game.

She scooped some food into her mouth and chewed. Sitting up ramrod straight, Abby pulled the T-shirt as tight around her front as she could get it, so it stretched over her breasts. Then, spreading her legs, she edged the hem of the shirt up enough so he could see a hint of the midnight blue panties she wore. Once she was satisfied with her position, she went back to eating, making sure to draw attention to her mouth with every bite.

Trent didn't say anything, but Abby didn't miss how he started eating a little faster. She smiled around her fork and reveled in the knowledge that she could push his buttons as easily as he could push hers.

As soon as he'd finished his food, he was on his feet and taking his plate over to the sink. When he turned around, he marched across the room and came to a stop hovering over her.

"I'm not done yet." While she was going for nonchalance, Abby didn't think she pulled it off.

Instead of speaking, Trent shifted her hair out of his way and stroked his fingers ever so gently along the back of her neck. It was both relaxing and stimulating at the same time. She leaned into his touch and forgot about the food.

"I thought you weren't done yet?" he asked when several minutes had passed and she hadn't taken a bite. There was a hint of teasing in his voice.

"I changed my mind," she whispered.

He grazed his palm over her shoulder and down the length of her arm until he covered her hand with his. Abby dropped her fork and tilted her head up to meet his gaze. Within a matter of seconds, he was hoisting her into his arms and kissing her.

Abby moaned as he lifted her. She figured they were going back to the bed, but she was wrong. He carried her into the bathroom and set her down on her feet next to the bathtub.

When she glanced at him with a curious expression, he shot her that wicked grin again. "Are you opposed to taking a shower with me?"

"No. I just thought . . ."

He tilted his head to the side. "You thought . . ."

She blushed and looked away.

Trent, of course, wasn't having that. He stepped forward and brought her body in line with his. "There's no need to be embarrassed, Abby. You can tell me anything." He ran the backs of his fingers over her cheek. "Although, I do love it when you blush."

Abby met his gaze. "I thought we were going to make love again."

"Oh, we are."

Her eyes widened. She looked over at the shower and then back at him. "In the shower?"

Trent's only response was a huge smile.

"I've never done it in a shower before. Is that even possible? I mean, won't we slip and fall or something?"

He laughed. "Don't worry, baby. I won't let you fall. I promise."

Then words left her mind altogether as he removed their clothing and showed her how good sex in the shower could be.

* * *

Saying goodbye to Abby wasn't easy, but they both had work to do. When Trent had promised to see her tonight, her answer of "you don't have to" made him feel irrationally angry. He'd felt compelled to kiss her within an inch of both their lives right there in her parking lot to prove that yes, he did have to. How could she possibly think, after last night, that he didn't want to be with her?

Once he arrived at work, the morning flew by. He barely had time to breathe, let alone ponder the previous night with Abby. There were emergency orders that had to be placed for the supplies that had been stolen. He'd paid extra to have them delivered the same day where he could. They'd had to rent the missing equipment again. Too many more days of that and he'd have to dig into his savings. The insurance would pay him back, but it would take at least a couple of weeks before he got that check.

The first truck with a load of mulch and gravel pulled up around eleven thirty. Given what had happened, he waved Joss off and went to meet the truck himself. Trinity shot him a look, but let it go.

He should have known that wouldn't be the end of it. She found him going over packing slips while munching on a sandwich. Waltzing into his office, she sat down across from him.

Trent raised an eyebrow when she didn't say anything right away.

"Something going on you're not telling me?"

"Like?" Trent took another bite of his lunch.

She huffed and held up a hand, ticking off the reasons. "One: You practically ran out to handle that delivery earlier. I get that you're on edge because of the break-in, but you can't do everything yourself. Two: You've been cooped up in this office, with the door closed, huddled over paperwork all morning. You never close your door. And three: You've barely spoken a word to me or the guys since you got here unless you needed something from us."

Trent shrugged, trying to downplay it. "Sorry. A lot on my mind, I guess."

"Uh-huh."

He took a bite of his sandwich and chewed. It gave him time to formulate an answer that wouldn't be a lie, yet would skirt around the truth. Unfortunately, until he could eliminate Trinity as a suspect, he had to play things close to the chest. He didn't want to believe she was capable of something like this, but he couldn't be sure. And until he was, he was keeping his mouth shut.

The best way to divert her attention, he decided, was to shift it to the personal. "I've been seeing my brother's ex."

Trinity's eyes widened. "You're dating Chris' ex-wife? Have you lost your mind?"

Trent shook his head. There's no way in hell he'd ever go anywhere near Carol. No way, no how. "No. Not his ex-wife. An ex-girlfriend. And how did you know it was Chris?"

She leaned back in the chair, settling in. "My amazing powers of deduction, of course."

He snorted.

"I saw Chris pull in last night as I was leaving. Besides, Paul doesn't have any ex-wives or girlfriends that I know about. And Gage, well, I doubt he'd care. Before Rebecca, that man went through women like he went through shirts."

That was true enough. Paul had married the only two women he'd ever dated: his high school sweetheart, whom he'd lost way too early to a drunk driver, and his current wife, Megan. Trent couldn't dispute her assessment of Gage's past relationships either. Then again, Trent doubted his baby brother would consider any of his trysts with women as relationships. Even in high school, he didn't have any long-term girlfriends.

"Yes, well, be that as it may, as you can probably guess, things are a bit complicated at the moment."

"I bet," she said. "How long were they together?"

"Almost two years."

Trinity whistled. "So we're not talking about a spring fling or anything. They were serious."

"High school sweethearts."

She shook her head as if to clear it. "Wow. And now you're dating her?"

"Yes."

Trinity thought about that for a moment. "I guess I can understand why you'd be preoccupied today, then."

He nodded and expected her to excuse herself.

She didn't.

"Have you heard from Detective Travers? Every one of the guys asked me when they came in this morning if we knew anything yet."

"No. Not since he left yesterday after taking our statements." Trent polished off the last bite of his sandwich. "From what Paul tells me, all the verifying takes time."

"I'm sorry," she said.

"About what?"

"I know this business is your baby. You have to be upset about the theft. I know I am."

He grinned. "I am upset. But I'm also a realist. While I might want to call Detective Travers every hour on the hour to ask for an update, I won't. He'll get back to me when he has something."

Trinity snorted. "You have more patience than I would."

"Maybe it's because Paul's a cop. He never talks about the details of his cases, but he's told me enough that I'm not expecting miracles."

Trinity stood with more force than necessary, drawing his attention. She took a step toward the door. "You'll let me know if I can do anything to help?"

"Of course."

She nodded and let herself out, closing the door behind her.

Trent breathed a sigh of relief. He hated suspecting her or any of his other employees. While what he'd told Trinity was true, that he wasn't expecting miracles, it didn't mean he was planning to sit on his hands and do nothing.

He picked up his cell phone and scrolled until he found Paul's number.

His brother answered on the first ring. "I was wondering if I'd hear from you."

Trent sighed. "Let me guess. Either Chris or Ma called you."

Paul laughed. "Both, actually."

"Do I even want to know?"

"Ma's worried. About all three of you. You know she's always thought of Abby as the daughter she never had."

"Yeah, I know."

"As for Chris, he's about what you would expect. Angry. Confused. Hurt."

Trent heard movement in the background and figured his brother was moving to a more private location. He waited.

"Can't say as I blame him. I don't know what I would do if . . ."

"Neither do I. Abby knows she didn't do right by him, but the past is the past and she can't change it." Trent ran a rough hand over his face. "You know they're planning a trip to New York this weekend, right?"

"Yeah. Chris told me. I understand why he wants to go, but I'm not sure his insistence they go alone is the best idea. Ma is having a fit about it. She wants either her or Elizabeth to go, too." Paul paused. "I think Chris is unsure how he's going to react and doesn't want anyone there to witness it."

Trent could only imagine his brother's reaction when he arrived at his daughter's grave. It was something he didn't want to think about too closely.

Paul cleared his throat and Trent knew from experience that meant something big was coming and he probably wasn't going to like it. "How serious are things between you and Abby?"

Trent didn't hesitate. "I've loved her since we were kids."

"Why didn't you ever say anything? Back then, I mean."

"Chris got there first, so I stepped aside. He was older and wiser when it came to women. I didn't think I had a chance with her," Trent said.

Paul didn't answer right away. "Just be careful. Both of you. I'm not going to tell you not to go after who you want because that would be like the pot calling the kettle black."

Trent chuckled.

"But Chris and Abby do have history. You can't change that. And if you two do end up together, you're going to have to figure out what that means not only for the two of you, but the rest of the family."

His brother wasn't telling him anything he didn't already know. "I know that, too. We're figuring it out."

"Good. I like Abby," Paul said. "And I think she could be good for you."

"Thanks."

"Anytime." He could tell Paul was smiling. "Now that we've gotten all the mushy stuff out of the way, what did you really call me for?"

Trent laughed. Leave it to his brother to cut to the chase. "How do you know I didn't call you to talk about all the mushy stuff?"

"Because if it weren't for Ma asking me to talk to you, I wouldn't even have brought it up," Paul said.

"I'm surprised she hasn't called me herself." In fact, Trent was downright shocked.

"Give her time. Chris called her about an hour ago. I'd say you'll be hearing from her before the end of the day."

"Wonderful."

Paul snorted. "You did bring it on yourself, little brother."

"That I did." Trent sighed. "That brings me back to the real reason I called, though."

"Lay it on me."

"Someone broke in and stole some tools, mulch, and some pea gravel from the business. I spent all day yesterday taking inventory and talking to a detective."

"What's he saying?"

"He thinks it was an inside job." Trent stood and walked over to the window. He could see the yard off to his right. All his guys were out on jobs at the moment, so it was empty. In a few hours, it would be bustling with activity as everyone returned from their respective jobs. "Everyone's a suspect at this point and I hate that I feel I can't trust anyone, not even Trinity."

"Do you think she'd do something like this?" Paul asked, completely serious.

"I don't know. I wouldn't think so. But then again, I wouldn't think any of my employees would."

"Don't you have cameras?"

"One. But it didn't get anything. I've put up some new ones and I'm the only one who knows they're there," Trent said. "A recommendation from Detective Travers."

"That's a good start. I'll e-mail you a few other things I'd recommend you do. But most importantly, you need to watch and listen. More often than not, the criminal will give themselves away. They'll do something or say something that doesn't fit with what they should know or do. It's their tell. You just have to be looking for it."

The brothers talked for another minute or two before Paul had to go. Trent appreciated his brother's advice, both regarding the theft and Abby.

Thinking about Abby made Trent want to hear her voice. He didn't stop to think before dialing her number. Then again, how much had he really stopped to think about in regards to her since he saw her sitting in the sun that morning outside her office?

"Hey." Her sweet voice whispered through the phone. His heart skipped a beat. He was beyond hope if all she had to do was say *hey* and it had him wanting to drop everything and rush home to her.

CHAPTER 17

ABBY'S HEART started racing when she saw Trent's number come across her phone. Max was in his office on a call, but he could come out at any moment, so she tried to keep her voice down.

"I hope I didn't call at a bad time."

"You didn't, but could you hang on a sec?"

He hesitated. "Sure."

She glanced into Max's office to confirm he was still engaged in his conversation. He didn't look as if he'd be finishing up anytime soon. That was good since she'd wanted to talk to Trent all day. The way she missed him when he wasn't with her should probably concern her.

With one last look over her shoulder, Abby hightailed it into the conference room where she could have some privacy. She shut the door behind her and released a sigh. As much as she loved Max, he was driving her nuts with his hovering.

"Abby? Is something wrong?"

She shook her head even though he couldn't see her. "No. I just didn't want to talk out at my desk."

"If you're sure."

"I am. It's been a little crazy today with a lot of people coming and going. I didn't want us to be interrupted." That wasn't a lie. There had been a lot of people in and out today, but that wasn't the real reason she'd wanted to take the call in the conference room. What she was really worried about was Max overhearing something and misinterpreting it.

"I didn't mean to bother you, if you're busy."

"It's fine. Really. If someone comes up to talk to Max, they can wait. He's supposed to be at lunch anyway, but it got canceled at the last minute." Abby pulled out one of the big chairs and took a seat. "How's your day going?"

"Not bad, so far. Of course, it would be going much better if we both would've blown off work and stayed in bed all day." He'd lowered his voice and it reminded her of the way he'd hummed in her ear as he'd slowly washed her body earlier that morning in the shower.

Abby felt her cheeks heat as she remembered everything they'd done a few hours earlier.

"You're blushing, aren't you?" he asked.

"Yes. You can't say things like that to me while I'm at work." She fanned herself with one hand, trying to get the coloring in her face to go away.

He laughed. "I love it when you blush, baby."

Whenever he called her *baby*, her belly did a little flip. If he kept up the flirting, she was never going to recover.

Abby knew she needed to change the direction of their conversation. "What all did you do today?" And before he could answer she added, "And don't say think of me."

Trent chuckled. "You know me too well."

Abby grinned. She did know him well. Even though they'd been apart for more than a decade, he was still the same amazing guy he'd always been. "I do. So don't give me a line, because I'll know."

He sobered. "It's never just been a line with you, Abby. I hope you know that."

"I do." That was the problem. If he was just giving her a line, she could pretend the feelings she was experiencing regarding him weren't real.

"Good," he said, and she could tell he was smiling again. "And to answer your question, it's been a fairly boring day up until about a half hour ago."

"What happened a half hour ago?"

He told her about Trinity coming into his office, and then about his phone call with his brother. She knew it would happen. The Daniels family was close like that. Seeing it happen and having her be the one on the opposite side of things, however, was an entirely different matter.

"Maybe us seeing each other isn't such a good idea," she said, even though she felt her heart breaking just thinking about it.

"Don't talk like that. Emotions are running high right now. Give everyone a couple of days to digest everything and I'm sure it will figure itself out."

"What if it doesn't?"

"It will."

Abby grinned. "Always so confident."

"In this I am."

"Why?" she asked. "You can't tell me that you have a shortage of women knocking down your door, Trent Daniels. I know better."

"Jealous?" She could imagine him waggling his eyebrows suggestively.

Abby rolled her eyes. "I'm just saying that I'm not the only fish in the sea."

"You are as far as I'm concerned." His tone was matter-of-fact.

How could he be so sure? They'd only spent one night together. Well, two nights if you counted him holding her in his arms the night before as she'd cried herself to sleep.

"Does that scare you?" he asked.

"A little." Not as much as it probably should have. "There are so many things—"

"We'll figure them out."

There was no use arguing with him. "And your family?"

"They want me to be happy."

Abby knew the rest without him having to say it. She'd seen it in his eyes the night before, felt it in every touch of his hands, every brush of his lips against her skin. Trent might like to flirt, but he was being dead serious. She was who he wanted and he would move heaven and earth to make it happen.

Her history with his brother was a huge stumbling block, as was the fact that she didn't technically live or work in Ohio. Her life, her career, was in New York.

"Abby?"

She blinked and cleared her throat. "Sorry."

"Where did you go?"

"Just thinking about all the things I have to do to this afternoon. I should get back. Max is probably off the phone by now." She hated to lie to him, but there was no reason to beat a dead horse. They'd talked about all this before.

"Okay. I'll see you tonight. Did you want to go out, or would you rather stay in?" he asked.

As tempting as staying locked inside her apartment was, she needed a change of scenery. "I think I'd like to get out of the house, if you don't mind."

"I'll pick you up at six thirty. Be ready."

The way he said it made her laugh. "I will."

Almost as soon as she'd disconnected the call, the conference room door swung open and Max barged in. "There you are."

She held up her cell.

A scowl crossed his face. "I guess I don't need to ask who it was."

She stood and made her way toward the door. Instead of answering him, she asked a question of her own. "Were you able to find out anything?"

He knew she was referring to the call he'd been on for the last hour and a half. "Yes. We've narrowed things down to the who. Now all we have to do is figure out the why."

"Emily?" Abby asked, referring to Max's father's personal assistant. Make that former personal assistant. She had made a mess of everything else. Why not this as well?

"Yes." Max ran his fingers through his hair in frustration. "I'm still trying to understand why Dad gave her so much control when she clearly had no clue what she was doing."

Abby shrugged. "Maybe he didn't think he had a choice."

"He could have called me."

"Sometimes it's hard to admit when you need help. Especially to the ones you love."

"That doesn't make me feel any better," Max said.

She tilted her head down and raised her eyebrows as if to say, 'so?'

He snorted. "You do nothing for my ego."

Abby waved her hand in front of her, dismissing his comment. "Like you need any help with your ego. It's big enough as it is."

He rocked back on his heels and grinned at her.

She rolled her eyes and exited the room.

Max followed. "Have you had lunch yet?"

"Have you forgotten so soon that I was in there on a personal phone call? Wow. Your memory's slipping."

It was his turn to roll his eyes. "Food, Abby. Have you eaten food?"

"I figured I'd just grab something out of the vending machines downstairs and eat at my desk."

"I'll take that as a no." He took hold of her arm and redirected her toward the elevator. "This way."

"Where are we going?"

"I'm starving. Both for food and for some decent company."

Abby halted in her tracks. "Hold on. If we're going out, I need to get my purse."

He waited for her to run back to her desk and retrieve her purse from one of the drawers.

"Got everything now?" he asked.

She was tempted to stick her tongue out at him. "Yes. Come on, let's go before I change my mind and decide I'm the one who needs some decent company." Abby delivered the last sentence with a smile.

He chuckled as he pushed the button for the elevator. "What would I ever do without you, Abby? You're the one who keeps me grounded."

She didn't respond, but her thoughts drifted to Trent. His business was here. There was no way he could move to New York. In fact, she knew that if he did, he would hate it.

It was then that she realized her feelings for him were just as strong as his were for her. Despite what was going on with his family, she was thinking about a future with him.

The elevator doors opened and she stepped inside. How had her life changed so drastically in such a short period of time?

* * *

Almost as soon as Trent hung up the phone with Abby, his mom called. He'd known it was coming, but that didn't make it any easier. "Hey, Ma."

"How are you doing?"

Her question caught him off guard a little. "I'm fine."

"Are you sure? You'd tell me if you weren't, right?" Paul was right. She sounded really worried.

"Of course."

She continued as if he hadn't answered. "Chris called me this morning. Well, Elizabeth called and made Chris get on the phone."

Trent's chest vibrated with amusement. He could see his sister-in-law doing that. She was extremely stubborn when she wanted to be.

"He told me about Abby and what happened. The baby. He also said you were there with Abby when she told him." His mom paused for a long moment. "I could tell there was something between the two of you when she was here Sunday for dinner. I may be worried about Chris and what he's going through right now, but that doesn't mean I'm any less worried about you."

"I'm fine, Ma," he said again. Compared to Chris his issues weren't even a blip on the radar.

"Are you? Really?" For some reason she didn't believe him.

"Yes. Other than being worried about Chris and Abby, I'm good." That wasn't entirely true, but his mom didn't need to know that. She had enough on her plate already.

"How is Abby? I thought about calling her, but I didn't know if she'd want to talk to me." The hesitancy in his mother's voice unsettled him. His mother was usually a rock, especially in uncertain situations.

"She's afraid we all hate her. I've been trying to convince her that's not the case."

His mom was quiet for several moments. "While I don't understand why she kept this to herself all these years, I don't hate her. I don't think your brother does either, as hurt and angry as he is right now." Her voice got quieter as she continued. "I remember what it was like to be twenty. I can't imagine being single and finding out I was pregnant. Maybe I would have done the same thing. I don't know. We can never know until we are in that position."

A smile pulled at the sides of Trent's mouth. His mom was an incredible woman. But he'd always known that. "Did Chris tell you the two of them are going to New York this weekend?"

She was quiet for too long.

"Ma?"

"Yes. Your brother did tell me. I understand why he wants to go, but I do wish he'd let someone go with them. I just don't want them to be alone. Either of them."

While Trent felt the same way, he tried to soothe his mom's fears. "Maybe he feels like it's something they have to do alone. I mean . . . it was their baby after all."

"You're not telling me anything I haven't told myself, son. Unfortunately, that doesn't ease my worry. I know your brother. He may seem like a tough guy on the outside, but inside he's a big softie and this has hit him hard."

That was true. The last time he'd seen Chris anywhere close to this was when he had walked in on his best friend in bed with his wife. It took a lot for Chris to lose his tough guy exterior, and Trent was pretty sure this was the biggest blow he had ever received.

"I should go," she said, although it didn't sound as if that's really what she wanted. "Your dad and I have some errands to run this afternoon and I've been on the phone for most of the day talking to your brothers."

Trent strolled over to the tall filing cabinet along the far wall, cradling the phone against his shoulder. "Tell Dad I'll be over Saturday to help with the flower beds."

"All right." She paused. "And Trent?"

"Yes?"

"I love you. I love all my boys and I always will. No matter what. Remember that."

He'd begun digging through the drawer, but he stopped when he heard the catch in her voice. "I know, Ma. We love you, too."

It was almost as if he could see her smiling through the phone. "Call me if you need anything." She hesitated. "And give Abby a hug from me."

"I will."

After saying goodbye to his mother, Trent returned his attention to the files in front of him. It was strange how the human brain worked and what triggered a memory. When his mom mentioned Chris and Abby's upcoming trip to New York, he'd started thinking about the city. The people. The cars. The cameras everywhere. It reminded him of the reason he'd had the security camera installed in the first place.

Three years ago, they'd had some mulch go missing. The only reason he'd noticed was that they were a much smaller crew back then and ten bags meant a lot more to the bottom line than they did now. He'd called a security company and had them install the camera.

What he was looking for now was the invoice from the security company. It would have a date on it. Something told him that was important. He didn't know why, but if he'd learned nothing else from his big brother Paul, it was to always follow your gut even if it didn't make sense at the time.

After spending almost twenty minutes searching through the filing cabinet, Trent moved into the storage room. He knew it was in the building somewhere. He only had to find it.

It took him almost two hours going through eight different boxes, but he found it. He scanned the papers several times, hoping something would jump out at him. What, he had no idea.

An hour later, he was no closer to figuring anything out than when he'd walked into the storage room. Trinity had come to check on him once. He'd made some excuse about wanting to double-check something for a client. She'd offered to help, but he assured her that he had it under control. He hated not being able to trust anyone.

Putting everything back in the boxes, including the paperwork he'd been staring at for the past hour, he ambled out of the back room with the date of March tenth seared into his brain.

"Find what you were looking for?" Trinity asked as he passed by her desk.

"Yeah."

She frowned and he realized that hadn't come out sounding all that confident.

"Just took longer to find than I thought it would."

Knowing he needed to get her mind off what he'd been doing, he asked for an update on the Keller job. She'd been putting some figures together for a new water feature they wanted to add.

At five thirty, he locked up and headed home. If he and Abby were going out, then he needed a shower and a change of clothes. While digging through boxes wasn't as dirty as field work, he felt as if he'd been coated in a layer of dust.

He got ready as swiftly as possible. Even though he'd spoken to Abby a few short hours ago, the desire to hold her close was increasing with every breath. In three days, she and his brother would be flying off to New York. He had no idea how that would go, and he wanted to solidify his position in her life before then. She needed to understand that he wasn't going anywhere.

It took him a little longer than normal to reach Abby's apartment. Two blocks from her place, a family of geese had stopped traffic trying to cross the road. Thanks to them, he was late.

He jogged up the sidewalk, but before he could knock, she pulled the door open. Abby was a vision standing there in a flowery dress full of pinks and purples. Her long hair fell around her shoulders in soft waves. He couldn't hold back any longer.

She squeaked as he crushed her against him.

"You're late," she whispered against his lips.

"Sorry." He bent his head down and kissed her, taking his time. "I'll try not to let it happen again."

Abby grazed her hands across his chest, making him reconsider the notion of going anywhere with her except straight to her bedroom.

He cleared his throat and took a step back before his thoughts could go any farther down that path. "You ready to go?"

She took a deep breath, which drew his gaze to her chest. The rise and fall of her breasts did nothing to help calm the desire racing through his veins.

"Yeah," she said. "Let me get my purse."

He waited outside, not trusting himself. If he crossed her threshold, they wouldn't be going anywhere tonight.

Abby emerged from her apartment a couple of minutes later with a small white purse slung over her shoulder.

"Ready?" he asked.

She nodded. "Ready."

CHAPTER 18

ABBY CLIMBED inside the cab of Trent's truck and waited for him to settle behind the wheel. She hadn't cried in almost twenty-four hours, and it was all thanks to him.

He put the truck in gear and reached for her hand. The look in his eyes made the muscles in her belly clench in the most pleasurable way. She released a contented sigh as he laced their fingers together and pulled out onto the road.

In some ways, Cincinnati had changed since she'd been gone. It others, it hadn't. The city still felt like home even though she hadn't called it that for over fourteen years.

When he started heading south, she figured they were going back to the riverfront. She wouldn't say no to another boat ride. Their first one had been fun and romantic. So when he turned into a parking garage instead of continuing on toward the river, she was intrigued.

He reached behind the seat and pulled out a folded up blanket once he'd found a parking spot not far from the entrance. Abby raised her eyebrow, but didn't say anything. Whatever he had in mind for tonight was fine with her, as long as they were together.

They met at the back of the vehicle and Trent took her hand again. She held on tight as they walked past the parking attendant out to the sidewalk. Once they were clear of the concrete structure, Abby saw the park. "Wow."

"They opened it a few years ago. I've driven past it, but I've never been down here myself." He squeezed her hand. "Never had reason to before now."

She felt the heat rising in her cheeks.

"Come on." Trent tugged on her arm. "Let's get moving before I change my mind and drive us back to your place."

Abby giggled, but followed him willingly.

They crossed the street and into the park. Even though it was the middle of the workweek, there were plenty of people about. Kids were playing, their squeals of delight sending a pang of regret.

Trent must have seen her reaction. "Do you want more someday?"

She turned her gaze from the children and looked at him. "Yes. Hopefully."

He released her hand and circled his arm around her shoulders. She took the offered comfort and leaned into his strength. While she wanted to have children again, it scared her. Abby didn't know if she could handle the possibility of losing another baby.

Trent brushed his lips against her forehead, and led them farther down the path toward a line of food trucks. "I thought we could get something from one of the trucks and enjoy a picnic on the grass."

She looked in the direction he was indicating and noticed a large grassy area not that far away. People were scattered around doing various things. Most were either reading or eating, but there was one couple playing Frisbee. "Sounds good."

It took them several minutes to decide what they wanted. She hadn't paid much attention to the food trucks in New York. Max tended to have more expensive tastes and more often than not she tagged along with him for lunch. When she looked at the offerings in front of her she was shocked at the variety. They had a little bit of everything. It was somewhat daunting.

In the end, they decided to try a truck that served Korean barbecue. It had been a while since she'd had barbecue at all, and the smell coming from the truck had her mouth salivating. The man at the window took their order and a few minutes later, he handed them each a nicely wrapped container of food.

With their dinner in hand, Trent and Abby found a quiet spot on the lawn. She held their food as he laid out the blanket. He took the containers from her and waited while she got comfortable before lowering himself down beside her.

The food was delicious. She couldn't believe it had come from a food truck. It was as good as any meal she'd had in a restaurant.

"What do you think?" Trent asked, pointing to her food.

"It's really good. I don't remember food trucks serving food like this when we were younger."

"They didn't. Things have really changed in the last ten years. I'm glad, though. Food trucks have saved my stomach more than once when I've been out on a jobsite."

Abby grinned. "I'm glad you found something you enjoy doing. I always worried that you wouldn't."

He leaned in, invading her space. "You worried about me?"

"Yeah."

Her eyes fluttered closed as he removed the distance between them. The feel of his lips grazing against her cheek caused her to sigh.

"You don't have to seduce me, you know. It's a pretty sure bet that you're going to get lucky tonight." She'd meant it as a way to lighten the mood. Otherwise, she was going to end up jumping him right there in the middle of a public park.

Trent lay down on the blanket, propping himself on one arm, a satisfied smirk on his face. He'd finished his food before she'd eaten half of hers. "What do you do back in New York when you're not at work? For fun."

"I don't get much downtime, to be honest. Being Max's personal assistant keeps me pretty busy. But when I do get some time, I usually read or go for a walk in the park." She didn't mention that most of those walks included a stroll by Kaylee's grave.

He was quiet for a while. "I'm supposed to give you a hug."

"What?"

"Ma asked me to give you a hug."

He said it as if it were the most natural thing in the world. Maybe it was fifteen years ago, but not now. Not after what happened.

"Abby?"

She looked up and met his gaze.

Trent took what was left of her food and set it off to his right before scooting closer to her. No words were spoken as they sat there, but the way he looked at her spoke volumes. He cupped the side of her face and rested his forehead against hers. "You need to let go of the guilt, Abby. It was a long time ago."

It was amazing how well he could read her. "What if I can't?"

He grinned. "Well then, I'll just have to stick around and remind you, won't I?"

Trent didn't give her a chance to respond before he kissed her. This one was so slow and deep that she could feel it all the way down to the tips of her toes. The way he took his time, not seeming to care about anything outside their little bubble, had her inching closer to him.

Something landed on their blanket, startling them both. They jerked apart.

A little boy was running toward them. He skidded to a stop a couple of feet away. The boy looked at them and then down at the ball resting in the crook of Trent's knees. "Can I have my ball back?"

Trent picked up the baseball and tossed it back to the boy. He caught it with little effort and mumbled, "Thanks," as he ran back across the field to where an older man waited for him. The man had a cheesy grin on his face which made Abby wonder if the ball had been misthrown on purpose. Considering how their kiss had probably looked to the outside world, she really couldn't blame the man if that's what he'd done. It was too easy to forget where she was when Trent was around.

She heard a snicker beside her and glanced over to see Trent trying his best not to double over in laughter.

"You know he did that on purpose, right?" he said when he noticed Abby staring.

"Yeah." She grinned. "I guess we did kind of get carried away there."

He picked up her hand and brought it to his lips for a soft kiss. "It seems to happen quite often."

"You've noticed that, too?" Although she'd phrased it as a question, she hadn't really expected him to answer.

Trent smiled and stood, not letting go of her hand. "Come on. Let's take a walk down by the river before we get any more balls thrown at us."

She laughed.

It took a few minutes to clean up their little picnic before they headed down toward the water. Trent had the blanket tucked under one arm as they walked hand in hand along the path. She loved the water. There was something soothing about it. If she was being honest, it was one of the things she'd missed most about living in New York. Although you were surrounded by water, the city swallowed you up. Here, even with the city right behind her, Abby still felt a connection to the water.

For the next hour, they strolled along the path, stopping every now and then to get closer to the river's edge. It felt normal and very peaceful. Abby knew she had Trent to thank for that. When she was with him, she could be herself. It was a good feeling. She only hoped it would last.

* * *

Trent couldn't remember the last time he'd had a more enjoyable evening. As they'd ambled along the riverbank, they'd talked some more about their time apart. He'd learned that Abby had gone back to school a few years ago and become a paralegal. Max had thought it might come in handy from time to time when dealing with clients.

It was such a beautiful summer night that they drove back to Abby's apartment with the windows down. Her hair was blowing in the wind and she kept trying to hold it down. He loved seeing her so relaxed.

Abby shot him a look from beneath her flying strands of hair. "Are you laughing at me over there?"

Of course her indignation only made his smile grow wider. "Nope."

Abby rolled her eyes and turned toward him. She rested her head on the back of the seat. "Thank you."

"For what?" he asked.

She just continued to stare at him and grinned.

When they arrived at her place, he helped her out of the truck and followed her up the walkway to her door. He was hoping she'd invite him in, but he had no idea what was going through that mind of hers.

Trent got his answer when she pushed the door open, reached for his hand, and encouraged him to come inside. She barely gave him time to shut the door and turn the lock before she fell against him, pushing him against the door. She gazed up at him for a moment and then placed a barely there kiss against his lips while drawing circular patterns on his chest with her fingers.

The sensations were completely opposite and it was short-circuiting his brain. He went to put his hands on her hips, to bring her closer, but as soon as his fingers grazed her skin, she backed away from him.

Abby strolled across the room, swinging her hips seductively. She glanced back at him for a brief moment before returning her attention to the bookshelf in front of her.

"What are you doing?" he asked.

Soft jazz music filled the room.

She came to stand in front of him again.

"Did you have a sudden desire to listen to music?"

"We need music to dance."

Trent raised his eyebrows and looked at their surroundings. "You want to dance? Here?"

"Uh-huh." Abby didn't wait for him to catch up to her way of thinking. She ran her hands up his arms, rested them on his shoulders, and began swaying her hips. He had no choice but to follow her lead.

Trent wasn't the best dancer, but he could hold his own. He held her close and moved them in a small circle.

Abby had rested her head on his chest and he wondered if she could hear the thunderous beating of his heart. She belonged in his arms. He never wanted to let her go. He was hoping he wouldn't have to.

"If you'd told me you wanted to go dancing, I could have found someplace that had a little more room."

She shook her head. "This is perfect."

He didn't argue with her. Although it would have been nice to have a little more space, he couldn't dispute the advantages. They were completely alone. To emphasize that fact, he lowered his hands and cupped her ass.

Abby tightened her grip on his shoulders before going up on her tiptoes. She brushed her lips along his collarbone, snaking her tongue out for a lick.

Trent chuckled and dug his fingers into her backside. "You'd better be careful. You're playing with fire."

"Oh really?" she asked, before nipping at the skin at the base of his neck with her teeth.

A hiss escaped his lips.

With one hand still firmly on her ass, he braced the other at the base of her neck and brought her mouth to meet his in a hard kiss.

Abby gasped and clung to him as he thrust his tongue into her mouth, taking what he wanted. He was so hot for her—so turned on. It felt as if his erection would rip through his shorts at any given moment.

He backed her against the nearest wall and slid his left hand under her dress until he found the edge of her panties. The lace scratched at his fingers as he worked them down her legs with little finesse. He didn't care how he did it. The only thing he cared about was getting them out of his way.

Finally, he let the material fall from his fingers. Abby kicked off her shoes and the panties that had bunched around her ankles.

As soon as she was free, he wasted no time going after what he wanted.

Abby moaned and arched against him as he touched her. She was more than ready for him, but he wasn't going to give in quite yet. There was a part of him that wanted to hear her beg for it—beg for him.

Trent covered her mouth again with his own, capturing each of her sighs and moans as he brought her closer to the brink. But he wasn't done with her yet. He didn't want her going over the edge until he was ready. So when he felt her begin to tense, he pulled back, dropping his hand.

"What?" She blinked as if trying to clear her head. Then, when what he'd done registered, she narrowed her eyes at him. "Why did you stop? I was so close."

Trent reached up and smoothed his fingers over her lower lip. "I know."

"Then—"

Before she could finish her sentence, he crushed his mouth over hers again. Seconds later, she was caught up once more in the sensual dance of their tongues. This time, however, Abby wasn't content to let him set the pace. She fisted her hand in his shirt and held it in a death grip.

The sides of his mouth pulled up in a smile.

"Something funny?" she asked, and kissed him again.

"Yes," he mumbled, not breaking their connection.

All amusement went out the window when she popped open the button on his pants and plunged her hand inside. He jerked his hips into her grasp.

"Not so funny when the shoe is on the other foot, is it?" She punctuated her question by giving him a little squeeze.

Done with the games, Trent released her and shucked his pants, kicking them out of the way. Then he took the hem of Abby's dress and lifted it over her head. He threw it behind him, not caring where it landed. The only thing left between them was her bra and that was swiftly removed and discarded.

Without the barrier of clothing, things escalated quickly. Trent palmed her ass and lifted her up off the ground. She wrapped her legs around his waist and held on while he carried her into the bedroom.

The sun was setting and the light coming through the windows gave everything an otherworldly feel. He laid her down on the mattress and hovered over her, running a hand down the length of her body. She was everything he'd ever wanted, and for the moment she was his.

Abby placed her hand along the side of his face and he looked up to meet her gaze.

"I know," she whispered.

He kissed the inside of her palm. "Do you?"

She nodded.

Trent wanted to ask her if she felt the same way about him, but he didn't. Instead, he covered her body with his and brought their mouths together for a kiss that was much different than the one they shared up against her wall. As the heat built between them once more, he slipped his hand between them and positioned himself at her entrance.

"Please," she begged.

He pressed his forehead against hers and looked into her eyes as he pushed inside. "Always."

Trent had no idea if she knew what he'd meant, but he knew and that was what mattered. Abby had always owned his heart and he knew she always would. Now it was up to her to decide if she would give hers to him in return.

CHAPTER 19

WHEN ABBY WALKED in to work on Wednesday morning, she had a goofy grin on her face. She couldn't help it. The night before with Trent was something she'd never forget.

It had been so much more than sex. Trent had a way of seeing past all the walls she put up to protect herself. He knew her. Maybe better than anyone else. Her entire body had responded to him, and even now she ached to have him inside her again. It was completely irrational for an independent woman such as herself, but she wanted him, and on some level she needed him as well.

Abby leaned back against the wall and daydreamed about the night before as she rode the elevator up to her floor. It had been a long time since she'd felt this way. Reality would come crashing through her good mood eventually, but until then she was going to enjoy it.

The elevator doors opened and she stepped out onto the executive floor. It didn't take her more than a few seconds to spot Max sitting behind her desk. "Something wrong with your office?"

He stopped rifling through the stack of papers and stared at her.

"What?" she asked, standing up a little straighter.

"I was going to ask you the same question." He sat back in her chair and brought his index finger up to press against his lips, studying her. "Something happened last night."

She turned on her heel and walked into the small break room down the hall. "I don't know what you're talking about. And you still haven't answered my question. Why are you at my desk instead of in your own office?"

Max followed her. He stopped right inside the door and stood with his arms crossed, leaning against the wall.

Abby pretended like she didn't notice. She removed a clean mug from the cabinet and poured herself a cup of coffee.

When she turned back around, the look on his face had changed. If she didn't know any better, she'd say he looked sad. "Just spit it out, Max. I've got work to do."

"I'm going to lose you, aren't I?"

It didn't take a genius to know what he was referring to. She peered down into her coffee and bit the inside of her cheek. "I don't know."

"You're falling in love with him." It wasn't a question.

Abby gripped her mug tighter and took a minute to gather her thoughts. When she looked up to respond, Max was no longer there.

Confused as to why he would take off in the middle of their conversation, Abby marched out of the break room and made a beeline for his office. He was standing, facing away from her, looking out the large bank of windows that framed the back of his office.

She placed her coffee down on his desk and walked over to him. "Max, what's going on? Did you find something out with the reports you've been working on?"

"No. I'm still waiting for the independent accounting firm to get back to me with their final analysis."

Abby placed a comforting hand on his arm. Had there been a new development with his father? "Then what is it?"

He sighed but didn't look at her. "I was sitting with my dad last night."

Her heart sank. "How's he doing?"

Max gripped the windowsill and leaned forward slightly, not taking his eyes off the Cincinnati skyline. "He went in for some tests on Monday. The cancer's spread even more than they'd thought. They don't—"

There was a catch in his voice and she knew he was trying to hold himself together.

"They don't know how much longer he has. The doctors told Dad to make sure he had his affairs in order."

"Oh, Max, I'm sorry."

He turned to her then and rested his forehead on her shoulder. A shudder moved through his large form as he released a ragged breath. "I guess I kept thinking—hoping—that he'd get better, you know?"

She placed a hand at the base of his neck, wanting to give him what comfort she could. "I know."

A knock sounded at the door and a throat cleared, drawing their attention. Max pulled away and turned once again to face the window.

Abby greeted their intruder. "Good morning, Phil."

The accounting manager averted his eyes and held up the file he was carrying. "I brought the report Mr. Collins requested."

Phil looked extremely uncomfortable, almost as if he'd barged into the office and caught her and Max in a compromising position. It made her wonder what kind of office gossip was going around. Abby and Max didn't exactly have a traditional working relationship, but they also tried to keep things professional while at work. Today was a rare occasion when they'd both allowed that to slip away.

Abby crossed the room and took the file. "Thank you, Phil."

It was a clear but polite dismissal. Max wouldn't want anyone to see him like this.

Phil hesitated for only another moment before backing out of the office. "Let me know if you need anything else from my department."

As if someone had lit a fire under his feet, he darted out the door.

With Phil gone, Abby closed the door and placed the file on Max's desk before rejoining him at the window. He glanced over at her. The short time it had taken her to deal with Phil had given Max a few moments to center himself. He gave her a half smile. "I wonder how long it will take for everyone in the building to hear about what Phil walked in on."

"If the look on his face was any indication, not long. I'm guessing we're going to be the topic of discussion over lunch today."

Max's mood shifted again. "Sorry for breaking down like that."

"You just found out some devastating news. I think it's allowed."

This time the smile that graced his face was genuine. "What did I ever do to deserve your friendship?"

She bumped her hip into his and he laughed.

"Thanks," he said.

"Anytime." Abby pushed herself away from the window and retrieved her coffee from his desk. Before she left his office, she met his gaze once more. "You know I'll always be your best friend, right? No matter what happens between me and Trent."

"I'm sorry. I didn't mean to rain on your parade. It was pretty obvious you were flying high on some post-sex endorphins."

Abby felt herself heat and her thoughts immediately went to Trent's comment about how much he loved to see her blush.

"See what I mean?" Max chuckled. "I'm happy for you, Abby. Really."

"But?"

He sighed. "But it means I'm going to have to find myself a new assistant when I head back to New York. The selfish part of me isn't happy about that."

"This thing with Trent is still new," she said, trying to lessen the blow. "And there's the whole issue with Chris and his family. I don't know what's going to happen yet."

"It'll work out. I've known you for fourteen years and I've never seen you with that look on your face."

"And what look is that?"

Max grinned and reached for the file Phil had brought him. "Like Trent Daniels took you on a trip to the moon and back."

Her face was on fire. She could only imagine how red she was.

Max laughed and flipped open the folder. "Enjoy it, okay, Abby?

You deserve to be happy. Even if it means I have to go through the extremely unpleasant task of finding someone to replace you."

While she was glad he was taking it so well, she was surprised he seemed okay with the possibility that she'd be staying in Ohio. "I thought you'd be more upset."

"Why's that?" He scanned over the papers in front of him.

Some people would get upset that he was carrying on such a serious conversation and working at the same time, but that was Max. She didn't hold it against him. "Because you don't like Trent."

Max met her gaze from across the room, completely ignoring the papers that'd had his attention moments before. "I stand by my original statement. If he breaks your heart, I'll kick his ass."

Before she could second-guess herself, Abby walked over to Max and gave him a peck on the cheek. "Thank you."

He waved her away.

Abby chuckled.

"Get out of here before someone realizes I'm just a big softie," he said.

Abby shook her head and reached for the doorknob. "Let me know what you need me to do. If your mom wants me to make any arrangements or call anyone, I can, even if it's after hours."

He nodded.

She went to her desk and booted up her computer. As she was waiting for everything to come online, it occurred to her that Max had never told her why he'd been at her desk.

Before she could decide whether to let it go or not, her cell phone dinged, indicating she had a message. Thinking it might be Trent, she scrambled to dig it out of her purse.

It wasn't Trent.

Do you have our flight information for Friday? I assume we will be flying out of Cincinnati.

The sender didn't have to sign it. She knew it was from Chris.

Yes. What is your e-mail address and I'll forward it to you? - Abby

Several seconds later, her phone dinged again and his e-mail address popped up on the screen.

Figuring there was no time like the present, Abby logged on to her e-mail and found the airline confirmation. Once she forwarded it to him, she sent him another text.

I sent you the confirmation. – Abby

Abby paused, unsure if she should say anything else. Were they meeting at the airport?

Before she could decide to say anything or not, she got another message.

I will pick you up at two.

She guessed that answered that question.

Okay. I'll be ready. – Abby

She leaned back against her chair and closed her eyes. It was going to be a very long weekend.

When Abby emerged from the office building, Trent hopped out of his truck to meet her. The moment she saw him her eyes lit up. "I didn't expect to see you here. Are you meeting with Max?"

"Nope," he said, rocking back on his heels. "I'm here to see you."

She wrinkled her nose in the most adorable way. "Why?"

He clutched his chest in mock pain. "Ouch. That hurts."

Abby gave him a playful shove. "That's not what I meant and you know it."

Not able to wait any longer, Trent pulled her against him.

"What are you doing?" She glanced around, nervous.

He pretended he didn't notice. "I'm answering your question."

Without any further discussion, Trent covered her mouth with his. He kept it chaste. They were, after all, outside her place of employment.

"I want you to have dinner with me tonight," he murmured against her lips, not letting her go.

"Okay," she said with a hint of confusion.

He clarified. "At my place."

"Oh."

Trent cocked his head to the side. "Everything all right?"

She nodded. "Yeah. I'm fine. It's just been a long day."

He leaned back against the hood of his truck and situated her between his legs. Abby scanned their surroundings again, but no one was paying them any attention. They were all too busy rushing to their vehicles.

When she realized he was waiting for her to elaborate, she sagged against him. "Max and his family got bad news about his dad. The cancer has spread even more than they thought. They aren't expecting him to make it much longer."

Trent ran his hands along her back. "I'm sorry. You said you were close to them."

She nodded again and looked down.

"Is there something else?" he asked.

"Chris," she whispered, not meeting his gaze.

"What about him?"

"I sent him the flight information today."

Trent knew there had to be more to it than that. "Did you talk to him? Did he say something?"

Abby gave him a half smile. "No. It wasn't anything he said. I'm just . . . I'm dreading this weekend."

Placing one finger under her chin, he tilted her face up so he could look into her eyes. "I can still go with you. It wouldn't take that much to move my schedule around. The hardest part would be getting the plane tickets."

She shook her head. "No. I need to do this on my own."

He frowned.

"I appreciate you offering, though." The halfhearted grin she wore told him more than her words. He knew she was unsure how the trip with his brother would go.

Trent brushed the back of his fingers down the side of her face. She was so precious to him and more than anything he wanted to support her.

Abby leaned into his touch, nuzzling her face into his hand.

"I'd do anything for you, Abby. All you have to do is ask."

She released a breathy sigh. "I know. I don't deserve you."

"Yes, you do." He ghosted his lips over hers once more. "Are you hungry?"

Abby shrugged. "I could eat."

"Good," he said, standing to his full height and guiding her around to the passenger side of the truck. "I'm starving."

She giggled when he opened the door with a flourish and helped her inside.

It didn't take long to reach his house. He was able to take some back roads and avoid most of the rush hour traffic. Throughout the drive, he kept glancing over at Abby. If Trent was being completely honest, he was slightly nervous about showing her his home. He wanted her to like it.

He pulled into the driveway and put the truck in park. Before he could turn the vehicle off, she was getting out. She stood a few feet away, taking in the three-bedroom ranch he called home.

Abby started up the brick walkway that led to his front door. He hurried to join her. She hadn't bolted yet. That had to be a good sign.

Trent unlocked the door and motioned for her to go first.

She took a tentative step through his front door, took a quick look around, and then whirled back to face him. "It's so clean."

He raised his eyebrows. "Were you expecting to walk into a pigsty?"

Abby pursed her lips. "Maybe. I do remember what your room used to look like."

Trent snorted. "Come on. I'll show you around."

The tour didn't take long. They were already in the living room and it opened into the dining room and kitchen. He'd converted one bedroom into a home office, although he rarely used it. The second bedroom had a full-sized bed and a few boxes. Trent couldn't remember the last time he'd been in there.

He skipped showing her his bedroom, figuring she'd get to see it later, and led her into the kitchen. She skimmed her fingertips along the edge of his counter while he removed the steaks he'd picked up earlier from the refrigerator.

"I'm not all that talented in the kitchen, but I can grill with the best of them."

"Works for me." Abby grinned and leaned back against the counter. "Need some help?"

Trent shook his head. "I took the easy way out and bought some salads at the grocery store. You could keep me company while I fire up the grill, though."

As soon as they walked out onto his deck, he heard her gasp. His backyard was pretty amazing, if he did say so himself. He'd worked hard to make it perfect. Every tree and flower had been handpicked by him and placed exactly where he wanted it.

He started up the grill and placed the steaks off to the side, allowing them to come to room temperature while the grill was warming up. "Do you like it?"

"It's beautiful." She kicked off her shoes and headed down the steps of his deck and onto the lawn. "You did it all yourself?"

"Yep."

Abby continued to stroll around his backyard while he cooked the steaks. She took her time looking at all the different elements he'd incorporated into his landscape. When she came to the small water feature he'd had specially designed for the space, she knelt down, dipped her fingers into the soft waves, and let the water trickle back down into the fountain.

A vision of her with a small child squatting beside her, playing in the water, hit him like a punch to the gut. She glanced up at him and he tried to smile back even though his throat was so tight it was difficult to swallow. He averted his eyes and focused on the steaks.

Trent heard her come up the steps, but he didn't look away from the meat. He still didn't trust himself.

Abby came to stand behind him and circled her arms around his waist. "What were you thinking just now?"

He shrugged, trying to brush it off.

She rubbed her lips along the back of his shirt, distracting him from his task. "Do I need to tickle it out of you like I did when we were kids?"

Trent released a sound that was somewhere between a snort and a laugh.

"Come on. Tell me what's wrong. You've listened to all my problems lately. Turnabout is only fair," she said, pressing her lips against the back of his neck, making him question if they needed to eat dinner at all.

He double-checked to make sure the steaks weren't going to burn, then twisted around to face her. "Nothing's wrong. Everything is right. You're here with me."

She didn't look convinced. "Then why did you look as if your mom had just made you eat an entire plate of broccoli?"

He chuckled. "I did, huh?"

She gave him a gentle slap on the chest. "Yes. And stop trying to change the subject."

Trent sighed. "I was watching you play in the water."

"And?"

"And I was picturing a child beside you." He paused. "Our child."

Her eyes went wide.

"Did I scare you?"

It was her turn to swallow hard. "Yes. A little."

Trent kissed her forehead and turned to flip the steaks, giving her time to process everything. He didn't want to scare her away, but he also needed her to know this wasn't a short-term fling for him.

"I'll go get the salads," she said, heading back inside. He wondered what was going through her mind.

She hadn't returned by the time the steaks were ready, so he piled them onto the clean plate he'd brought out with him and went to find her.

When he pushed open the sliding glass door, he found Abby had set the table. She was in the process of pouring them each a glass of iced tea.

He placed the steaks down in the center of the table and reached for her. Abby melted into his arms and burrowed her face into his chest.

"Tell me what you're thinking."

"That's really what you want? With me? Even after everything?" she asked.

Trent lifted her chin and waited until she was gazing up at him. "I've always known what I want, baby. I've just been waiting on you."

CHAPTER 20

On Friday morning, Abby was still trying to come to terms with all that had happened in the last week. She'd gone from telling one brother that years ago she'd had—and lost—his child, to having another declare that he wanted to spend the rest of his life with her. Granted, Trent hadn't come out and asked her to marry him or anything, but the implication had been clear.

She was at her desk going through her e-mails when Max popped his head out of his office. "Can I talk to you for a minute?"

"Sure." Abby made sure any sensitive items were put away, and then headed into his office.

"Close the door," he said as soon as she entered.

Abby did as he requested, his tone causing her anxiety to skyrocket. "What's going on?"

"I just hung up with my mother."

Over the last two days, Jacob Collins' health had declined rapidly. He'd gone from talking and laughing to coughing and stuttering. It had been such a drastic change that Abby had backed out on her plans with Trent the night before so she could go see Max's father.

"He didn't want to get out of bed this morning, so she called the nurse," Max said.

"And?" From Max's expression, Abby knew it hadn't been good news.

"She thinks his body is shutting itself down."

Max's eyes filled with moisture and Abby rushed across the room to give him a hug. He wrapped his arms around her waist in a vise grip. A wave of emotion vibrated through his body as he clung to her.

"Do you want me to cancel my flight? I can stay if you need me." As much as she wanted to do right by Chris, Max needed her. If he wanted her to stay . . .

Max sat up and straightened his shoulders. If Abby hadn't known him as well as she did, she might have been fooled. "I appreciate the offer, but you need to go."

She opened her mouth to protest, but he cut her off.

"There's nothing you can do here. All we're going to be doing is sitting beside his bed and keeping him company."

Abby knew what he said was true, but she was filled with guilt. Max had been there for her in her darkest time. "Are you sure? I think Chris would understand."

"No." He shook his head and stood. "You go. Do what you need to do. All this will be here when you get back."

She shot him a quizzical look. When she'd first brought up her impending trip with Chris to New York, Max hadn't exactly been jumping for joy.

Max must have realized the direction of her thoughts. He sighed and walked over to the window, something he did when he was stressed. "I'm still not a fan of the guy, but I figure if you're going to continue to see his brother, you two are going to have to work through your issues."

"Yes."

He removed his suit jacket from the back of his chair and slipped it on, pulling at the cuffs of his shirt. "I'll have my cell on me if you need anything today, or even this weekend."

"Don't worry about me. I'm a big girl. I can take care of myself." He needed to be focused on his family right now.

Max grinned but it didn't reach his eyes. She knew he was hurting.

He gave her a swift hug, picked up his briefcase, and strolled toward the door as if he didn't have a care in the world. "I'll see you on Monday."

Abby wished there was something else she could do, some way she could make this easier for her friend, but she knew there wasn't. She knew what it was like to lose a parent.

After Max left, she was inundated with phone calls. It was as if someone had sent out a memo or something. Everyone wanted to talk to Mr. Collins as soon as possible. She must have told at least two dozen people that he had a family emergency and would be out of the office for the rest of the day.

By the time lunch rolled around, Abby was ready to get out of the office. She made sure all the phones were forwarded and that everything was locked up tight before making her way downstairs. They were still going through all the paperwork the previous assistant had left. Either she'd been skimming money, or she was extremely bad at math. Max had enlisted the help of an independent accounting firm to help make sense of everything, but even they were having issues. Most of her records were paper, so they had to match everything up one by one. It was taking time.

The drive back to her apartment took less time than usual. Since it was the middle of the day, she hadn't had to worry about rush hour traffic. She was still getting used to driving everywhere again. Living in New York for so long, she didn't drive regularly anymore. It was easier to take the subway.

She didn't waste any time once she arrived home. Chris would be on her doorstep in two hours and she needed to be ready to go.

As she packed a small suitcase with enough clothes for the weekend, Abby realized that something had shifted within her over the last two months. New York no longer felt like home. This was a trip—her home was in Ohio.

The reason for the shift was at the forefront of her mind. Trent had assured her that he understood why she couldn't see him last night, saying they would have plenty of time when she got back. She thought he'd be upset, or at least unhappy, if for no other reason than because her plans involved Max. He hadn't.

She zipped up the suitcase and set it by the door. No, Trent had been wonderful about it, like he'd been about her trip this weekend.

Sighing, she ambled into the kitchen. They wouldn't land in New York until dinnertime, so Abby needed to eat something. She only hoped she would be able to keep it down. The closer it came to the time Chris was to arrive, the more nervous she became.

By the time he knocked on her door at one fifty-five, she'd managed to choke down most of the sandwich she'd made. She threw the rest of it away and went to get the door.

Chris stood on the other side in jeans and a T-shirt. His hair was sticking up in all different directions as if he'd been running his fingers through it. He looked nervous yet determined.

"Hi."

He cleared his throat. "Are you ready to go?"

"Yes." She grabbed her suitcase and stepped outside. When she set her luggage down on the sidewalk to lock up, Chris reached for it. "You don't have to do that. I can get it."

Chris ignored her and loaded her suitcase into the backseat of his truck.

She shook her head but didn't argue. If he wanted to get her bag, then she'd let him.

Neither said anything as Chris drove them south toward the airport. He parked the truck in long-term parking and they took the shuttle to the terminal. This time he let her carry her own bag.

It took them almost forty minutes to get their tickets and go through security. Once that was done, they found their gate and waited for their flight. They had roughly an hour before takeoff and Chris hadn't said anything to her since they'd left her apartment.

His silence unnerved her, but she knew she had to deal with it. If all he did all weekend was stand stoically beside her, then so be it.

As it turned out, Chris waited until they were thirty thousand feet in the air to say anything else. "Are you staying in Ohio?"

It had been so long since he'd spoken that she jerked at the sound of his voice.

"Once your assignment or whatever is done."

Abby closed the magazine she'd been pretending to read. "I don't know. I haven't decided yet."

He nodded and looked out the window again.

It was on the tip of her tongue to ask why he'd wanted to know, but she didn't. Abby was pretty sure she already knew the answer.

Instead, she closed her eyes and tried to think about pleasant things. Her mind floated back to the last night she'd spent at Trent's house. They'd finished their dinner, and then searched his movie collection.

A smile tugged at her lips when she remembered how little of the movie they'd actually watched.

She must have fallen asleep, because the next thing she knew the flight attendant was waking her up. "Could you bring your seat into the upright position? We're preparing to land."

"Sure," Abby mumbled.

She righted her seat and looked over to where Chris was sitting next to her. He hadn't moved. He was still staring out the window.

"We can take a cab to the hotel," she said as the plane came to a stop on the runway.

"Don't you have an apartment here?"

"I do, but I'm subleasing it since I'm in Ohio for an extended period of time."

He nodded but didn't say anything more.

With their luggage in tow, they weaved their way through the airport and out to the passenger pickup area. There were people everywhere, coming and going. It took them a while to get a taxi, but eventually they made it to the front of the line. While Chris put the luggage in the trunk, Abby gave the cab driver the address to the hotel. Even though it had cost more, Abby had chosen a hotel in Brooklyn. It would be an easier commute to the gravesite that way.

Abby had booked them rooms on the same floor of the hotel to make it more convenient. She'd considered getting them connecting rooms, but thought better of it. Chris wasn't exactly her biggest fan right now, and he might want a little more distance between them.

They came to her room first. He paused when she stopped in front of her door.

"This is me."

Chris looked at the door, and then down at her. His brow furrowed slightly, but he didn't say anything. He'd said maybe ten words to her since they'd left the airport.

"Do you want to meet for dinner?" she asked.

He turned his head to look down the hallway. "Okay. I'll come by your room in about an hour."

"All right." Even their breakup hadn't been this awkward.

Chris nodded, then continued on to his room roughly five doors down. He slipped his keycard in the slot and entered, leaving her standing alone in the hall.

Abby let herself into her room. She dropped her suitcase right inside the door and strolled over to the window. So much had changed since she'd last been in New York, yet the city itself hadn't changed at all. That should have been comforting, but it wasn't.

* * *

Trent was attempting to distract himself with work. After everyone else had left for the evening, he'd stayed at the office to go over old security footage. He'd been hoping to find something that would tie the missing mulch from before to the more recent thefts.

Much to his disappointment, nothing major had stood out to him. The only thing of interest he'd seen was when the camera had caught Trinity and her boyfriend getting busy against one of the sheds. Trent remembered having to sit down and have a rather awkward conversation with her. She'd apologized and explained that they'd had a big fight two weeks before and that her boyfriend had stopped by to say he was sorry. Lucky for Trent, he'd been paying extra special attention after the mulch had gone missing and had captured their reconciliation on camera.

When he could no longer justify hanging around the office, he locked up and headed over to his parents' house. Trent knew that eventually he'd have to go home, but he was putting it off. All he kept thinking about was Abby being in New York with Chris and here he was in Ohio, sitting on his hands.

He parked his truck along the curb—the driveway was already occupied by Elizabeth's car. Trent hadn't realized she would be there.

Just then, she came around the side of the house. She grinned. "Hey. I didn't know you were stopping by tonight."

"Same here. I figured you'd be at home waiting for Chris to call."

Elizabeth strolled over to her car and removed a book from the center console. "He called me about a half hour ago."

Trent waited to see if she'd leave him hanging. Abby had texted him to say they'd landed in New York, but that was the last he'd heard from her.

"He said the hotel they're staying at is pretty nice. There was even a piece of chocolate on his pillow." She seemed rather amused by that bit of information. Trent wondered if his brother had said something more about the chocolate that Elizabeth wasn't sharing. Then again, if he had, that was probably information Trent was better off not knowing.

He cleared his throat as they walked toward the backyard. "Did he say how he and Abby are getting along?"

Elizabeth stopped and glanced over at him. "I got the impression that they haven't said much to each other. Of course, I'm sure that has a lot to do with Chris."

Trent placed a hand on her arm. "What do you mean?"

"I don't want him saying anything he's going to regret later. Abby hurt him. More than I think any of you know." She hesitated. "Chris and I had just started talking about trying to have a baby a few months ago."

"That's great," Trent said, genuinely happy for them.

The smile didn't quite reach her eyes.

"What is it?"

She shook her head and sighed. "You know what happened with my first husband. That he used to knock me around."

He nodded. While Trent didn't know the details, he'd known it had been bad enough for her to risk her life leaving the bastard.

Elizabeth inhaled sharply. "I don't want to go into the details, but getting pregnant might not be all that easy for us. So this . . . now . . ."

Trent was beginning to see the connection. He pulled Elizabeth in for a hug. "I'm sorry."

She leaned into him for a few moments, and then took a step back. "Something tells me Abby is going to be in all our lives for the foreseeable future. Chris is going to have to deal with that, and learn to move past what happened. I'm guessing he's taking that to the extreme and not saying much of anything."

A small smile tugged at Trent's lips. "Sounds like my brother."

Elizabeth chuckled. "Doesn't it, though?"

He spent the next two hours helping his dad weed the flower beds and trim some bushes. It felt good to get his hands dirty. He hadn't been out with the guys since the theft and he missed it.

Trent had figured at some point during their work in the yard his dad would use the opportunity to have a heart-to-heart with him, but he didn't. Other than a few comments here and there about the plants themselves, his dad remained quiet. It was odd. Then again, maybe his father realized that Trent would rather work than talk at the moment.

When they had all the weeds plucked and the bushes tamed, the two men went inside to cool off. They found his mom and Elizabeth huddled together at the dining room table over some fabric.

"There you are." His mom made it sound as if they'd wandered off or something. "We wanted to ask your opinion."

Elizabeth held a piece of blue fabric against her shoulder. "What do you think of the color?"

"For what?" Trent asked.

"Curtains." His mother scraped the chair against the floor as she got up and went to the refrigerator. "Elizabeth is thinking of making some curtains for the spare bedroom."

"Looks good to me," his dad grunted, only half-paying attention.

He was more concerned with the two glasses of lemonade his wife was pouring.

"Me, too," Trent agreed. He wasn't exactly sure what type of input they wanted from two guys who knew nothing about décor. That was more Abby's thing.

Elizabeth wasn't deterred. "You don't think it should be darker or lighter?"

Trent pulled out a chair and sat down, thanking his mom for the glass of lemonade she placed in front of him.

Marilyn retook her seat next to Elizabeth. "I think it will work fine. Just add a few dark blue accent pillows in the room and it will be perfect. I might even have some fabric you can use for those as well, if you're interested."

The two women went on to talk about patterns and fabric swatches that meant nothing to Trent. It was seriously enough to make one's eyes glaze over.

After a few minutes, his dad caught Trent's gaze and tilted his head toward the living room. Nodding, they both stood.

"Where do you think you're going?" his mom asked.

Mike bent down and kissed the top of his wife's head. "We're going to see if there's a game on. Give you ladies some privacy."

To her credit, all she did was give them a look that said she wasn't fooled as they hustled out of the room.

Trent didn't end up leaving his parents' house until after nine. He and his dad had settled on watching some preseason roundup, since there wasn't a game worth watching on television. There was footage of his younger brother, Gage, throwing the football to one of his teammates during spring training.

It had been a way to kill time, but eventually he had to give up and go home.

He was climbing into bed that night when his phone beeped, notifying him of a text message.

Are you awake? – Abby

Yes. Everything okay? – Trent

The next thing he knew, his phone was ringing.

"I'm sorry to call so late," she said as soon as he answered the call. "I just wanted to talk to you. Hear your voice, I guess."

"I'm glad you called." He'd been worried about her all day. "How are things going in New York?"

"Not too bad, I guess. Chris isn't saying much. I'm trying to go with the flow and not push him."

Trent leaned back against the headboard and stretched out his long legs. "Probably wise."

"How are things there? Any news on your thief?"

"I'm not sure you could say it's progress, but I spent some time tonight going over some old surveillance footage. Not much there, other than I got to witness my office manager making out with her boyfriend again." He shivered at the memory.

"She was making out with her boyfriend at work?" Abby asked.

"It was a few years ago, and we talked about it after it happened. Apparently they'd had a big fight a couple of weeks before and he came by to apologize."

"Sounds like a nice apology."

He laughed. "Yeah."

"So if it was years ago, what made you go back through all that video?"

"The reason I put the cameras up in the first place was because we had some bags of mulch go missing. It didn't happen again, so I figured whoever it was, they were either satisfied with what they got the first time around, or saw the camera and thought better of it."

"Makes sense."

"Then about three weeks ago, we had some mulch disappear again. I was hoping that maybe I'd see something on the video I'd missed the first time around." Trent shrugged even though she couldn't see him. "It was a long shot, but I was hoping."

"You don't think . . ."

She didn't finish her sentence.

"I don't think what?" he asked.

"Never mind. It's none of my business."

"Abby, what is it? Tell me."

"Well, I was just thinking. I know you said you don't think Trinity would do something like that, but what about her boyfriend? Is she still seeing him? He's obviously been there, and if they were in the yard fooling around, chances are that he'd at least have an idea of where everything is. Maybe not as good as you or the rest of your employees, but enough. And if they got caught, I would think Trinity probably told him about the camera."

A smile spread across Trent's face. "It makes sense. I hadn't thought about it that way before."

She was quiet for several moments. "I hope I'm wrong."

So did he. Because if Abby was right, if it was Trinity's boyfriend—or ex-boyfriend for that matter—his office manager was going to blame herself. Even if she didn't have anything to do with it.

CHAPTER 21

On Saturday morning Abby went about her routine of getting ready, her thoughts more on her conversation with Trent last night than on what she was doing. They'd talked on the phone until almost midnight. It had been nice to hear his comforting voice on the other end of the line, even if he was six hundred miles away.

They'd made plans to go see a football game. With everything going on, Trent asking her to go to a game had struck her as funny and she'd dissolved into a fit of laughter. He'd patiently waited for her to get herself back under control, and then changed the tone of the conversation completely by saying he missed her.

Abby sat down at the end of her bed and sighed. Things with Trent were getting really serious, really fast. Logically she knew she should walk away, but the thought of doing that made her heart ache.

She turned the television on and flipped through the channels. Today was the day. She was taking Chris to see Kaylee's grave. He'd be there to pick her up any second.

A knot formed in her throat thinking about visiting her daughter's grave with Chris. He'd been so quiet last night when they met for dinner.

The news droned on about some jewelry store robbery that had happened overnight. She was only half paying attention, too worried about how the day would go.

There was a knock at the door—two sharp raps. Chris. He'd done the same the night before.

She turned the television off and tossed the remote on the bed before making her way over to the door and looking through the peephole. Chris stood in the hallway, looking as uncomfortable as she felt.

She unlatched the chain and opened the door. "Morning."

He shoved his hands in his pockets and nodded. "Are you ready?"

"Yeah. Just let me grab my purse."

They stopped in the hotel restaurant for a quick breakfast. Chris was as stoic as he had been the night before. She tried to give him his space, but it would have been easier if he'd yelled at her. The silence was getting to Abby.

He walked beside her as they made their way to the subway station, and then stood next to her until they reached their stop. After they climbed the steps up to the sidewalk, it was three blocks to the cemetery. He glanced around at their surroundings, but said nothing until they were a block away. "Wait here. I'll be right back."

Chris didn't wait for her response before jogging to the crosswalk and across the street.

She didn't know what had come over him until she saw where he was going. Across the street there was a vendor selling flowers. He returned a few minutes later with a pink carnation in his hand.

Moisture clouded her vision and she turned away, trying to keep it together. "You ready?"

"Yeah."

Chris stayed right behind her as Abby made her way into the cemetery. She led him over to the children's section. It was flanked by two tall oak trees. She remembered the first time she'd seen them, the day she buried Kaylee. The way they were positioned made it seem as if they were standing guard over the children's section of the cemetery.

She walked past the imposing oaks into an entirely different world. The children's section was different from the main cemetery. Each grave still had a gravestone, but there were also small statues of animals peppered throughout. She zeroed in on the statue of the baby lamb standing next to her mother. Instinctively, she wrapped her fingers around the pendant she wore around her neck.

Before she could chicken out, Abby put one foot in front of the other. Chris followed close behind, letting her lead.

Stopping in front of Kaylee's tombstone, she knelt down and ran her fingers over the engraved letters that spelled out Kaylee Alice Daniels.

Chris sucked in a loud breath directly behind her. "You gave her my name."

Abby didn't look at him. She couldn't because there was a huge knot in her throat. All she could do was nod.

"Thank you," he whispered.

She looked up to see tears streaming down his cheeks. Seeing him so emotional broke the last little hold she'd had on her own. She placed two fingers to her lips, pressed them gently against Kaylee's tombstone, and then stood. "I'll give you a minute alone."

Abby turned to go, but Chris grabbed her hand, stopping her.

Once he seemed sure she wasn't going anywhere, Chris lowered himself down until he was eye level with Kaylee's little tombstone. He placed the flower on the little ledge at the base and bowed his head.

Abby wasn't sure what to do. She felt as if she was intruding on a private moment, but he'd wanted her there, so she stayed.

After a long moment, he raised his head and mimicked her action from before, pressing two fingers to his lips before placing them over their daughter's name. He held them there for several moments before standing and immediately wrapping his arms around Abby. She felt him shudder as he buried his face in the crook of her neck.

A heartbeat passed before she returned his embrace. "I'm sorry I didn't tell you about her," Abby whispered. "If I could go back . . ."

He took a deep breath and released her. Tears flowed unchecked down his cheeks. "I know."

For the first time, she wondered if maybe they would get through this eventually. She knew it would take time for him to forgive her, but Abby could handle that. Heaven knew it had taken her a long time to forgive herself—to admit that maybe, just maybe she hadn't done anything wrong—that Kaylee's death hadn't been her fault somehow.

Several more minutes passed before he wiped the moisture from his cheeks and turned to leave as suddenly as he'd hugged her.

She followed him out, staying a few steps behind.

When he reached the sidewalk in front of the cemetery, Chris turned to the right. The subway station was to the left. Abby had no idea where he was going. She considered leaving him to his own devices and heading back to the hotel, but then she remembered how he'd reached for her hand.

Staying a few steps behind, Abby followed him down the sidewalk. After a while, she wondered if he had a destination in mind or if he was mindlessly taking a stroll through Brooklyn.

They'd gone several blocks before he turned and walked through a door. She'd fallen a little behind and rushed to catch up. When she entered the small café, she found him seated at a table in the corner.

"Did you want to be alone?"

"No."

Nodding, she pulled out the chair across from him and sat down.

Almost immediately, a server approached their table. "What can I get ya?"

"I'll take a coffee," Chris said.

The woman looked to Abby.

"The same. Thank you."

Chris made no effort to start up a conversation while they waited for their drinks, so Abby sat there and waited. The ball was in his court.

The server placed their coffees in front of them along with a few little packets of sugar and some half-and-half. "Let me know if you need anything else."

Abby took two of the sugar packets, ripped them open, and dumped them into her coffee. All the while, Chris made no move to add sugar or cream to his. Instead, he rotated the ceramic mug between his fingers several times, appearing deep in thought.

"I'd like copies of the pictures you have," he said without looking up.

"Of course."

He took a sip of his coffee and stared out the window. "Are things between you and Trent serious?"

Abby almost choked on her drink. Hot coffee went flying from her mouth and onto the table in front of her.

Chris handed her a napkin. "Are you okay?"

"Yeah. Sorry." She used the time it took to clean up the mess to try and figure out how best to answer his original question. Out of all the questions she thought he'd ask her, that hadn't been near the top of her list. She'd been sure he'd ask about Kaylee or even her life in New York, not her relationship with Trent. Although, now that she thought about it, she shouldn't have been surprised. "I don't know. We haven't been seeing each other that long."

The look he gave her spoke volumes. She'd seen it many times when they were younger. It was his 'I'm not buying what you're selling' look.

Laying the dirty napkin to the side, Abby met his gaze across the table. "What if it was? Would you be okay with that?"

He studied her for a long minute. "Yes. I would."

"You would?" She stared at him with wide eyes.

Chris leaned forward, resting his elbows on the table. "I want my brother to find someone who can make him as happy as Elizabeth has made me. If you're who he wants, then . . ."

"Then?"

He looked out the window again, and then back at her. "Then I'm okay with that."

Neither of them said anything more as they finished their coffee. For the first time, Abby allowed herself to really imagine a possible future with Trent. Could it work? If Chris was able to accept it, then maybe the rest of the family would as well. She felt as if a huge weight had been removed from her.

When the server came by with their bill, Chris swiftly pulled out his card and handed it to her. Abby opened her mouth to tell him he didn't have to do that, but Chris cut her off. "My treat."

She bit her tongue and accepted the gesture for what it was. "Thank you."

They took the subway back to the hotel. Some of the awkwardness had dissipated, but they had a long way to go before things between them were mended.

He walked her up to her room like he'd done the night before.

"Do you want to meet later for dinner?" she asked as she dug her keycard out of her purse.

"No. I think I'm just going to order room service tonight."

She opened the door to her room and stepped inside. "I guess I'll see you in the morning, then."

He gave her one short nod. "Good night, Abby."

"Good night."

It was only two thirty in the afternoon, but Abby was exhausted. She secured the door, dropped her purse on the nightstand, and kicked off her shoes before falling onto the bed. Her eyelids felt heavy, as if she'd pulled an all-nighter. She closed her eyes. Before she knew it, she was asleep.

Three hours later, her phone rang, waking her. Abby bolted up and scrambled to reach the phone before the call went to voice mail. She almost fell off the mattress and face-planted into the floor in the process. "Hello?"

"Is this a bad time?"

Abby smiled at the sound of Trent's voice. "No, not at all. I just woke up from a nap, actually."

"Long day?" he asked.

"Yeah. You could say that." She strolled over to the desk and sat down.

He knew she and Chris were visiting Kaylee's grave today. "How'd it go?"

Abby rubbed her forehead. "It wasn't as bad as I thought it would be. W-we went to a café after and talked."

Trent didn't respond right away. "A good talk?"

"Yeah. I think so." She picked up a pen and began doodling on the hotel stationery. "Tell me what's going on in Ohio. How did you spend your day off?"

"I didn't."

"What do you mean you didn't?"

"I worked today. Had to help some of my crew remove a stubborn tree." He proceeded to tell her how they'd tried everything to get this tree out of the ground. At first, they'd attempted to save it, but that proved to be impossible. In the end, they'd had to climb the tree, remove the larger limbs, and then cut the thing down. "And don't even ask about the stump."

He was so animated telling the story—adjusting his voice, pretending to be members of his crew—that Trent had her giggling and completely forgetting about the stress of the morning.

Eventually, her stomach growled, reminding her that she hadn't eaten anything since breakfast. She called down for room service while Trent dialed for a pizza. They continued to talk until she started yawning.

"I should let you get some sleep," he said. "When do you get back tomorrow?"

She knew he was right. "Our plane leaves at ten, so we should land in Cincinnati around eleven."

"Do you need me to pick you up?"

After she'd finished eating, Abby had moved to the bed. She relaxed back against the pillows. "I don't think so. Chris drove us, so I'm assuming he'll drop me off back at my apartment."

"Call me if you need me, all right?"

"I will." She paused. It was on the tip of her tongue to tell him she loved him, but it didn't feel right to say something that monumental over the phone. "Good night."

"Good night, baby. I'll see you tomorrow."

* * *

Trent dragged his butt out of bed and tried not to think of the hours he had to kill before Abby's plane landed. He made breakfast, threw in a load of laundry, and even went for a run. Unfortunately, when he looked at the clock, it was still only ten forty-five.

Throughout the morning, he kept thinking about their conversation the night before. It was in the tone of her voice as she'd told him about her day and her talk with Chris. She hadn't sounded as though she were about to jump off a cliff like she had the night before.

But more than that, the thing that kept replaying in his mind was a random comment she'd made regarding how it had felt strange being back in New York. She said it didn't feel like home anymore. Trent knew he was probably reading too much into it, but he was hoping that meant Ohio was home to her now. That she was considering staying there with him. Having a future with him.

He checked his phone, confirming she hadn't called or sent him a text, and then went to shower. She would call him after she landed, or once Chris dropped her off at her apartment. Stalking his phone wasn't going to make it happen any quicker.

Irritated with himself, he stripped out of his clothes, and stepped into the shower. He'd pushed himself on his run, trying to get rid of some of his excess energy. The water felt good on his overworked muscles.

Trent rested his hands on the tile wall and stretched out his back. He closed his eyes as the water beat out a rhythm on his back and shoulders. Memories of the shower he'd shared with Abby that first morning they'd made love filled his mind—the feel of her soft, wet skin as he rubbed soap up her torso to cup her breasts.

His body began to react to his erotic musings and he reached down to take care of his growing problem when his phone rang.

The sound made him jerk and he bumped the top of his head on the tile. "Ouch."

He rubbed the spot on his head he'd hit and bent to turn off the water. The phone rang again as he snatched a towel off the counter. He did a quick swipe over his body and rushed to answer it. "Hello?"

"Good morning, son." His father paused, and then chuckled. "Yep. It's still morning. Time seems to be getting away from me today."

Trent glanced over at the clock. It was eleven thirty-five. Still no call from Abby. "You still have a few minutes of morning left."

His father laughed again. "Your mother has had me working on her honey-do list. Sometimes I think she stays up late at night just to dream up stuff for me to do."

Trent grinned when he heard his mother's voice in the background. He imagined her standing there with her hands on her hips, chastising her husband for his comment. It was a familiar sight.

"All right, all right," his father mumbled.

Trent couldn't help but smile at his parents' antics.

"Anyway," his father said, talking to Trent once more, "your mother wanted me to call and see if you would be coming over for dinner today." He paused. "Abby's welcome as well."

Trent glanced at his cell phone, which was still deathly silent. "I don't know."

"You know your mother is going to want a better answer than that."

Yeah, he could see his mother's reaction if his dad came back with a response like that. Next thing Trent knew, his phone would be ringing again and this time it would be his mom.

"Tell her not to plan on us being there." If Trent hadn't heard from Abby in the next hour, he was going to head over to her place and wait there until she got home. There was no way he'd be able to have lunch with his family without Abby there with him. He also knew that chances were the moment he saw her he wasn't going to be able to keep his hands off her. It had been three and a half days since he'd seen her.

"All right. Well, you know you're always welcome if you change your mind. Both of you."

"Thanks, Dad."

Trent hung up the phone and went to find some fresh clothes to put on. He'd managed to pull on a pair of shorts when there was a knock on his door.

Given it was a Sunday, he had no idea who it could be. He didn't bother to look before wrenching it open. If it was someone selling something, he had no problem telling them to go away.

But it wasn't a salesman standing on his front porch. It was Abby.

She glanced up at him with a shy smile, wringing her hands in front of her. "Hi—"

Before she was able to get anything else out, he scooped her up and dragged her inside. He kicked the door closed behind them and, in the next breath, his mouth was on hers.

She released a low moan and kissed him back as if they'd been apart for months rather than days.

"I missed you," he whispered against her lips.

"Missed you, too."

"Are you hungry?" he asked between kisses.

She tilted her head to the side to give him better access to her neck. "Not for food."

Trent met her gaze and saw the same need he felt staring back at him. He set her feet on the ground, took both her hands in his, and began walking backward down the hall toward his bedroom.

Abby followed him step for step until they were next to the bed. He pulled her roughly against him, holding the back of her head exactly where he wanted it before tasting her again.

Clothing was removed and kicked out of the way as they touched and kissed. He unhooked her bra while she impatiently worked his underwear over his hips. When his boxers got snagged against the edge of the bed, Abby huffed and pushed down so hard he lost his balance. They both went tumbling onto the mattress, her sprawled on top of him.

His chest vibrated with his amusement, but it died swiftly when Abby reached down and took hold of his erection.

Trent cupped the back of her head and brought her mouth to his so he could devour it. He plunged his tongue into her mouth, taking what he needed from her as she stroked him until he could barely stand it.

"Need you," she moaned.

He flipped them over and kissed his way down her chest. When he reached the top edge of her panties, he looped his fingers into the sides and gradually slid them down her legs. He tossed them on the floor with the rest of the clothes and drank in the sight of her lying naked before him. "You are beautiful, baby."

She reached for him and he went willingly.

With one hand, he made sure she was ready and then positioned himself at her entrance. The love he felt for her overwhelmed him as he pushed inside. Abby looked up at him with such openness he couldn't hold it back any longer. He brushed his lips against hers and whispered, "I love you, Abby."

Abby placed her palm over his heart. He knew she could feel it pounding in his chest. She held his gaze. "I love you, too."

Trent swallowed. As much as he'd longed to hear her say those words to him, he had to be sure. "Do you?"

She nodded. "Yes. I've known for a while. I was just afraid to admit it."

He placed a soft kiss on her lips. "You don't ever have to be afraid with me."

Her fingers tangled in his hair and she lifted her hips, causing him to sink deeper. The look in her eyes held all the raw emotion he felt.

Trent placed a hand on her waist to still her for a moment. He needed her to understand the depth of what he felt for her. This wasn't casual for him. It never had been. "You know I'm never going to want to let you go."

She smiled and scraped her nails along his scalp, sending delightful tingles coursing through his body. "That's what I'm counting on."

Forgetting about everything else, he took her face in both his hands and kissed her hard. He flexed his hips and thrilled when he heard her suck in a breath.

As he picked up his pace, he rested his forehead against hers. Her eyes glazed over as they both edged closer and closer toward the climax they were seeking together. He felt her muscles pulse, and snaked his hand between their bodies to help push her over that final peak.

Her orgasm triggered his own and he collapsed beside her on the bed, more contented than he could ever remember being in his life. Trent pulled her into his arms. She cuddled against his side.

Before he knew it, her soft breathing told him she'd drifted off to sleep. He kissed the top of her head and adjusted the blanket over them. When she woke up they'd talk more, but for the moment he was going to enjoy having her in his arms.

CHAPTER 22

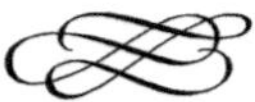

THEY WERE LYING in bed a while later, Abby with her head resting on Trent's shoulder, tracing lazy patterns on his chest. When they'd woken up from their nap, they'd made love again. Trent made her feel as if she were the most precious thing in the world.

"What are you thinking?" he asked, pressing his lips against her forehead in the lightest of kisses.

Abby tilted her head up to meet his gaze and felt her cheeks heat. "I was thinking about before."

He raised one eyebrow in question.

"I can't believe you were inside me when I told you I love you."

Trent kissed the palm of her hand before placing it over his heart. "I thought it was pretty perfect myself."

She giggled and shoved against his wall of solid muscle. "Of course you do."

The next thing Abby knew, Trent had flipped them over, pinning her to the mattress with his weight. "Are you saying you disagree?"

As he spoke, she could feel him pressing against her thigh. Surely he wasn't ready to go again so soon? They'd already made love twice. Not that she was complaining or anything, but weren't guys supposed to need recovery time?

Trent ran the tip of his nose along her neck, down to her shoulder. She sucked in a breath as heat began blooming anew in the pit of her stomach. He placed a kiss to her collarbone and gazed up, his eyes full of desire. "You need to stop looking at me like that."

"Like what?" she asked.

He pushed himself up on his elbows until he was hovering above her. "Like you'd be perfectly fine with me spreading your legs and pounding you into the mattress."

His statement was so blunt and unexpected she threw her head back and laughed. "So romantic."

"Just being honest, baby."

Abby sighed. "I love it when you call me that."

"Good," he said, pressing his lips to hers.

She threaded her fingers through his hair, trying to deepen the kiss, but he pulled away and climbed off the bed. Sitting up, she watched as he bent to pick up his pants from the floor. He was facing away from her, so she got a nice view of his fine backside.

"I can take a picture for you if you'd like."

She blushed. "Sorry."

Placing his hands on the mattress, he brought his face level with hers and smiled. "Don't be embarrassed. You can look at me all you want."

He gave her a quick kiss, and then walked toward the door.

"Where are you going?" she asked.

Instead of answering her question, he asked one of his own. "Have you eaten lunch?"

"No. Chris and I ate a big breakfast at the hotel before we left." It felt a little weird to be mentioning Chris when she was in Trent's bed.

"Are you hungry?"

Right on cue, her stomach growled.

He chuckled. "I'll take that as a yes."

Abby shook her head, stood, and stretched. "Do you mind if I grab a shower?"

His gaze traveled down her naked body and back up. "Want some company?"

Walking backward toward the bathroom, she sent him a flirtatious grin. "Sure. I can always use someone to wash my back."

Trent got an evil smirk on his face and rushed toward her. She squealed when he knelt down and tossed her over his shoulder like she weighed nothing.

"What do you think you're doing?"

He landed a sharp smack on her ass and laughed. "Making sure you don't have a dirty back."

Forty minutes later, they were clean and dressed. Well, sort of dressed. Abby had thrown on one of Trent's T-shirts and he'd slipped on a clean pair of loose-fitting shorts. He kept sending her looks that made her wonder just how long they'd be keeping them on.

She leaned against the counter while he dug some leftovers out of the refrigerator and set them on the counter. There was everything from green bean casserole to Chinese food. "Quite the assortment."

Trent licked some sauce off his thumb and she tried not to think about what his tongue had done to her in the shower. "Sorry. I know it's not all that impressive."

"It's fine." She placed a spoonful of macaroni and cheese on the plate he handed her. "I don't need anything fancy."

"That's good, 'cause I'm a pretty simple guy."

By the way he was looking at her, Abby knew he was talking about more than food. "I like simple."

He cupped the back of her head and rubbed his thumb back and forth along the skin behind her ear.

A shiver rippled through her and she leaned into his touch. She knew she needed to do something fast or the food would be forgotten, so she said the first thing that came to her mind. "I'm surprised you didn't want to go to your parents'."

"Dad called earlier. He wanted to know if we were coming today."

"Oh." She guessed the cat was out of the bag that she and Trent were seeing each other, then. "What did you tell him?"

He dropped his hand and went to put her plate into the microwave. "I told him I didn't know, but not to count on us."

"We could've gone," Abby said. "If you wanted to."

Setting the timer, he hit the start button and the microwave hummed to life. "What I have in mind for this afternoon might be a little difficult with an audience."

"Is that so?"

The only response she got from him was a boyish grin. It was full of promises that Abby had no doubt he could fulfill.

Trent reached around her to get a plate of his own and began piling it full of the assorted leftovers, acting like the sexual tension she'd just felt had been all in her imagination.

They curled up on the couch and flipped through the channels until they found a movie to watch. It was just starting to get good when her phone rang. She'd left it in her purse, which was still on the floor by the door.

When she saw Max's name on her caller ID, all the euphoria she'd been feeling drained from her body. "Hey."

Max didn't speak immediately, and she was filled with dread. He wouldn't have been calling if it wasn't important. "I'm sorry to bother you. I know you just got back."

"Don't be silly. You know you can call me anytime." Trent had abandoned his food and had come to stand next to her.

"It's just . . ."

"What, Max? Did something happen with your dad?"

She heard Max release a shaky breath. "Yeah. Mom went to wake him up this morning and he wouldn't respond. She called the nurse. She's still here. She said he probably won't wake up."

"I'm sorry." She felt Trent's hand press against her lower back. Knowing he was there warmed her heart and caused her pulse to race at the same time. "Do you need me to come to the house?"

"I can't ask you to do that. You're probably with Daniels and I mean—"

"You didn't ask. I offered." Before Max could come up with another excuse, she continued. "I'll be there as soon as I can."

Abby hung up the phone and turned to face Trent. Before she could say anything, he framed her face with his hands and pressed his forehead against hers. "Do you want me to come with you, or would you rather go alone?"

"You'd come with me?"

He held her gaze for a long moment. His eyes said it all.

She grinned and traced the outline of his lips with her fingertips. "Have I told you how much I love you?"

"Not for at least the last half hour or so." He placed a kiss on her forehead and lowered his hands to her arms.

Abby sighed. "I need to go home and change into clean clothes. Everything in my suitcase is dirty."

He hummed his agreement, but he didn't release her.

Another minute passed, and she was starting to forget why they couldn't continue. "Trent?"

"When we stop by your apartment, go ahead and pack an overnight bag."

Abby raised an eyebrow. "Good to know you think I'm easy."

"Ah, baby. Easy is not the word that comes to mind when I think of you."

"And what word does come to mind?" she asked.

Trent gazed into her eyes and with one of the most serious expressions she'd ever seen from him, he said, "Mine."

Maybe she should have bristled at the intense feeling of possession she felt rolling off him, but it had the opposite effect. She wanted to be his. Now, and for as long as he would have her.

* * *

Trent held Abby's hand as they climbed the steps leading to the Collinses' door. She'd been solemn looking out the window as they drove to the Collins family's estate east of the city. It was a drastic difference from the laughing woman he'd thrown over his shoulder a few hours ago.

She rang the doorbell and a few moments later Max opened the door. There were bags under his eyes and his hair looked as if he'd been running his fingers through it. To put it bluntly, the man looked a mess.

As soon as she saw him, Abby released Trent's hand and wrapped her arms around Max. Trent tried to tamp down the jealousy he felt seeing her in another man's embrace. Logically, he knew they were only friends—Abby had made that clear over and over and he'd not seen anything to make him think any differently. That didn't, however, change his natural male response to watching another man put his hands on her.

Taking a deep breath, Trent moved closer.

Max noticed they weren't alone and let his arms drop to his sides.

"How's your dad doing?" Abby asked.

"He started moaning about a half hour ago, so the nurse gave him morphine for the pain. That's all she can really do at this point. Make him comfortable."

"Is your mom with him?" she asked.

"Yeah. So are Uncle Frank and Aunt Lillian." Max glanced in Trent's direction, and then turned his attention back to Abby. "Come on in. Mom will want to see you."

The foyer to the Collinses' house was grand and elegant with lots of grays and blues. Max headed down a hallway to the left of the foyer. Trent and Abby followed.

"Are you okay?" she whispered to Trent when Max turned right.

Trent gave her hand an encouraging squeeze and nodded. He didn't want her to be worried about him at a time like this. While he didn't quite understand her friendship with Max, he accepted it. "How about you?"

"Scared. Nervous." She glanced at the door Max had disappeared into, and then took a step closer to Trent. "Are you sure you're okay being here? I mean, I know my friendship with Max makes you uncomfortable. You don't have to—"

He cut her words off with a kiss. "Don't worry about me. I'm a big boy. I can handle watching you comforting your friend."

She gave him a skeptical look.

Trent pretended to be shocked. "Are you doubting me?"

Abby narrowed her eyes at him.

He wasn't deterred. Trent tucked a strand of hair behind her ear and whispered, "Because you've seen me naked, I'm pretty sure you know just how big of a boy I am."

A shiver rippled through her body, and the corners of her mouth lifted slightly. "No problem with your ego, is there?"

Trent pressed a kiss in the hollow behind her ear. "Are you saying I'm wrong?"

Before she could respond, Max reappeared and motioned for them to come in.

Trent wasn't sure what he'd expected. He didn't have a lot of experience with death and dying. The last person in his family to die was his grandmother, but he'd been six at the time. He didn't remember much apart from going to the funeral.

Then again, his grandmother had died from a heart attack. It had been sudden. She hadn't suffered. The man lying in the hospital bed in front of him was clearly suffering. His skin had almost no color to it and there were dark circles under his eyes. He looked frail, breakable. It was difficult to imagine that six months ago this same man had been running a business.

Abby went to sit next to a woman that was huddled in the corner, who Trent assumed was Max's mother. She appeared to be lost as she stared at her husband with a blank look on her face. A sob erupted from deep in her throat when Abby sat down beside her.

Max placed a hand on his mother's shoulder, and then went to stand beside his father's bed. Trent felt as if he was intruding. Maybe tagging along with Abby hadn't been the best idea. He didn't even know these people.

Abby looked up at him and held out her hand. "Katherine, I'd like you to meet Trent Daniels."

The woman blinked as if only now registering his presence. He wondered how much this woman knew of Abby's past with his brother.

An awkward silence filled the air. Trent was at a loss as to what he should say. The standard "nice to meet you" didn't seem to fit given the circumstances.

Max cleared his throat. "Mom, when's the last time you ate something?"

Katherine shook her head. "I'm not—"

"You need to eat." Max left his father's bedside and came to stand in front of his mother. "Starving yourself isn't going to help Dad. And it isn't what he would want."

She hesitated, and then nodded.

Without missing a beat, Max glanced over to Abby. "Can you stay with her while I go make something?"

"Of course."

Max straightened up and met Trent's gaze. "I could use some help."

"Sure." Trent gave Abby's hand a reassuring squeeze before he followed Max back down the hallway and into the kitchen.

Max strolled over to the coffeepot sitting on the counter and poured two cups. "Cream or sugar?"

"Just sugar," Trent said. "Thanks."

He took a sip of the offered coffee and waited to see what Max would do next. Trent doubted the man actually needed his help.

Several minutes passed before Max finally spoke. "Do you love her?"

Trent paused with the mug halfway to his mouth. It made him bristle a little to have this man ask his intentions toward a woman he'd been in love with for half his life. "I do."

Max nodded. "She's not coming back to New York with me."

It wasn't a question, so Trent didn't bother to reply.

"I don't know. I guess a part of me always thought she'd be there no matter what. That I wouldn't have to worry about her finding someone she wanted to share her life with." Max shot him a weary smile. "Selfish, I know."

Trent didn't know what to say, but he felt he needed to respond. Like it or not, Max was Abby's closest friend. He'd been there for her when she'd had no one else. "I'll do everything I can to make her happy."

Max lowered his gaze and stared at the cup that contained his coffee. "I'll hold you to that. She's had a lot of disappointment in her life. First her mother. Then her father. Your brother. The baby. I don't want to see her hurt again."

"Neither do I." As they stood there talking about Abby, Trent had to wonder how she would feel about the conversation. Would she be glad they were coming to a sort of understanding, or would she rail on them for talking about her as if she weren't the strong, independent woman they both knew her to be?

Before Trent could think too long on the subject, Max stood. "We should see what's in the refrigerator. Uncle Frank went to the store yesterday. I'm sure we can whip up something edible."

Frank must have figured they wouldn't feel like cooking. Most of what he'd bought only had to be heated. They followed the warming instructions and loaded it onto a tray before heading back to the room.

Max hesitated outside the door.

"You all right?" Trent asked.

Max straightened his shoulders and marched inside without saying a word.

CHAPTER 23

TRENT STAYED CLOSE to Abby as she visited with Max's mother. He was an outsider and he was okay with that. He might never be fully accepted in the part of her life that included these people.

Max was seeing the nurse out. There wasn't any more she could do for now. All they could do was wait. They would call her when something changed.

When Max strolled back into the room, he met Trent's gaze across the room. In a strange way, having Max ask Trent's intentions toward Abby helped to ease the jealousy he felt. The way Max had approached the conversation was more like that of a big brother, rather than someone who was romantically interested.

Abby hugged Katherine, stood, and walked over to hug Max. For the first time, Trent didn't feel like punching the other man. "You'll call me if anything changes?"

"Of course," Max promised.

She was quiet as they made their way outside. When they reached his house, he grabbed the bag of clean clothes she'd packed when they'd stopped by her apartment earlier out from behind his seat. By the time he rounded the truck, she was already waiting for him by the door.

Trent followed her inside. She went to the refrigerator and began removing containers. He figured she must be hungry—he knew he was. He grabbed some plates and laid them on the counter. She moved with quiet efficiency, completely focused on her task. Her silence bothered him, but he decided to wait her out.

It wasn't until they were halfway done eating that she spoke. "Max told me Jacob had gotten worse. I guess I was fooling myself into thinking it wasn't as bad as he said."

There was something in her tone that made him think there was more to it. "Did seeing him today remind you of your dad?" Abby had come home for a surprise visit and found her dad collapsed on the floor. She'd called for an ambulance, but by the time it arrived, he was gone.

"He was just lying there, not moving, not opening his eyes."

Abby had experienced too much death in her life. First her mother. Then her father. And even her child. She needed some joy.

"Why don't you finish your food and we'll turn in early?" He leaned in as if he was confessing some secret. "I could probably even be persuaded to give you a relaxing back rub."

Her lips turned up a little. "Just a back rub? No straying hands?"

Trent shrugged. "Not really sure I can make a promise like that. I am a guy, after all."

Abby lowered her head, but he was fairly sure he saw her smile.

He let it go and took his empty plate to the kitchen. A few moments later, she did the same. It was only the third time she'd been in his home, but already it felt as if she belonged.

When she put her plate next to his in the dishwasher, he closed it with his hip and tugged her into his arms. "I love you, Abigail Hoffman."

This time he got a genuine smile out of her.

Trent brushed his lips against hers and she sighed.

He took both her hands in his and led her down the hallway to his bedroom. She lifted her arms over her head while he worked her shirt up her torso and let it drop to the floor. Her bra fell to the floor moments later. He wasn't trying to make it sexual, but it was impossible. The look in her eyes had him longing to be inside her.

When he reached between them to unbutton her shorts, Abby's hands got there first. She popped the button and lowered the zipper before wiggling her hips ever so slightly to work the material down her thighs.

Trent lowered his gaze to take in the sight of her standing before him in nothing but a minuscule pair of satin panties. He had to remind himself that this was about comforting her. There would be time later to make love to her.

He cupped the side of her face. "Lie down on the bed. I'll go get some lotion from the bathroom."

Digging through one of his bathroom drawers, he found a bottle of lotion Trinity had bought for him last winter. It was her ritual to buy all the guys lotion. She said there was no excuse for dry, chapped hands. The guys all groaned about it, but most of them used their gift, including him. It was going to come in handy tonight.

Trent palmed the lotion and took a deep breath, trying to settle his libido down before he waltzed back into the bedroom. But all the breathing in the world wouldn't have been enough to prepare him for the sight that welcomed him. Abby had done as he'd asked. She was lying in the middle of his bed, facedown, her hair fanned out over the pillow, and her barely covered ass beckoned him. He moved toward her without even thinking.

Abby must have heard him because she turned her head so she could meet his gaze. "Am I in the right position?"

He nodded and knelt on the bed. "Perfect. Just relax and enjoy."

She shot him a skeptical look, and then lowered her head on her hands and closed her eyes.

After squeezing some lotion in one hand, he set the bottle aside. He rubbed his hands together to warm up the liquid, and then went to work on her shoulders. She was tense. It took some effort, but as he continued to knead and caress her skin, he felt her start to relax.

"You're really good at this," she mumbled.

He grinned and continued to work his way down her body, loving the way she felt under his hands. When he reached the edge of her panties, Trent debated whether or not to skip to her legs. If he began massaging her backside, he was almost certain it would lead to a lot more than a back rub.

Shifting his weight, he moved to make it easier to access her legs. That was when he noticed a damp patch between her legs. Trent swallowed and did his best to ignore the growing discomfort in his pants. He was a grown man, not a sixteen-year-old boy. He could keep his urges under control.

That was until he ran a hand up the back of her leg and she opened her legs a little to give him better access. Before he could think about what he was doing, the tops of his fingers grazed the seam of her panties. She released a soft moan that went straight to his groin.

"Baby, you're killing me here," he said through gritted teeth.

She turned slightly to look at him, her eyes dark and full of desire. "You can remove my panties if they're in the way."

He looked at her with all the intensity he felt inside, wanting her to understand that her panties were the only thing keeping him in check.

Her only response was to lift her hips.

Deciding not to fight it, Trent looped his fingers into the sides of her underwear and shimmied them down the length of her legs. Without the thin covering, he could smell her arousal. All he wanted to do was dive in and taste her, but instead he retrieved the lotion and picked up where he'd left off.

This time, however, he didn't keep it as innocent as he had before. When he inched up her thighs toward her sex, he made sure to tease her sensitive skin. He did it several times before he removed his shirt and bent down to add his mouth to the action. Starting at her calf, he placed little kisses all the way up her leg. He repeated the process over and over again until Abby was lifting her hips and arching her back every time he came near the junction between her legs, silently begging him for more.

Eventually, her patience ran out. "Trent, please. I can't take it."

He skimmed his nose across her thigh and up over the swell of her luscious backside. "What can't you take, baby?"

"The teasing. I can't take any more. I need you."

Trent placed a firm kiss to her lower back and stood. He shucked his shorts and underwear, then rejoined her on the bed. Slipping a hand between her legs, he made sure she was ready for him.

Abby spread her legs, giving him unguarded access to her. She arched her back, wordlessly telling him with her body what she wanted.

He positioned himself between her legs and held onto her hips as he eased inside her. Making love to Abby was the single best thing Trent had ever experienced in his life. There was something about being with her that made him feel as if everything in his world made sense.

There'd always been something about her that had drawn him in. At first, it was how comfortable he felt around her. Then, as he grew and became aware of her as a woman, it became much more. Finally being with her, no walls between them, made things feel more potent than ever. This was how it was meant to be between them.

Trent enveloped her in his arms as they both came down from their climaxes. He held her close, tucking her head beneath his chin. "I want to ask you something."

She nuzzled closer.

"How would you feel about moving in with me?"

She lay there as their breathing returned to normal, not saying anything, but he knew she'd heard him.

"Are you serious?"

He lifted her chin so she could look at him. "I want you to marry me, too, but I figured this would be a good first step."

Her eyes went wide as she stared back at him. He didn't know if it was panic or shock. Either way, he wouldn't take it back. He wanted her with him. Always.

* * *

Abby was speechless. She opened and closed her mouth several times. He had to be joking. They'd been seeing each other for what, two weeks? It wasn't more than a month ago when he walked up to her in front of the Collinses' corporate office.

It was too soon. Couples didn't start dating and then two weeks later move in together. It hadn't been long enough. Had it?

Her head was spinning. Not only did he want her to move in with him, he wanted to marry her, too.

Trent looked at her as though what he'd proposed was the most natural thing in the world. There was no question, no second-guessing. He knew what he wanted. It had always been that way with him.

She needed to think logically about this because he was waiting for an answer, but it was way too easy to let fear grip her. It felt as if someone had taken hold of her chest and begun to squeeze.

"Breathe, baby," Trent whispered.

Abby tried to follow his instructions. She took a ragged breath in and let it out slowly.

How would his brother and the rest of his family feel if they got married? Yes, Chris had said he was okay with Abby and Trent dating, but dating and marriage were two different things. Ever since that night in Fort Lauderdale with Chris, she'd played it safe. Could she take a chance with Trent? Should she?

She regulated her breathing and the vise grip on her chest eased. Was it the thought of moving in with Trent, of marrying him that was causing her to panic, or was it her fear of what others might think? When she'd gone to New York, it was the thought of him supporting her that had given her peace. She loved him. Not like a teenager who was young and naive and didn't understand life, but as a woman who knew heartache and pain and wanted someone to share her life with —someone who would stand by her no matter what. "I don't know what to say. Can I think about it?"

He kissed the tip of her nose. "Of course."

"Thank you." Abby sighed and rested her head on his chest.

Trent ran his fingers through her hair and down her back, making her tingle in all the right places. "Take all the time you need. I didn't ask to freak you out, it's just that I know what I want. I let you go once before because I was too scared to say anything. I won't do that again."

She understood that. "It's not that I don't want to be with you. I hope you know that."

His chest vibrated under her cheek. "Considering what we just did . . ."

Abby playfully shoved at his chest, which only made him laugh harder.

He rolled them both over until she was lying beneath him. "The offer stands. Both offers."

Abby swallowed.

"I feel you tensing again."

It wasn't as if she could deny it. "I'm just not sure we're ready. We've only been dating for two weeks."

"So we'll take our time. As much time as you need. I won't push," he said, skimming his fingers down the side of her face. They'd made love not fifteen minutes ago and she could already feel the need for him building once more.

She glanced up at him with a doubtful look on her face.

He chuckled. "Okay, I won't push *much*."

"I guess that's all I can ask."

They lay there for several minutes, enjoying the feel of each other's bodies. With every brush of his fingers, the heat between her legs increased. It was getting harder and harder to think.

Deciding she could ponder the future of their relationship later, Abby tilted her head up and pulled his mouth down to hers. His lips met hers with an eagerness that only fueled the fire within her. She wrapped one arm around his neck and snaked the other between them. His flesh grew in her hand as she made her intentions clear.

Trent didn't hesitate to go with the flow. He pumped his hips into her hand and plunged his tongue into her mouth.

Things escalated quickly after that. He moved her hand out of the way and guided himself home. Abby's eyes rolled back into her head and she let the sensations take over. Until she could figure things out, this would have to be enough.

The sound of his alarm woke her the next morning. She groaned and snuggled herself closer to his warmth. "What time is it?"

Trent chuckled. He kissed the side of her head, and started to get up. "Five thirty. Go back to sleep."

She heard his feet hit the floor and rolled over to see his naked form barely outlined by moonlight coming through the window. "Why are you up so early?"

He padded over to his dresser and dug out a clean pair of boxers. "I need to get in early this morning."

Abby propped herself up on her elbows. "Why?"

"I've been thinking about what you said." He walked back to the bed and sat down.

With the fog of sleep, her brain wasn't computing what he was trying to say.

Her confusion must have shown on her face, so he explained. "What you said about Trinity's boyfriend. I think you might be right. I wanted to pull some other tapes and talk to her when she comes in."

"Do you really think that's a good idea? I mean, shouldn't you just tell the detective and let him handle it?"

Trent shook his head. "I doubt he'd bat an eye, let alone look into it based on a gut feeling."

"You have video."

"From three years ago." He stood and headed toward the bathroom.

She lay there for a few minutes before she gave up on any notion of going back to sleep. Throwing off the covers, she headed into the bathroom to join Trent for his morning shower. If they both had to be wide awake before dawn, they might as well have a little fun.

An hour later, Abby stood alone in Trent's kitchen, sipping a cup of coffee. He'd given her a long kiss goodbye before he left for work at six twenty-five—a little later than he'd planned, thanks to their shower activities. It felt very domesticated and Abby had to admit that she could get used to it. Maybe living together wouldn't be so bad.

Not wanting to think too hard about it until she'd had a few more cups of coffee, Abby finished cleaning up their breakfast and gathered her things. She'd brought clean clothes with her, but all her work clothes were still at her apartment. At least her stop at her place would be quick. All she had to do was change, put her hair up, and slap on a little makeup.

As it turned out, it took her a little longer at her apartment than she planned.

Abby had several messages on her voice mail. She'd been so focused on getting to Trent and then going to see Max's father that she hadn't thought to check it.

One of the messages was from Marilyn Daniels. She wanted to meet Abby for lunch. There were a few from Max, but since she'd seen him the day before she wasn't worried about most of them. The last one from him, however, was from early this morning. He wasn't going to be coming in to work today. His father's condition hadn't improved and he didn't want to leave his mother alone.

She'd call Max back once she got to the office and make sure to take care of anything on his schedule that needed to be rearranged. The message from Marilyn was a different story. Abby knew she couldn't avoid her forever, so before she could lose her nerve she picked up her phone and dialed.

"Hello?" Marilyn's voice came through the phone loud and clear. It was obvious she'd been up for a while.

Abby tried to steady her nerves. "Hi. It's Abby. I hope you don't mind me calling so early."

"Of course not. I'm glad you called. I was a little worried when you didn't return my message. But then I thought maybe you were with Trent." At least she didn't sound upset with the idea of Abby being with her son.

"I was. I'm sorry. I didn't even think to check my voice mail when I stopped home yesterday."

"Don't worry about it." Abby heard some movement in the background. "I was hoping maybe you'd be free for lunch today."

"Sure." It wasn't as if Abby could refuse her. Without Marilyn and Mike, her childhood would have been much different. If the woman wanted to yell at Abby for what she'd done, she would take it and not complain. "What time?"

"Whatever time works for you. One of the joys of being retired. My schedule is an open book." Marilyn laughed.

"All right. How about one o'clock?" With Max out for the day, she didn't need to worry with scheduling her lunch around his.

"That sounds perfect."

They decided to meet at a restaurant about a mile from Abby's office. Marilyn beat her there and had reserved a table for them. Abby sat across from the woman who had been her second mother and prayed Marilyn could find it in her heart to forgive her.

"You look happy," Marilyn said once they were alone.

Abby blushed. "I am."

The server came to take their order, saving her from having to say anything else. She decided to keep it simple and went with the lasagna and a salad. Considering the workout she'd been getting lately, Abby wasn't all that concerned with the calories or the carbs. She had no doubt they'd burn them off later.

Alone again with Marilyn, Abby felt her anxiety begin to creep up once more. She knew she had to say something. "I know you know about Kaylee and I'm sorry I didn't say anything back then. I know it's not an excuse, but I was scared and I didn't know what to do."

She looked up expecting to find judgment in the older woman's eyes, but instead she saw understanding. "I know. Chris called me last night and told me about your trip. It meant a lot to him that you gave her his name."

Abby cleared her throat, not wanting to tear up in the middle of the restaurant.

Marilyn reached across the table and covered Abby's hand with her own. "Don't let what happened years ago with Chris come between you and Trent. I want my boys to be happy."

Abby didn't know what to say. She'd expected Marilyn to at least give her a stern warning. Instead, it sounded as if she was getting the woman's blessing.

After squeezing Abby's hand, Marilyn released it and picked up her napkin. "We didn't get to talk much when you were at the house. Tell me all about your time in New York. What's your life like there? It has to be quite different living in the big city."

As she started telling Marilyn about her job in New York with Max, her anxiety began to ease. Abby had missed this. She'd missed Marilyn and all the Daniels family. Could they really accept her now, even after everything? If Marilyn's reaction was anything to go by, then, yes, they could.

By the time they hugged goodbye in the parking lot a little after four, Abby was feeling much better about her future—and more specifically, her future with Trent.

Without overthinking it, Abby made a left turn out of the restaurant parking lot instead of a right. She had a sudden urge to see him and she didn't want to wait until later tonight. Even though moving in with him was a huge step, it was what she wanted. She wasn't going to let fear keep her from what she wanted anymore.

CHAPTER 24

Even though Trent had gotten to work almost an hour later than he'd planned, he still had enough time to pull the footage he wanted. He'd heard Joss and Kevin come in a little before eight, and Trinity peeked her head in about eight thirty, asking if he needed anything. He assured her he was good and went back to what he'd been doing.

He'd only met Trinity's boyfriend once, and he hadn't been impressed. Billy, if Trent remembered his name correctly, struck him as arrogant and completely self-centered. His cocky attitude had left a bad taste in Trent's mouth, but he had to assume the man had some redeeming qualities if Trinity was dating him.

Trinity strolled in two hours later with two steaming cups of coffee. She held out one for him.

"Thanks."

"You're welcome." She sat down in the chair across from him and stretched her legs out in front of her. "What has you concentrating so hard in here, Boss?"

He took a sip of the coffee she'd brought him. Trinity took better care of him than he deserved. Things between them had been strained since the robbery and Trent knew it was entirely his fault. "Just a lot on my mind."

"Still seeing Abby?" she asked.

Trent grinned despite the serious conversation that was looming. "I am."

Trinity tilted her head to the side. "Wow. I've never seen you this way about a woman before. So it's serious?"

He couldn't seem to wipe the smile from his face. "I told her I want to marry her."

Trinity almost choked on her coffee. "But you've only been dating for like . . . two weeks."

"It's not like she's a stranger. We grew up together."

"Still," she said, "I mean, that was years ago, right? Shouldn't you wait a while and see how things go? Billy and I have been dating for five years."

It wasn't a great segue to what he wanted to talk to her about, but it would do.

"How are things with you two, anyway?" He was going for casual, but he had no idea if he pulled it off.

She glanced down into her coffee for a long moment. "We're good."

"That sounded convincing," he said, his voice laced with sarcasm.

Trinity ran her index finger around the rim of the paper cup she was holding. "Can I ask you something?"

Trent opened his mouth to answer in the affirmative, but she spoke again before he could get anything out.

"Do you get jealous of the people Abby works with? The guys, I mean?" Her eyes were pleading, as if she was hoping he'd say yes.

"Sometimes." Trent tried to keep it vague. He didn't want to go into his feelings about Max and Abby's friendship. Besides, he was trying to move past that.

Trinity placed her cup on the edge of his desk and leaned forward, resting her elbows on her knees. "But why? Do you not trust her? Has she given you any reason to think she's been or would be unfaithful to you?"

Trent raised an eyebrow. "Are we talking about me and Abby or you and Billy?"

She opened her mouth, hesitated, and then said, "Billy thinks you and I are having an affair."

It took a couple of seconds for Trent to figure out how best to respond to that. "Why would he think that?"

"I don't know." Trinity ran a hand through her hair in frustration. "I'm sorry. It's not your problem. I shouldn't be telling you this."

"It's fine." In fact, it was more than fine. He'd been around his big brother, Paul, enough to know that every criminal had a motive. Jealousy was as good as any. And if Billy viewed Trent as a personal threat to his relationship, it wasn't out of the question that he'd target Trent's business.

"No, it's not. I just . . . I don't know who else I can talk to." She sighed. "Things will be good for a while. Great, even. Then I don't know what happens. I'll come home and he'll be sitting at the kitchen table with this look on his face. The next thing I know, we're screaming at each other."

He recalled they'd had a big fight three years ago, hence the make-out session he'd caught on tape. It might be the connection he'd been looking for. "Did you have a fight like that recently?"

"Yeah." She slumped back in her chair, defeated.

"When, exactly?" It wasn't the most sympathetic response, but he needed to know.

"It was a few weeks ago." She paused. "Things are good again, so I know I shouldn't complain. But it keeps happening over and over again. I tell myself that couples fight. It's normal. But then I think, is it really?"

"Couples do fight." Trent got up from behind his desk and went to stand in front of Trinity. "But if it's a trust issue . . ."

"I don't know what to do."

There was a level of desperation in her voice, which made what he was about to say that much harder. "Trinity, this most recent fight you had, was it a big one?"

"Yeah. Probably the biggest we've had. He called me a lying whore and stormed out of the house." Tears welled up in her eyes.

He fought the instinct to comfort her. "When was that, exactly?"

She blinked, clearly confused by his question.

Trent hated being the bad guy, but he figured it would be better coming from him than from Detective Travers. "Was it before or after the break-in?"

"It was the night before." She stiffened as she caught up to his train of thought. "No. Billy wouldn't do that. He—"

"I'm not saying he did, but, Trinity, someone broke in and stole a lot of equipment and supplies. Someone who knew how to avoid being seen by the security camera." He knelt down in front of her and softened his tone. "I have a hard time believing that one of my employees would steal from me, which is what Detective Travers believes."

She stared back at him with wide eyes.

He understood her disbelief, but he needed her to understand his thought process. "As far as I know, Billy is the only other person who knows his way around the yard."

"There are the delivery drivers," she whispered.

"I've contacted all our vendors and let them know of the theft. I asked them to check with their other clients to make sure that there haven't been any other problems on our route. There haven't been." Trent let that sink in for a moment. "You said yourself that Billy thought the two of us were having an affair. Would that make him angry enough to want to steal from me?"

She didn't answer right away. "I don't know."

Trent knew that a big part of her world might come crashing down very soon. He rested a hand on her arm. "I'm sorry. I hope I'm wrong. But I need to give this information to the police. Especially now that I know the timeline fits."

Trinity nodded.

"Can you do me a favor?" he asked. "I need you to keep this to yourself for now. If Billy did do this, if you say anything to him, he might run—or worse."

"I don't want to believe he could do something like this." The way she said it made him think that while she didn't want to believe it, she was seeing the same pattern he had. She glanced down at the floor, then back up at him before admitting, "Two days before the mulch went missing, we argued about you, too. He'd seen us talking in the parking lot when he came to pick me up from work." She turned to look at him. "Do you think he did that, too?"

"Remember when I caught you two making out on the security camera?"

"Yeah."

"Mulch went missing not long before that. And you told me the reason you were all over each other was because you were making up after a fight."

She gasped and put her hand over her stomach. "I think I'm going to be sick."

Trinity took several deep breaths and he waited for her to calm down some before he continued. "I could be wrong. I hope I am."

"I'm sorry, Trent. It's my fault. If I hadn't brought him here—"

"You can't blame yourself, Trinity. The only thing you did was fall for the wrong guy." And whether or not Billy was the one behind the theft, Trent still believed he was the wrong guy for her. Yes, Trent might be jealous of Max and Abby's relationship from time to time, but he didn't pick fights with her about it. He trusted her and she hadn't given him any reason to believe she was being anything less than honest with him.

"What happens now?" Trinity asked, bringing him back to the here and now.

"Just go about your day like normal. I'll call Detective Travers and give him this new information. That's all we can do for now."

"Normal." She inhaled slowly and then let it out. "I can do that."

"Don't worry," Trent said, standing. "Everything will work out. You'll see."

Trent hoped he was right. The last thing he wanted was for Trinity or anyone else he cared about to get hurt.

Alone again in his office, Trent called Detective Travers. The sooner this case was closed, the better it would be for everyone.

Ten minutes later, he hung up the phone, frustrated and slightly pissed. His conversation with Detective Travers hadn't gone as well as he'd wanted. The detective wasn't happy Trent had been poking his nose around the case and in no uncertain terms told Trent to let him do his job.

The sound of a delivery truck's air brakes releasing brought Trent's head up. He looked out the window in time to see the driver hopping down from the cab of his truck.

Joss headed for the door, but Trent stopped him. "I've got this one." He needed to work off a little steam.

Trent greeted the driver by name as he approached the gate. "How've you been, Eddie?"

"Oh, can't complain. I get paid to sit on my ass."

Both men laughed as Trent pushed the metal gate out of the way. He stepped aside and waited for Eddie to drive the loaded truck into the yard, then went to get the forklift.

It took a good half hour to unload the twenty pallets of sod they'd ordered. Almost half of it would go out to a jobsite tomorrow. The rest would follow soon after.

Eddie handed Trent the paperwork once everything had been unloaded. "You ever find out who broke in?"

Trent signed his name and handed the clipboard back. "Not yet. The police are still looking into it."

Eddie nodded and hoisted himself back into the cab of his truck. "Well, I hope they catch 'em soon."

"Me, too."

Trent followed behind Eddie as he drove out of the yard, and resecured the gate. The sun had come out from behind the clouds and it was beating down on him. Trent looked at his watch and was surprised to see it was almost one. He made his way back inside.

"Did Trinity go to lunch?" he asked when he noticed she wasn't at her desk.

"I guess," Joss said. "She got a phone call and said she had to go take care of something."

The hairs on the back of Trent's neck stood up. While he had no reason to think something was wrong, he couldn't shake it. "Did she get the call on her office phone or her cell?"

"Her cell. Why?"

Trent walked to the window and looked outside. Her car wasn't in the parking lot. Trent prayed she hadn't gone and done something stupid, but he wasn't going to take any chances. Marching into his office, he opened the bottom drawer of his desk and opened his safe. Anyone who stole thousands of dollars' worth of equipment because they suspected their significant other was cheating on them wasn't someone he trusted to have a level head.

He reached inside and extracted his 9mm. He checked the magazine, racked the slide, and then tucked it into the back of his shorts.

* * *

By the time Abby pulled up in front of Trent's office, it was almost four thirty. She found a spot in the shade and called Max. While she wanted to see Trent as soon as possible, she'd be a bad friend if she didn't check in to see how Max's dad was doing.

The phone rang twice before a very weary sounding Max answered. "Hey."

"Hey. I wanted to see if there had been any change?"

"No. He's still hanging on. The nurse says it's only a matter of time." Max paused. "At least he doesn't seem to be in pain anymore."

"I'm sorry. I wish there was something I could do." A part of her felt guilty. Her life finally appeared to be coming together while his was falling apart.

"How was work today?" he asked, changing the subject.

"Quiet. I canceled your appointments for the rest of the week."

"Probably a good idea."

"An envelope came from the accounting firm you hired. I can bring it over in the morning," she said.

"That's all right. They called me earlier. We were right. Emily was just that bad at basic math. She kept transposing numbers and it was screwing everything up. An accounting nightmare, but nothing that can't be fixed."

"I guess that's good news."

Max released a loud breath into the phone. "Yeah. One less thing I have to worry about right now."

"Call me if you need anything?" She knew Max wasn't big on asking for help.

"I will."

Abby tucked her phone into her pocket and grabbed her purse. The afternoon had turned muggy and the sun beat down on her as she made her way up to the front entrance. A business suit was fine for an air conditioned office, but she couldn't imagine being outside on a day like today for very long in her dress pants, long-sleeve blouse, and jacket.

For a brief moment she thought about going home to change, but the desire to see Trent, to tell him what she'd decided, was too strong. She'd endure a little discomfort. Besides, she was kind of hoping he'd be helping her out of her clothes before too long.

A blast of cold air hit her in the face when she walked through the door. It felt good—a direct contrast to the heat outside.

She was enjoying the change in temperature so much that it took her a few moments to notice the office was empty. Trinity wasn't at her desk. Neither were the other two guys who worked in Trent's office. It was only four thirty. Where was everyone?

Abby was about to call out when she heard a crashing sound coming from the back room. The sound was followed by a gruff voice she didn't recognize. Whoever it was, they sounded angry.

Something was wrong. She knew it in her bones.

Making a split-second decision, Abby removed her heels, afraid they might make too much noise and tip off whoever it was, and hid them beside a filing cabinet. They would also hinder her if she had to move fast.

Abby tiptoed across the room, drawing closer to where she'd heard the noises. As she got closer, she heard more voices. One was clearly a man and he sounded angry. He must have been the one she'd heard before. The other was a woman's voice. Trinity. She was pleading with the angry man.

She heard Trent next. His voice was calm for the most part. She only heard a hint of fear mixed in there, but his words caused her heart to clench in fear. "Just put the gun down and we can talk."

Someone was holding them at gunpoint? Why? Who was he?

"No more talking. I think you've talked enough," the angry man said. His tone sent shivers up her spine.

Abby backed away as quietly as possible and ducked into Trent's office. Her first thought was to call 911 and then look for some sort of a weapon. She wasn't leaving while Trent was being held at gunpoint, but she wasn't stupid enough to hang around with no way to defend herself either.

As she reached for the phone, however, she heard a buzzing sound. Lowering herself to the floor, she crawled around the desk until she found the source. Trent's cell phone. He must have dropped it.

She snatched it up and saw Paul's name on the screen. "Paul?"

There was a pause before he answered. "Abby?"

"I think Trent and his employees are being held hostage in one of the back rooms." Her panic factor had ratcheted up significantly. Nothing could happen to him. Not now.

Paul's voice changed and she knew he'd switched from a concerned brother to cop mode. "Where are you?"

"I'm in Trent's office. His phone was on the floor under his desk."

She heard Paul curse. "Have you called 911?"

"I was about to."

He hesitated. "Do you still know how to shoot?"

It was only then it dawned on Abby that Trent must have a gun somewhere in the office. "Yes."

"Bottom right-hand drawer. The code is his birthday," Paul said.

Abby pulled open the drawer. There in the back was a safe. She typed in Trent's birthday and the lock clicked open. She lifted the lid, expecting to find a gun inside, but it was empty. "It's not here."

"He must have it on him. At least, I hope he does."

So did she. Because if he didn't, then chances were that the gun was in the possession of whoever had them hostage.

She was still running that over in her mind when Paul interrupted her thoughts. "Abby, I'll stay on the line with you, but I want you to get the phone off Trent's desk and check to make sure it has a dial tone. And stay behind the desk as much as you can. I'd tell you to get the hell out of there, but one, I don't think you would listen, and two, there's always a chance whoever it is would hear you."

"I'm not leaving him." Abby reached for the phone and then crouched down behind the desk with it cradled in her lap. She picked up the receiver and breathed a sigh of relief when she heard the dial tone. "It's still connected."

"Good. Call the police. I'm right here with you, okay, Abby?"

Her hand shook as she punched in the three numbers. She knew she needed to stay calm. Freaking out wasn't going to help Trent.

CHAPTER 25

Billy had one hand wrapped around Trinity's forearm, his fingers digging into her flesh, and his other held a gun that he kept pointing at Trent, Joss, and Kevin. For the last ten minutes, Trent had been trying to think of a way to defuse the situation. Billy had caught him off guard. Trent had been on the phone with a client demanding to know why it was taking so long to get the special brick pavers they'd ordered, otherwise he would have taken action as soon as the man walked through the door.

As it was, they were now trapped in the storage room with stacks of boxes and only one way out—a door that was being blocked by Billy. No one was going to come looking for them anytime soon. Best case scenario, they had another hour at least before anyone began to wonder where any of them were.

Trent knew he was going to have to make his move soon. He'd been trying to talk Billy down, but then Kevin had panicked and tried to make a run for it. His actions had sent Billy into a fury. He was waving his gun around, his finger on the trigger.

Trinity was barely holding it together. She was scared. Trent only hoped she didn't do something stupid. This wasn't her fault. No, they had Detective Travers to thank for this.

The detective had taken Trent's information and stopped to have a chat with Billy about the break-in. Whether the detective got any useful information from Billy or not, Trent didn't know. Billy had called Trinity and convinced her to meet him for lunch. Almost three hours later, they both showed up at the office—Trinity with a black eye, busted lip, and her clothes ripped to the point that Trent wondered if Billy had sexually assaulted her as well.

Trent took a small step forward and to the side, away from Kevin and Joss, trying to redirect Billy's attention. He looked about a second away from shooting Kevin and that was the last thing they needed.

It worked. Billy swung his arm around until Trent was looking down the barrel of Billy's gun, only about four feet separating them.

Trent held up his hands in surrender. "You don't want to shoot any of us."

"Oh, I don't know about that. Seems like a pretty good option to me." Billy's eyes were wild. The hope of talking him down seemed to be dwindling away.

Billy flexed his fingers on the gun. He released Trinity's arm long enough to wrap his arm around her neck. Her mouth opened and she gasped, struggling to get air into her lungs as he compressed her airway. Something had to give soon.

Trent could feel his gun pressing against his back. He'd considered reaching for it a dozen times but the timing hadn't been right. He was a decent shot, but he wasn't a sharpshooter. It was too risky to try and shoot Billy while he had Trinity. And that wasn't even taking into consideration Billy's itchy trigger finger. One wrong move from any of them and he had little doubt Billy would shoot.

"Just let Trinity and the others go and we can talk. I'm sure we can figure this out," Trent said. He was trying to remember all the stuff Paul had told him over the years. His brother had been involved in a few hostage negotiations, but Trent's adrenaline was getting the best of him, making it difficult to remember Paul's advice.

Billy shifted the gun again, pointing it at Trinity's head. This wasn't going the way Trent wanted it to.

"Not much to figure out. You've been screwing my girlfriend. I took what was due me and now you sic the cops on me."

Trent knew there was no use trying to convince Billy that he and Trinity hadn't ever slept together. And Trent doubted saying he had a girlfriend of his own would do any good either. The man was clearly unhinged.

Trinity's face was red and her lips were beginning to turn purple. If Trent couldn't get Billy to loosen his hold soon, she was going to pass out.

Trent ran through his options. None of them were all that great.

Kevin moved again, drawing Billy's attention. At the same time, Trent saw Trinity's eyes roll into the back of her head. Trent knew this was it. He was going to have to act and it would have to be fast. He only hoped he was fast enough.

Out of the corner of his eye, Trent saw Joss reach behind him for what looked to be some sort of old accounting equipment. He wasn't sure what the man was planning on doing, but it didn't matter. If Billy felt threatened, he was going to start shooting.

Trent knew he couldn't wait any longer. He couldn't think about the fact that in mere seconds he might be shooting—killing—another human being. There were three other people in this room besides himself and he cared about them. They all needed to survive this.

His moment came sooner than he'd anticipated. Trinity slumped in Billy's arms as the lack of oxygen caught up to her. The dead weight caused Billy to lose his balance and he lowered his gun to compensate.

Trent didn't hesitate. He couldn't. It was his one chance and he had to take it.

Reaching behind his back, he pulled his gun out of his waistband and brought it to eye level. He took aim and fired.

* * *

Abby nearly lost her lunch when she heard the gunshots.

Paul and the 911 operator heard them, too.

"Stay where you are," they said in unison. It was as if they both knew that her first instinct would be to go check to see if anyone had been hurt—if Trent had been hurt.

"A patrol car is thirty seconds out," the dispatcher said.

"Paul?"

The dispatcher knew that she had a friend on a cell phone. "I'm here, Abby. Just take some deep breaths. The police will be there any second. It's going to be fine."

"But what if it isn't?"

"It will be. You'll see." He said it with such confidence. She wondered if he truly believed that or if he was only trying to be brave so she wouldn't go into hysterics.

Abby heard the front door creak open. "Someone's at the door."

"There are officers on scene. Just stay where you are. They need to secure the scene."

She heard more footsteps in the main room, and then there was shouting. "Drop your weapon!"

"I have to go out there. I have to make sure—"

"No," Paul and the dispatcher said in unison again. It was like she was getting admonished in stereo.

"Stay where you are," the dispatcher added. "When the officers ask, respond to them and do what they tell you."

"She's right," Paul said in her other ear.

She didn't want to stay put, but she trusted Paul. If he thought she should stay where she was for now, then she would.

Abby had no idea how much time passed. It felt like hours, but in reality it was probably only a few minutes. More people could be heard entering. More people were talking, shouting.

A flash of white appeared in the doorway. "Anyone in here?"

"Yes." Abby's throat constricted so much it was difficult to get that one word to come out.

"The officer is there with you?" The dispatcher's voice jarred Abby out of her fog.

"Yes."

"Okay, I'm going to hang up now."

"Okay." Abby let the phone drop from her fingers, not bothering to put it back its cradle as she crawled out from behind Trent's desk.

The officer walked toward her, weapon lowered but still at the ready. "Are you the one that called 911?"

Abby nodded.

The officer motioned for Abby to come toward her. "Let's get you out of here."

"What about—"

The radio on the officer's shoulder crackled to life. "The scene is secured. We have one down and another needing medical attention."

"Trent." His name came out as a plea of desperation. She needed to see him.

The officer grabbed hold of her arm as she started to rush out into the main room. "Ma'am, you can't go in there."

Tears stung her eyes. "I have to know if Trent's okay. I have to . . ."

The woman didn't waver. "We need to get you outside. Then we can get things sorted."

It wasn't what Abby wanted, but she nodded.

The officer gave Abby's arm a small squeeze before letting her go. "Stay behind me."

All Abby could see as they made their way through the main room were police officers, at least ten of them. Most of them were focused on the back room where she knew Trent had been. Was he hurt? Had whoever it was shot him?

She was guided to a waiting ambulance. "They're going to check you out and make sure you don't have any injuries."

Again she nodded to the officer. Abby felt as if she was in a haze.

A man about her age hopped off the back of the ambulance and smiled at her. She smiled back out of habit as she hugged her arms around her waist.

It was then she heard muffled shouting. She glanced down and realized she still had Trent's cell phone clutched in her hand. "I'm here. I'm here. Sorry."

"What happened?" he asked.

"I don't know. They won't tell me anything." The paramedic held a bright light up and shone it in her eyes. "They wouldn't let me go . . ."

When Paul spoke again, reason had returned. "It's a crime scene, Abby. They have to be careful that evidence isn't contaminated."

The female officer who had escorted her out reappeared and placed a gentle hand on Abby's forearm. "You were asking about the owner, Trent Daniels, right?"

"Yes." Abby held her breath, trying to prepare herself for the worst.

"He's all right. They'll be bringing him out in a minute to get checked."

Abby took her first real breath in what felt like hours. "He's okay," she translated back to Paul.

"Good. Now take a deep breath and let the paramedic examine you. They're going to want to take everyone's statement, so you'll have to go down to the police station."

"Thank you. For staying on the phone with me." Abby had no idea what she would have done if Paul hadn't been there to coach her through everything.

"Anytime."

Abby shoved the phone in her pocket and tried to answer the paramedic's questions as best she could. He gave her a bottle of water and a blanket, saying he was concerned she would go into shock, and left her to sit on the back of the ambulance. They brought Joss out of the building looking shaken, but he didn't look hurt. The same paramedic that looked her over began assessing Joss.

An officer hovered nearby as she sipped on her water. Abby didn't know if that was because they feared there really might be something wrong with her or because they didn't want her leaving the scene. Maybe it was a little of both.

She got her first glimpse of Trent several minutes later. He was ushered out of the building and taken to another ambulance at the opposite end of the parking lot. An officer was with him and he appeared to be unharmed.

As a paramedic checked him over, a man in a suit strolled up to talk to him. It took her a moment to realize that the man must be a detective.

Time seemed to stand still as she observed their conversation. She was too far away to hear what they were saying, but she honestly didn't care about that. Abby concentrated on the way Trent moved his hands and how he held himself.

Abby was so focused on watching Trent that she didn't notice when another man approached her. She jumped and spilled some of her water when he said hello.

"Sorry," she muttered.

"My name is Officer Manns. I'll be escorting you to the station so the detective can take your statement."

Paul had mentioned that. She stood and followed the man to his cruiser. He opened the door for her and she slid inside. Even though she knew she wasn't under arrest, it still felt as if she must have done something wrong to be sitting in the back of a police cruiser.

Trent turned to look at her as she drove away. She couldn't read the expression on his face. It was somewhere between relief and regret.

When she arrived at the police station, she was taken to a nice-sized room with a table and several chairs. There were two bottles of water on the table and some small bags of snacks.

She took a seat and less than a minute later a tall man with sandy blond hair walked in. He pulled out the chair across from her and took a seat. "Hello. Miss . . ."

"Hoffman. Abigail Hoffman."

He smiled and wrote her name down. "I'm Detective Kent. I need to ask you a few questions about what happened today. You were the one to call 911?"

"Yes." Abby took a deep breath and launched into the explanation of how she'd come to Trent's office to surprise him only to realize her boyfriend was being held hostage.

He asked her a few more questions to clarify the order in which things had happened, thanked her for her cooperation, and then handed her a business card. "If you think of anything else, don't hesitate to call me."

She took the card and shoved it into her bra. There wasn't anywhere else to put it since she'd discarded her jacket somewhere in Trent's office when she'd been waiting for the cops to arrive.

When she had finished giving her statement, Detective Kent walked her to the front of the station. She turned the corner and saw Mike and Marilyn Daniels waiting.

"Abby!" Marilyn rushed over to her and pulled her into a bone-crushing hug. "Are you okay?"

Mike came up beside his wife and stood with a concerned look on his face as Marilyn doted on Abby.

"I'm fine. But I don't know where Trent is. The last time I saw him, he was talking to a detective."

"He's giving his statement," Mike said. "Paul said it's standard procedure."

Marilyn guided Abby to a row of chairs along the wall and sat down. Mike lowered himself into the seat next to his wife.

"How are you so calm?" Abby asked them.

Marilyn grinned. "I raised four boys. I've learned not to stress about things I can't change. Besides, Paul says this is normal. I trust his judgment."

Abby didn't like waiting, but she didn't see that she had much choice.

An hour passed and they were still waiting. Abby's leg was bouncing up and down and she didn't care. What was taking so long? At least two dozen police officers had passed by them with barely more than a glance. Marilyn had done her best to ease Abby's tension. She'd even called Paul again and had him tell Abby personally that this was all routine. It didn't help. Not in the slightest.

"Ma? Dad?" It wasn't the voice she'd wanted to hear. When she looked up, Chris and Elizabeth were headed their way.

Mike stood. "Did Paul call you?"

Chris nodded. "We came as quick as we could. Is Trent still in there?"

"Yes. It's been over an hour, so I'm hoping it won't be much longer."

Chris gave his mom a hug and then took a seat next to them.

Abby got up. She had the sudden need to move around. Sitting still was slowly driving her insane.

She'd made it down to the end of the hall when Trent came around the corner. Detective Kent was with him, but she barely spared him a glance before she shot down the hall and ran into Trent's arms.

"Hey," he whispered into her hair as he wrapped her in his warm embrace.

She glided her fingers over his head and down the side of his face as she held his gaze.

The detective cleared his throat. "You're free to go, Mr. Daniels. We'll be in contact with you if we have any more questions."

Trent nodded.

As soon as the detective walked away, the rest of his family descended. They all hugged him. Trent returned the show of affection, but kept one arm firmly around Abby's waist at all times.

"Let's get out of here," Mike said. "I'm starving. What do you all say we blow this joint and go grab a bite to eat?"

There were a few chuckles, and then everyone was moving. She went along even though she wasn't sure she would be able to eat anything.

Trent and Abby slid into the backseat of his parents' vehicle. He pulled her close to his side and she snuggled into him.

"What are you in the mood for, son? I'd say after the day you've had, the choice is yours."

"Anywhere's fine, Dad." Trent answered his father, but he never took his gaze from Abby. He kept stroking her hair and brushing his lips against hers.

Mike drove to a steak house a few miles away and they all piled out of the car.

Dinner wasn't bad. Abby ate more than she thought she would. Now that she could see that Trent really was safe, her appetite returned.

Everyone had questions. They wanted to know what had happened, who the guy was, and why he'd targeted them. When it came out that Paul had stayed on the phone with her through the whole thing, Trent commented that he was going to owe his big brother an extra Christmas present this year.

Abby was just glad Trent was all right. He'd sworn to her and his mother that there wasn't a scratch on him. While she believed that he was physically unharmed, she had to wonder how he was doing with the rest of it. Trent had killed a man. Even though his life and those of his employees had been in danger, she couldn't imagine what that would be like.

His main concern seemed to be for Trinity. She'd been taken to the hospital to make sure nothing was broken and that there was no internal bleeding. Trent had called her on the way to the restaurant. The doctors had bandaged her up and sent her home with some medicine for the pain. It would take a little while for her to heal, but she was going to be okay.

On the way back out to the car, Chris walked over to them. "We're going to head home."

Trent embraced his brother. "Thanks for coming down."

"Anytime." Chris looked over at Abby. "Take care of him."

Abby grinned. "I will."

Chris smiled back and waved goodbye. It was the first time Abby felt as if maybe, one day, things would be back to normal between them.

Mike and Marilyn drove Abby and Trent back to his office so they could get their vehicles. Trent stood off to the side as Abby opened the door to her car.

"Follow me home?" he asked.

She looked him dead in the eye before lowering herself into her seat. "If you think I'm letting you out of my sight, Trent Daniels . . ."

He gave her one of those smiles of his that had her heart racing. She wanted to rip off his clothes right then and there.

Trent leaned down and gave her a lingering kiss. "I'll see you at the house."

The drive back to his place—which would soon be her place, she reminded herself—only took a few minutes. It was late and most people were already home for the evening.

She parked her car in the garage beside his and followed him inside. They made their way down the hall to his bedroom. He pulled his shirt over his head and tossed it into the hamper. "I need to take a shower. Do you want to join me?"

Abby tilted her head to the side. "Did you miss what I said earlier about not letting you out of my sight?"

She hummed when he bent down to nuzzle her neck.

"I didn't forget." He placed one arm under her legs and lifted her into his arms. His mouth found hers once more as he strolled into the bathroom.

Trent lowered her feet to the floor again outside the shower. He tucked a strand of hair behind her ear before reaching to turn on the water.

All the love she felt for him surged through her with an undeniable force. He had changed her life in more ways than one. Trent had given her back the family she thought she'd lost because of a stupid decision she'd made. He'd shown her that she didn't have to give up on love—that she deserved it.

She took a step forward, closing the distance between them, and caressed the side of his face. "I love you."

Trent kissed the inside of her palm. "I love you too, baby. Always."

"Did you mean what you said last night? About us living together, I mean?" she asked.

"You know I did." He placed a kiss on her wrist and then continued down the length of her arm. It was hard to remember what she'd been about to say.

"I think I want to."

Trent halted his movement and met her gaze.

"I want to move in here with you. That's . . . that's what I was coming to tell you today." She swallowed. "And then we can talk about the other."

He dropped her arm and cradled her face between both his hands. "You won't regret it, Abby. I promise."

Abby didn't think she would either. Trent made her feel as if the future was full of possibilities and she never wanted to let that go. Not ever.

EPILOGUE

ABBY STOOD at the railing of the paddleboat, looking out at the Ohio River. The wind whipped her hair around her face as they made their way along the water, but she didn't care. Today she was officially becoming a member of the Daniels family.

It was hard to believe that less than a year ago she'd been living in New York. The life she'd had there seemed a world away. Ohio was her home now. Trent was her home.

Max leaned against the railing beside her, squinting against the sun. "You ready for this?"

She smiled. "More than ready."

"No cold feet?" he asked, giving her shoulder a bump. Max had softened considerably toward Trent and the Daniels family in general. He still wasn't a big fan of Chris, but Abby wasn't sure that was ever going to change.

"Nope. Not even a little."

Max placed his hand over hers and squeezed. "I'm glad you're happy. Trent . . . he's . . . he's a good guy."

Abby narrowed her eyes a little. "Are you feeling okay? I mean, you don't have a fever or anything?"

He chuckled and shook his head. "I just want you to be happy,

Abby."

"What about you?" She leaned into his side and wrapped her hand around his bicep. "When are you going to find some nice girl to settle down with? Maybe that new assistant of yours?"

Max rolled his eyes. "You need to stop playing matchmaker."

"I like Amber."

"Considering you're the one who picked her out, I would hope so," he commented.

"Yes, but you hired her. You could have rejected my recommendation." She looked up at him with mischief in her eyes. It was one of the things she missed about not being Max's assistant. She couldn't tease him like she used to.

"While that might be true, today isn't about me. It's about you." He glanced down the walkway that led to the back of the boat. The captain, who was performing the ceremony, stepped into view, catching Max's gaze. "I think that's our cue. Last chance to back out."

Abby nodded to the captain and ran her hands down the front of her white dress. She'd picked a lightweight dress that came down to her ankles. It reminded her of the beach. All she needed was one of those large-brimmed hats. "I'm not backing out."

Max grinned and offered her his arm. "Let's get you to your groom, then."

Threading her hand through his arm, she let him lead her down the walkway that ran along the side of the paddleboat. Abby and Trent had decided that instead of a church wedding, they would have the ceremony on the same paddleboat where they'd spent their first official date. It had been the beginning of their romantic relationship. Why not have it be the place where they began their marriage as well?

Everyone who meant something to Trent and Abby were waiting at the back of the boat. They turned as she and Max came into view, their faces lit with happiness.

Abby looked through their friends and family until she found Trent. He was standing to the right of the big paddle wheel, next to the captain. When their gazes met, his smile widened. She still had to pinch herself some days to believe he was really hers.

As she took those final steps toward him, she thought back to the conversation they'd had two nights ago. They'd gone to one of their favorite restaurants and had sat next to a young family. The couple looked to be around their age and they had two kids under the age of two. For the first time since Kaylee's death, Abby felt something more than the loss of her baby when she saw the happy family. She'd laced her fingers with Trent's across the table and asked him if he was ready to start trying for a little one of their own.

He responded by bringing her hand to his lips and placing a tender kiss on it. "We can start tonight, if you want."

They didn't, of course, because she was still on birth control, but they both agreed that she wouldn't be refilling her prescription. She couldn't wait to see Trent hold their baby in his arms. He'd be a wonderful father.

Trent reached for her as she drew near, not waiting for Max to place her hand in his.

"Impatient?" she asked.

Trent rubbed his thumb over her ring finger. "Very."

The captain chuckled. "If you're ready to begin . . ."

Everything else seemed to fade away as they said their vows and before she knew it, they were being pronounced husband and wife. He pulled her into his arms and gave her a kiss that wasn't entirely chaste. Laughter bubbled up from deep inside as they both came up for air. She couldn't remember the last time she was so happy.

* * *

Trent stood near the dock. Abby had gone to find Max so she could say goodbye. They'd socialized with their friends and family for close to four hours as the boat cruised along the Ohio River, but he was ready to get her alone. They were spending the night at a hotel in Covington, and then catching a flight tomorrow morning for St. Thomas. He couldn't wait.

Gage snuck up behind Trent and slapped a hand on his back. He turned to face his youngest brother, but found himself surrounded. Gage wasn't alone. Chris and Paul were with him.

"You guys going to jump me or something?" Trent asked with a smirk.

"Not at all," Gage said. "Just thought we could impart some brotherly advice before you head off on your honeymoon. You know, since we all have the marriage thing down pat."

Trent laughed. "Oh really? Is that why I saw Rebecca giving you the stinkeye earlier?"

Gage shrugged, unfazed. "Foreplay, man. Foreplay."

Paul rolled his eyes. "More than we needed to know."

"Hey. What can I say? I know how to keep her satisfied."

"Do you two need a time-out?" Chris asked with amusement.

Trent caught sight of Abby. "You'll have to excuse me. I need to get my bride alone and away from you yahoos."

"Don't do anything I wouldn't do," Gage shouted as Trent helped Abby off the boat and back onto dry land.

"*Is* there anything you won't do?" Paul asked Gage.

Trent didn't hear Gage's response. He was too busy trying to get Abby to the parking lot and his truck.

"In a hurry?" she asked.

"The sooner we get to the hotel, the sooner we're alone, so yes."

It only took them ten minutes to get to the hotel, which in his way of thinking was still too long. He found a spot in the parking garage, and went to help her out of the vehicle. Luckily, he'd checked them in and dropped their bags off in their room before heading over to the boat. All they had to do was go to their suite.

Abby's eyes lit up when she walked into their room. There was a nice-sized sitting area, a table big enough for four, and a view of the Cincinnati skyline.

"It's beautiful," she whispered, making her way over to the window. It was dusk and the city was starting to light up.

He strolled up behind her and wrapped his arms around her waist. "I'm glad you like it, but you haven't even seen the bedroom yet."

She laughed.

"What can I say, baby? I'm unable to resist you." He placed a kiss on her neck.

Abby leaned into him. "Do you ever think how things might have been if you'd said something back in high school? I keep thinking that I'm so happy right now. What if I could have had that for the last fifteen years?"

He knew he could brush her question off, distract her, but he knew Abby. If he did that, she'd let it eat at her. "I don't know. Maybe. We were young. Now we've grown up. We know what we want." Trent turned her around to face him. "All I know is that I have you now and I don't intend to ever let you go, Mrs. Daniels."

She grinned. "I love the sound of that."

"So do I." Trent stepped back, taking hold of both her hands. "What do you say we do a little celebrating? I think maybe I need a little practice on the baby making. You know, just so we do it right when the time comes."

"You don't think we've had enough practice yet? We've been practicing a lot." She followed him toward the bedroom, despite giving him sass.

"There's no such thing as too much practice."

"Oh, really?" she asked.

To prove his point, Trent bent down, tossed her over his shoulder, and marched toward the bedroom.

***

Are you READY FOR MORE from Sherri Hayes? **Get her standalone office romance, Strictly Professional, and start reading today!** Turn the page to read Chapter 1 of Matthew and Cali's story.

Sign up HERE or at www.sherrihayesauthor.com to make sure you don't miss any of Sherri Hayes' new releases.

CAN'T WAIT FOR SHERRI'S NEXT BOOK?

Let her know by leaving a review and telling her what you liked about
WHAT MIGHT HAVE BEEN (DANIELS BROTHERS #4)

BUY IT TODAY

Chapter 1

Cali Stanton gave her appearance one final appraisal in the full-length mirror. It wasn't an image she was used to. Not anymore, at least.

She'd spent over an hour getting ready, making sure her hair and makeup were just right before donning one of her new power business suits. Normally she left her hair down or pulled it back into a ponytail, but today, to give herself a more professional appearance, she'd twisted her reddish-brown hair up off her neck and secured it on top of her head with a clip that scraped against her scalp as she adjusted it.

To add to her tailored appearance, she slipped her feet into a pair of three-inch black pumps. The saleswoman had assured her that they would go well with her sleek black pantsuit, and they did. The fabric of the suit hugged her curves and the heels made her legs look long and elegant.

Sighing, she ran a hand down the front of the suit. "Ready or not, here I come."

Cali grabbed her matching handbag from the bed and made her way downstairs. Her father's house was huge. It was a far cry from the small dwellings she'd inhabited for the past two years in Africa with Doctors Without Borders. The vast amount of extra space was taking a while to get used to, even though she'd grown up here.

As she descended the large central staircase, Cali could hear Jessie in the kitchen. Cali smiled as she thought of the older woman. Jessie had been her dad's housekeeper for over twenty years. She'd seen Cali through the tough years after her mother's death and stuck by her side during her not so tame teenage years. Jessie was like a mother to Cali and she was glad to have the older woman back in her life again.

Jessie glanced up when Cali entered the kitchen, and smiled.

"Good morning."

Taking an exaggerated step back, Jessie gave Cali a thorough once-over before whistling her approval. "My, my. Don't you look like something this morning?"

Cali blushed. "Thank you."

She walked over to the counter and took a seat. Jessie placed Cali's breakfast in front of her and once again she felt her love for the older woman surge. She hadn't asked Jessie to make her breakfast this morning but she had anyway.

Digging in to her food, Cali asked, "You don't think it's too much, do you?"

Jessie waved her comment away. "No, no, of course not. But you *will* make a statement. Maybe you can give some of those stuffy businessmen a run for their money."

Cali laughed. "Somehow I doubt that. I'm just hoping I'm able to hold things together until Dad's well enough to come back."

Jessie's face became serious. "I don't know what I'm going to do with that man. He's not twenty anymore."

"I know," Cali said. "I don't know what possessed him."

"I'll tell you what possessed him. He's feeling his age, that's what. You came back just in time. It's a midlife crisis or something. Trying to learn to water ski at his age." Jessie shook her head in dismay.

Cali didn't know how to respond, so she said nothing. She agreed with Jessie. A midlife crisis was the most logical conclusion because it wasn't like her dad to be so adventurous.

Forty minutes later Cali stood outside Stanton Enterprises. She took a deep breath and marched through the large glass doors that led into the first floor lobby. Situated in the center of the room was a massive reception desk. A smaller security station was nestled into the far corner. Both desks had an occupant who looked up at her entrance.

Since it was already after nine in the morning, most of her father's employees were already at their desks working. That left the large lobby area feeling even bigger and impersonal.

Her shoes clicked on the tile floor as she walked toward the receptionist. The woman stood. "Good morning."

"Good morning." Cali plastered a smile on her face. "Could you let Lisa Morgan know that Cali Stanton is here?"

Shock crossed the woman's face a moment before she went into action and reached for the phone. "Oh. Oh, yes. Of course."

While the receptionist called Lisa, her father's assistant, Cali took another look around the lobby area. The office hadn't changed much over the years. In fact, the only thing she noticed beyond a fresh coat of paint on the walls was the addition of several security cameras. Cali wondered if that had anything to do with what her father had shared with her last night over the phone. Not that he'd told her much, only that something was going on and that his heads of security, Matthew and Jason, would fill her in.

The elevator doors opened and she pushed thoughts of whatever mystery situation awaited her out of her mind. Her father's assistant glided elegantly into the lobby. Lisa made walking in four-inch heels look easy. Her legs looked a mile long and her long brown hair curled against her shoulders, bouncing with every step she took.

Lisa skipped the formalities and hugged Cali. "It's good to see you again."

Cali returned the embrace. Over the years, she'd gotten to know Lisa well. "Same here."

Taking a step back, Lisa grinned and motioned toward the elevators. "Shall we?"

They made their way up to the top floor where her father's office was located. Lisa gave her a brief tour and then left her alone in her dad's office. She sat down behind the imposing desk—the desk that would be hers for the next three months—and tried to take it all in.

One week ago, she'd been standing over a tiny cot examining a young boy with deep cuts covering his entire body. He'd been unconscious when a group of villagers had brought him into the makeshift hospital the night before. No one knew what had happened, so Cali and one of the nurses cleaned the boy's wounds and made sure he was comfortable. They were watching him closely for any sign of infection.

She'd felt someone approach her from behind and figured it was Rachael Michaels, one of her fellow doctors, so Cali hadn't turned around to look.

"How's he doing?" Rachael asked.

"No fever, which is good, but he's not out of the woods yet."

She came up beside her and placed a hand on Cali's shoulder. "I'll finish up here. You have a call."

Cali knew only one person would make an unscheduled call to her in the middle of Africa—her father.

She stood and handed the wet towel she'd been using to wash the young boy's wounds to her colleague. The sun beat down on her as she exited the small hut where the boy was being treated and trudged through the heat over to the small rundown metal shack that housed the only working phone. Chad, one of the locals, handed her the phone as soon as she entered.

"Thanks," Cali said as she placed the grungy handset that looked as if it had been around for at least thirty years to her ear. "Hello?"

"Cali? Cali, honey, is that you?"

"Yes, Dad, it's me. Is everything all right?"

"No, sweetheart, it's not. I need you to come home."

Cali collapsed into the beat-up wooden chair Chad had recently vacated. "Come home? Dad, what's going on? What's wrong?"

He released a sigh followed by a low moan.

She'd been a doctor long enough to know that he was in some level of pain. "Dad?"

"I kind of went and did something stupid."

She tensed. "What did you do?"

He hesitated. "I went waterskiing with Henry."

"You what?" Cali's voice reverberated through the small metal building.

"I know, I know. Stupid, right? Not something a man my age should be doing. I've already heard it all from Jessie."

Cali tried to tamp down the fear running through her body. "What happened? Were you hurt?"

"Well..."

"Dad?"

Her father released another sigh followed by a more pronounced moan. She closed her eyes and gritted her teeth as she awaited his response.

"I broke my hip and a couple of ribs. The doctors say I'm going to be out of commission for about three months."

"Oh, Dad." Cali's voice was laced with disapproval.

He pretended not to hear her. "So that's why I need you to come home. I need you to run the business while I'm away. Look after things."

"Dad…"

"Now listen to me, Cali. I know you've told me that you don't want to take over for me when I retire. And although I'm not happy about that, I will respect your wishes. However, at the moment there are some things going on and I would feel much better with someone I trust watching over my interests."

"What about Peter? I thought you were grooming him to take over?" She was grasping at straws and she knew it, but the last thing she wanted to do was travel halfway around the world to run her dad's company. Even if it would only be for three months.

"Peter is very good at what he does, and maybe someday I'll feel confident turning the business over to him, but he's not ready. He's not family." Her father paused. "You're the only family I've got, Cali. I need you for this. Only you."

The guilt trip was working. "I don't know…"

Alvin Stanton turned on the charm. "Please? Your old man needs you."

Cali giggled.

Her father knew he'd won.

"How soon can you get here?" he asked.

She thought about it for a moment, going over the logistics in her head. "I can get a ride into town tomorrow and catch the bus from there. It will take me most of the day to reach the airport so… I should be able to make it back to Chicago by Thursday or Friday."

"Call me when you have your flight information. I'll make sure someone picks you up from the airport."

"Okay, Dad." She arose from her seat, her mind going to all the things she needed to get in order before she left the next day.

"Cali?"

"Yes?"

"I love you, sweetie."

Her lips curled up into a soft smile. "I love you, too, Dad."

The phone on the desk buzzed, startling her. She placed a calming hand on her chest and pushed the intercom button like Lisa showed her. "Yes?"

"Matthew Andersen is here to see you." Lisa's voice came through clear and confident.

"Who?" Cali asked.

"Mr. Andersen. Head of security."

Well ... nothing like jumping in with both feet.

"Send him in."

Cali stood and straightened her suit jacket. She could do this.

The door opened and a man not much older than her entered. He strolled confidently across the room and offered her his hand. The most intriguing blue eyes she'd ever seen stared back at her.

She cleared her throat as her gaze drifted over his dark hair and broad shoulders. "You must be Mr. Andersen."

For a moment, she didn't think he was going to answer. "And you must be Ms. Stanton."

They stood there for a moment, and the air around them felt heavy and charged. She felt warmth rushing to her cheeks and looked away.

Swiping her hand back, she attempted to collect herself and hurried back behind the desk. It didn't matter that she could still feel the burn of his palm against her skin. Or that the way he seemed to own that suit he was wearing reminded her how long it had been since she'd had a man in her bed. She had a job to do and it didn't include fooling around with one of her father's employees.

Cali cleared her throat. "Um ... why don't you take a seat, Mr. Andersen?"

He lowered his tall frame into the offered chair.

She retook her own seat and placed both her hands in her lap.

They sat in silence for several moments. He seemed to be assessing her. For what, she had no idea, but Cali wasn't sure she liked it.

"My father said there were some things you needed to discuss with me." She attempted to sound as businesslike as possible.

"Yes." He paused. "What did Alvin tell you?"

Cali tried not to let his brisk tone bother her. "Not much. Just that he needed someone he could trust running his company right now." She gathered up her courage and leveled a look at him Cali saved for her most difficult patients. "What's going on?"

***

Matthew Andersen had seen pictures of Alvin's daughter before. Pictures of her when she was little and even one from when she'd graduated from medical school. None of those had prepared him for the woman sitting in front of him.

When security had called to let him know the boss' daughter was here, he'd been dreading the encounter. Alvin had called him to say that he wanted his daughter, Cali, to be brought up to speed on the current situation. She had no idea what was going on—what she was walking into—and Matthew didn't have time to hold her hand. But that's what he was going to have to do because it was part of the job.

Of course, his brother Jason had blown off the meeting in typical fashion. Jason didn't like what he referred to as the 'suit and tie' part of the job. He was much better with the hands-on aspects where Matthew thrived on the technical and theoretical side of things. Jason preferred to be out in the action, while Matthew liked to work alone.

As Matthew sat across from Cali Stanton he recalled exactly what his brother had said when he'd gone to get him. "The last thing I want to do this morning is entertain a pampered princess."

Looking at her sitting across from him at her father's desk, Matthew wondered if his brother would have the same opinion upon meeting her. Cali did have that air about her that said she came from money, but there was also something else. An edge that he couldn't quite explain. He'd done his research on her and knew she was twenty-eight and had been working as a doctor with Doctors Without Borders for the last two years. And while he knew working outside the US had its challenges, he couldn't imagine what she would have seen for him to be getting such a vibe from her. But Matthew had learned long ago to trust his instincts and something told him that she wasn't a pampered princess as his brother had suggested.

The black pantsuit she wore wasn't any different than what most of the other women in the office wore, but it had him struggling not to squirm in his seat. Her jacket hugged her waist and had a V-neck that plunged low enough to give a hint of the skin beneath. The reddish hair he remembered from the pictures was pulled away from her face and into some fancy hairdo that left a few stray curls caressing her face. He wanted to twirl the hair around his finger and see if it was as soft as it looked.

Then there were her eyes. They were brown with a hint of copper. He could easily get lost in them.

That thought brought him up short. This was his boss' daughter. His boss for the foreseeable future. He had no business thinking about how soft her hair was or how easy it would be to slip her jacket off her shoulders and . . .

Matthew shifted his focus to the window behind her in an attempt to clear his thoughts. He had a job to do and, damn it, he was going to do it.

For roughly the next hour, Matthew explained the situation to her. She took it better than he thought she would. After all, it wasn't every day you found out people were threatening violence to you and your company.

Cali listened closely to what he had to say, stopping every now and then to ask for clarification. While he could see concern in her eyes, he didn't see panic. That impressed him. Although Matthew understood why Alvin had wanted his daughter to run things in his absence, he was aggravated with the old man as well. Being thrown into a situation like this was no place for a woman like Cali Stanton. Once word got out that she was running the company, Matthew had little doubt that the threats her father had been receiving would transfer to her.

As Matthew left Alvin's office, the danger threatening his new boss bothered him more and more. It wasn't often something rattled him, but by the time he returned to his office, his frustration boiled over. He slammed his door shut, marched over to his desk, and fell into his chair.

Two knocks sounded on his door. Matthew ignored them. He didn't want to deal with anyone right now.

Unfortunately, his brother wasn't known for leaving well enough alone. Jason opened the door and gently closed it behind him. Matthew leaned his head back and closed his eyes, willing his brother to go away.

He should have known better.

"Meeting with the princess didn't go well, I take it?"

Matthew ran a hand over his head and met his brother's gaze. "Don't call her that."

His brother raised both eyebrows but didn't comment on Matthew's outburst.

Matthew reached for his keyboard and logged in to his e-mail, doing his best to ignore Jason's scrutiny. "The meeting went as well as could be expected. She didn't have the slightest clue about what's been going on. I still can't believe her father didn't warn her."

"Well, at least now she knows."

"Yeah." Matthew glanced down at a Post-It note on his desk. "How are things looking for Friday?"

His brother hesitated. "Good. Everyone's keeping their ears to the ground. I'll be notified if they hear something."

Matthew nodded, pushed away from the desk, and stood. "I'll stop by your office later. I need to get the security clearance finished for Ms. Stanton."

Without waiting for Jason to grill him about his unusual behavior, Matthew side-stepped his brother and strolled out the door.

GRAB YOUR COPY OF STRICTLY PROFESSIONAL

ALSO BY SHERRI HAYES

<u>Finding Anna</u>

Slave (Finding Anna, Book 1)

Need (Finding Anna, Book 2)

Truth (Finding Anna, Book 3)

Trust (Finding Anna, Book 4)

Finding Anna Boxed Set (Books 1-4)

Indulge: A Finding Anna Novelette

Change (Finding Anna, Book 5)

<u>The Daniels Brothers</u>

Behind Closed Doors

Red Zone

Crossing the Line

What Might Have Been

Daniels Brothers Box Set (Books 1-4)

<u>Serpent's Kiss</u>

Welcome to Serpent's Kiss

Burning for Her Kiss

One Forbidden Night

Longing for His Kiss

Claiming His Kiss

Tangled In His Embrace

<u>Liberty Crossroads</u>

Seducing Janey

<u>**Strictly Professional**</u>

Strictly Professional

A Christmas Proposal

ABOUT THE AUTHOR

Sherri picked up her first romance novel when she was twelve and immediately she was hooked. She would stay up reading long after everyone else in her house had gone to bed, needing to see the hero and heroine get their happily ever after. But Sherri never imagined becoming an author.

At the age of thirty, all that changed. After getting frustrated with the direction a television show was taking two of its characters, Sherri decided to try her hand at writing an alternative ending to give the characters the happy ending they deserved.

Since then, writing has become a creative outlet that allows her to explore a wide range of emotions, while having fun taking her characters through all the twists and turns she can create.

patreon.com/SherriHayes
facebook.com/SherriHayesAuthor
bookbub.com/authors/sherri-hayes